SPINSTER SISTER

Lawless Ladies, Book One

Elise Marion

ARE YOU SIGNED UP FOR DRAGONBLADE'S BLOG?

You'll get the latest news and information on exclusive giveaways, exclusive excerpts, coming releases, sales, free books, cover reveals and more.

Check out our complete list of authors, too!

No spam, no junk. That's a promise!

Sign Up Here

www.dragonbladepublishing.com

Dearest Reader;

Thank you for your support of a small press. At Dragonblade Publishing, we strive to bring you the highest quality Historical Romance from the some of the best authors in the business. Without your support, there is no 'us', so we sincerely hope you adore these stories and find some new favorite authors along the way.

Happy Reading!

CEO, Dragonblade Publishing

PROLOGUE

Kent, 1813

HELENA MONTGOMERY FLINCHED when the heavy blunder-buss exploded in her hand. The recoil jolted her wrist and sent vibrations along her arm. She stumbled but was balanced by a pair of hands gripping her shoulders.

"Steady, Helena," murmured Wilhelmina Barrington, giving her a consoling pat. "Relax your elbows, and don't forget to breathe. You are in control."

"Tell that to the gun," she muttered, walking to the long, rough table laden with various weapons, bullets, and gunpowder.

"I thought this would be easier," said another of her friends—Lady Cecilia Finch. She stood beside Helena, struggling to stuff her paper-wrapped ball into a flintlock. "The men make it look so effortless."

Helena nodded her agreement, trying not to draw attention to the fact that she was better at loading than Cecilia. Learning to shoot wasn't something she had ever expected to do. Amid the typical feminine pursuits of watercolors, needlepoint, and the pianoforte, the sport of shooting ranked rather low on the list of priorities.

However, none of those achievements had ever done her any good. She had been taught from a young age what a lady's place ought to be. She was to be quiet and demure, refined and poised in order to snag the perfect husband. Her first year on the Marriage Mart had ended in bitter disappointment, as none of the eligible men had displayed any interest in her. Another year passed, then another, and another, forcing Helena to give up entirely.

She simply wasn't marriage material. The quietness and modesty that were supposed to cultivate the interest of the opposite sex weren't assets for Helena—they were curses, manifesting as mortifying shyness and lack of social grace. She wasn't a wallflower... she was more like a stem—plain and unremarkable and always unnoticed.

Helena had resigned herself to the idea of being a spinster for life. Several seasons without a single offer had placed her firmly on the shelf, and she'd made her peace with that. She had her family, who were tight-knit and loving, as well as a group of dear friends. Her life was fulfilling because she strove to make it so.

But all that had changed with the death of both her parents. Now, being an unwed spinster with two younger siblings to care for and no fortune had created a desperate situation.

And desperate times called for desperate measures. Thus, the shooting lesson.

"Come on, ladies!" Wilhelmina bellowed, marching along the grass behind the cluster of women trying—without success—to land their shots at the center of their wooden targets. "Straighten those backs and steady those hands. We can do this!"

Mina was a force of nature—a tall, willowy slip of a woman with dark, flashing eyes and a determined chin. Unlike the rest of their group, she wore a pair of breeches and knee-high boots, a coat, and shirtwaist complementing her slender figure. Her skin was a toasted shade of sienna, and the braid hanging over one shoulder was comprised of thick, coiled spirals. She looked more like a general marching off to battle than the daughter of a duke. It was here, at her secluded house in Kent, that Mina was determined to turn them all into proficient marksmen.

Cecilia threw down her flintlock with a frustrated grunt. Her cornflower-blue eyes welled with tears as she blew a loose strand of honey-hued hair out of her face. "That's it. I can't do this. I'll simply have to rob carriages with a knife or a set of sharp knitting needles. This…this *thing* is impossible."

"Not *so* impossible," chimed in Euphemia Green. The eldest of their set and a widow, Effie was tall like Mina and gracefully built, with a head full of glossy, chestnut locks and eyes such a pale blue, they resembled a clear river. "Think of it as a game. It's rather fun, really."

Helena could hardly believe the smile stretching across Effie's angular features or the glee in her eyes as she pointed her pistol and fired, landing her shot just right of center.

"Effie, you're a natural," Mina declared. "Come, help Cecilia with her form. Cee-Cee, there will be no tears or hysterics. We have decided we aren't helpless, remember?"

With a sniffle, Cecilia allowed Effie to place the gun back into her hands. While the two murmured over the proper techniques, the fifth woman of their tight circle of friends sidled over, hands braced on her hips.

"Could she have possibly yelled that carriage robbery bit any louder?" Selina Russell grumbled, rolling her eyes. "We're going to be dragged off to Newgate before we've even begun."

Mina darted a gaze at the house looming over them—a quaint, two-story cottage where she lived with her infirm mother and a handful of servants. "No one can hear us with these guns firing off every few seconds. Besides, my staff are discreet. We're safe here."

Selina's indigo eyes, enhanced by inky-black hair, sooty lashes, and swarthy skin, met Helena's—wide and filled with unspoken words. They were all guests of Mina's for the week and very aware of their friend's dire situation. The house belonged to Mina's mother outright, but money for servants and even the barest of human comforts was dwindling by the day. Their friend might be reduced to poverty before long. But then, weren't they all in such dire straits?

The sudden and devastating deaths of Helena's parents had shattered the illusion of security she'd been surrounded by her entire life. The lovely townhouse she lived in might not be her home much longer, and all the things her family had collected over the years would fall out of their grasp and into the hands of the creditors. Their country home in Yorkshire had fallen into disrepair, with the barest skeleton of staff keeping it from collapsing onto itself. No one lived there, and the few tenants who depended on the land for their living had taken up other pursuits. They had families of their own to feed, after all.

As the eldest sibling, Helena was left shouldering it all. Her brother, Henry, was still a student at university and not yet wise in the ways of the world. His male pride had him ready to leave school and seek employment to care for their family, but Helena would hear none of it. Henry's education was too important to be thrown away, even if he was the only male left in the family. Harriett, the baby sister, had just reached the age of coming-out and was even more dependent upon Helena than their brother.

With their parents gone and the true state of their finances exposed, there would be no money for new gowns for Harriett's season—which was truly a shame. As a beautiful and accomplished young woman, Harriett could make a splendid match. The kind of union that would see the Montgomery family connected to a wealthier, more powerful one.

And thus had been born the plan to secure Harriett a wealthy and preferably titled husband. However, a husband couldn't be caught with nothing, and the youngest Montgomery sister's beauty wasn't nearly enough. She needed a coming-out and a wardrobe fit for a fine lady. She needed money that Helena just didn't have.

"Why did we let her talk us into this?" Selina whispered as Mina stepped away to watch the other two ladies shoot at their targets. Effie's guidance had steadied Cecilia a bit; now, their friend could at least point the weapon without fainting.

"Because we're desperate," Helena replied. "All five of us.

There *is* nothing else to do, short of becoming…Haymarket strumpets."

Selina's sprite-like face lit up with a teasing smile. "Whores, Helena, they're called whores."

Helena's cheeks flamed hot. Which, she decided, was a perfectly natural reaction for a well-bred woman when one mentioned such delicate subjects. Selina was high-spirited and outspoken and hardly ever blushed.

"Yes, well," Helena replied with a sniff. "I don't want to become one, but one must put food on the table, mustn't one?"

"And outfit one's sister for a season," Selina said with a sigh. "Poor Harriett used like delicious bait in a world filled with hungry sharks."

Helena gave her paper-wrapped ball a sharp jab, shoving it down the barrel of the blunderbuss. "Harriett *wants* to make a match. All the better if one of those sharks can learn to love her while also offering a massive fortune. She isn't bait, Selina. She's simply a means to an end for the good of us all. Harriett will find the husband she wants, and in the process, my family will be saved from destitution. But for her to make a match, we need money, and we've already decided there are only so many ways we can go about making ready funds."

"Yes," Mina said, having returned to overhear the last bit of conversation. "And it will work."

"We'll be caught," Cecilia whined, throwing her gun down and wringing her hands.

"No one will believe five women are capable of such a scheme," Mina argued. "That's why it's the perfect plan."

"She's right," Effie agreed. "I don't like this any more than the rest of you, but I have a son to think of and no other prospects."

"It doesn't quite feel right, does it?" Helena asked, giving voice to her own reservations. She was determined to go through with this but was no less afraid than Cecilia and Selina. "Robbing people?"

"Taking from those who take from others without a second

thought," Mina interjected, her plump upper lip curling into a sneer. Venom threaded through her words, and Helena could hear the pain her friend tried to conceal beneath such bravado.

Her father might have been a duke, but her mother was a former servant and black as well. Mina's illegitimate birth had placed her among the lowest of the low in society, and no one ever let her forget it. "We won't take from anyone who can't afford to lose a few baubles or pounds and pence here and there."

That only made Helena feel marginally better. She came from a family of landed gentry, which had placed her on the fringes of the *beau monde* her entire life. Any invitations they had received had been due to her father's connections. A baroness had sponsored Helena's debut, and that first season had offered her a glimpse into a glittering world of excess and privilege. The people of the *ton* were slaves to their vices. The ladies never wore the same gown twice to public functions and dripped with jewels. The gentlemen gambled their fortunes away on a whim and showed their wealth in carriages and horseflesh. She had seen mountains of food go to waste at balls and opulent gowns thrown into scrap heaps.

Mina was right; the people they planned to target with their daring scheme wouldn't die for the loss of a pocket watch or snuffbox. But the ladies standing around her—and Helena as well—might be reduced to starving if they didn't act fast. Mina's suggestion had filled them all with horror at first, but a little cajoling and convincing had brought them all around.

They were going to be highwaymen. Or rather, highway-women, but that was a term Helena was sure didn't exist. The dangerous world of carriages on dark roads in the middle of the night was strictly a man's domain. At least, it had been until five fast friends had decided to change that.

"We can do this," Helena said, feigning confidence she did not feel. But if Selina or Cecelia cried off, she didn't think she could muster the courage to go through with it herself. Either they were in this together, or they wouldn't do it at all. "It's like

Mina said last night, the theatrics of a highwayman are what really matter. With the proper costuming and intimidating weapons, people will hand over their valuables without a fuss. Really, this shooting practice is only a precautionary measure. I doubt we will actually have to *shoot* anyone."

"But you will be ready if you must," Mina insisted.

"Oh, God," Cecilia groaned, pressing a hand to her throat. "I think I'm going to be sick."

"Steady, Cee-Cee," Effie murmured with motherly affection. "We are in this together."

Effie extended one hand, lifting her eyes to meet each of their gazes one by one.

Mina placed her own hand atop it and smiled. "Together."

"Together," Helena agreed, adding her hand.

Reluctantly, Selina came next, and then Cecilia.

"Come on then," Mina encouraged with a decisive nod. "We still have much to do if we're going to be ready for the start of the season. Lots of carriages coming and going from London, all ripe for the picking."

Steeling her spine as well as her resolve, Helena turned toward the targets and lifted her blunderbuss. She took a slow, deep breath and remembered all that Mina had taught her. Releasing the breath, slow and steady, she pulled the trigger—this time managing to stay on her feet when the blunderbuss kicked, and the report echoed through the air. Birds squawked and scattered in the distance, and then a heavy silence followed as the other women gaped at her with slack jaws and furrowed brows.

Her bullet had hit the target dead center.

CHAPTER ONE

London, two months later

"ALL RIGHT, HARRIETT. Remember your lessons, steps light, chin up, shoulders back. Don't use your real smile, or your cheeks will ache within an hour. You have your fan?"

Helena twisted her trembling hands together as she looked Harriett over from head to toe. They stood in the entrance hall of their townhouse, waiting for a footman to hire a hackney. There was no money for a coach and four, or even a gig and one. However, Helena's secret nighttime activities had earned enough money to keep them stocked with tapers and coal and to purchase a few new gowns for Harriett. They weren't much but were new and made in the latest mode of fashion. It would be enough until Helena could commission more.

Harriett flashed her stunning smile and snapped open a painted fan—one borrowed from Helena. "I'm as ready as I'll ever be, sister. Do calm down."

Helena plucked at a loose thread on Harriett's gown. It was the typical, pure white of a first-season debutante, with a modest neckline and puffed sleeves. Minimal beading adorned the bodice, and a spill of delicate gauze overlaid the silk skirt. White gloves and their mother's pearls completed the ensemble, turning Harriett into a fashion plate. Her hair had been smoothed atop her head, with clusters of fat spiral curls at her ears. Light rogue gave her lips and cheeks a youthful blush—not that Harriett's beauty needed much enhancement. She had been born with everything Helena had not.

Harriett's hair was gleaming mahogany, whereas Helena's hair couldn't decide if it wanted to be blonde or brown. They had both inherited their mother's deep brown eyes, and Helena would consider them her best feature. They were dark chocolate from a distance, but prisms of amber and gold leaped out from within once one drew closer. The sisters shared the same heart-shaped face, but Harriett's was angular and defined with high cheekbones, while Helena's was round with plump cheeks. While both were short of stature, Helena outweighed Harriett by a stone, and that difference made one sister look rounder while it made the other look taller and more graceful.

Here was a young lady who had everything it took to catch a high-society husband.

"You look beautiful," Helena said. "And I cannot calm down. This is your first official ball, Harriett!"

Her sister let out a giggle, pressing a hand over her chest. The closed fan now hung from her wrist. "I have to admit being a bit nervous. It all seems to be happening so fast."

Helena took hold of Harriett's hands and gave them a gentle squeeze. "I know how you feel, but after tonight, you will find your footing. You are lovely and witty and so easy to like. You'll be the jewel of the season. I know it!"

Harriet bit her lip, looking uncertain. "I hope the season goes well. You've been so good to me—to Henry and I both—and if I can find a good husband—"

"Don't think of that," Helena blurted, though it was all she could think of herself. Worrying about their future was her job, and Harriett was too young to carry such a burden. "I want you to put it all from your mind and simply enjoy yourself. The right man will come, and I hope he will be someone you might come to love. That is what I want you to set your mind and heart on."

"But what about—"

"The rest will come, Harriett," Helena soothed, raising her sister's gloved hands and pressing a kiss to her knuckles. "I have faith that it will, and so must you."

Harriett blinked, her eyes glistening with tears, causing Helena to grow emotional as well. The sudden appearance of their brother broke the spell, and they pulled apart, sniffling and fanning at their damp eyes.

"Ho there, what's this?" Henry bellowed, bouncing off the bottom step. "Did someone die? You two look positively miserable."

Harriett jabbed their brother in the side with her elbow. "It's nothing you would understand, Henry. Don't worry, everything is fine."

Henry was good-natured and still filled with the foolish notions of young men. He laughed often and never frowned, reminding Helena so much of their father. Like Helena, Henry was flaxen-haired and brown-eyed, his looks plain but pleasant. A dimple in his left cheek made him handsome when he grinned.

He was home for only a few weeks from Cambridge, and his presence would help ease Harriett's path through society. Their parents had been gone for six months now, but the mourning period had been cut short to afford Harriett this chance. Henry had made several influential friends at university and would be able to make the necessary introductions. By the time he left them again, Helena would be ready to take over as both chaperone and critic of potential suitors.

"Well, won't I be the luckiest man at the ball this evening?" Henry said, puffing out his chest like a proud papa. "Escorting two such stunning women in on my arm. The pair of you look like fine catches!"

Harriett preened while Helena snorted and rolled her eyes.

"Don't be ridiculous, Henry. Tonight is about Harriett. I've already had my chance to catch a husband. The consensus seems to be that I am not marriage material."

Henry sighed and gave Helena a playful flick on the tip of her nose. "Stop grousing and say thank you. Self-deprecation is an abominable trait, and you know you look lovely in pink. If I say you look beautiful, you look beautiful."

Helena's smile was genuine as she returned her brother's teasing assault, tapping the tip of his nose. "Thank you, Henry. Oh, look, the hackney is here! Hurry now. We don't want to be late!"

"I thought being late was fashionable," Henry remarked, offering each sister an arm.

"Only up to a certain point," Helena argued.

They made haste to the hired coach, and Henry helped the ladies inside before climbing beside Harriett. Helena stared out through the parted curtains, her mind drifting away. After the ball, she was to meet Mina, Selina, and Cecelia for a trip to the edge of town, where they would set about their illicit business. She wasn't certain why a sudden case of nerves had overwhelmed her. To date, she and her friends had overtaken and robbed seven carriages successfully. The first time had been, by far, the most harrowing, with Helena flinching at every sound and feeling as if she might retch.

Mina had turned out to be right, as she often was. People were so overwhelmed when confronted with dark figures wearing hooded cloaks and black masks, and carrying deadly weapons, that they never hesitated to hand over their valuables. The five of them had agreed that even on nights when only some of them could participate in an excursion, all the profits would be split evenly. Each of them had a desperate need, and their closeness made it easy to be charitable about such things.

Rings, snuffboxes, watches, brooches, tie pins, purses filled with coins and pound notes—all were pocketed and used to ease the burdens of life grown too difficult to bear. Mina and Effie were knowledgeable about the kinds of seedy establishments where pilfered jewelry could be sold without questions being asked. The amounts earned and split between them weren't exactly a king's ransom. They would have to continue their dangerous activities until their circumstances improved, which Helena hoped would happen for her sooner rather than later.

The majority of the money she'd earned—or rather, stolen, but she wouldn't think too much about that—had gone toward preparing Harriett for the season. The rest had been used to keep the most persistent of the creditors at bay. Tonight, she hoped for a haul good enough that she might pay their dwindling staff. The most loyal of their servants had remained, doing their best to keep the house presentable, the hearths warm, and their bellies full.

Helena and Harriett might have taken to sleeping in the same bed to conserve coal and share warmth, and their meals might be a mundane repetition of toast, eggs, chicken, and tea, but they were sheltered and fed, and it was enough for now.

Between Helena and the lady's maid she shared with Harriett, older gowns had been torn apart and sewn together to look new for Helena. Just because she wasn't searching for a husband didn't mean she shouldn't look her best. Her job would be to stand beside Harriett and help gain the notice of suitors. No man wanted a young lady who came with a drab mouse of a sister. Lace, ribbons, and the few scraps of fabric they could afford had been used to create an adequate wardrobe for her. No one had to know that underneath the gowns, her chemises were worn and frayed and that her stays were limp with age. On the surface, they looked like passably respectable gentry. Helena was counting on Harriett's beauty and personality to do the rest.

It was easy to keep Henry stylish, as menswear constricted itself to few colors and austere trimmings. A couple of new shirts and cravats were enough to make him look like the other young bachelors.

Perhaps her nerves weren't for her own sake. Thus far, the highway robberies had been carried off with little difficulty, the only danger being that of exposure. But they were careful, and they were smart, and those things would be their saving graces.

Helena was anxious because tonight could be the start of the end of it all. The future beyond Harriett's wedding was uncertain, even if it did offer the hope of relief from struggle and worry. What if Harriett's husband was a horrid man who didn't care about the pains of his wife's struggling relations? What if he thought of a spinster sister as a burden—one great enough to be sent away to some lonely, solitary life in the country?

What if she grew old alone, watching Harriett grow her family in happiness and love?

Jealousy wasn't like Helena. She liked who she was, even if others couldn't appreciate it. She ate as many cakes as she liked with no thought to her figure because why would God create food if not for it to be enjoyed? She cherished her friends, for they loved her in a way no one else did. More importantly, they accepted her. There was no reason to be envious of her sister, who would spend the next few months performing before the judgmental eyes of society.

Helena had been in Harriett's position and wouldn't want to repeat the experience again. Harriett, on the other hand, had been made for such a time as this. She was the kind of woman who set ballrooms ablaze with talk and drew gazes of admiration everywhere she went. She enjoyed meeting and talking to new people, and she loved to dance.

Everyone must play their part, and Helena had discovered what hers was. There was nothing left to do but carry on and pray for the desired outcome.

Besides, how hard could it be to help her sister find a husband? She had, after all, robbed carriages by moonlight. This would be child's play by comparison.

A STUFFY LONDON ballroom was the last place Lord Sebastian Radcliffe, Earl of Stratford, wished to be. If he had his way, he would be enjoying a few hands of cards at his favorite gaming hell or enjoying dinner and drinks at one of his clubs. Perhaps a night at the theater might be in order, with a lovely female companion of questionable morals on his arm. However, those were the pursuits of a bachelor without a care in the world, and that title no longer applied to Sebastian. He might still be unwed, but the cares of the world had landed on his doorstep a few short months ago, changing life as he knew it.

All his life, he'd been preparing to step into his father's shoes, and with the death of the previous earl had come the time to put aside the pursuits of a boy and become a man. Sebastian's father had been a slave to his vices; the Radcliffe family and the people depending on their multiple estates for their livelihoods had suffered as a result. Sebastian had been a witness to the pain it caused his mother to watch her husband openly flaunt his mistresses or stagger about in a drunken stupor. Rumors of untoward behavior in the presence of young debutantes, and cheating at cards, still made the rounds after the old earl's death.

Everyone had expected no different from Sebastian. Because of that, he'd made it his life's mission to become everything his father hadn't been. The Stratford title was an old one, and the Radcliffe family descended from a long line of nobility. His father might have sullied his own legacy, but Sebastian would see the dignity of his family's name restored—hopefully while his mother was still living. The dowager countess had opted to remain home for the evening, but Sebastian would return to her filled with stories of the ball: the decor, the music, the food, and especially the young ladies.

He had put off this inevitable step long enough. The first year following his father's death had been spent managing estate affairs and making improvements for the people who were now his tenants. He had left his steward and land agents in charge of his affairs, and returned to London just in time for the start of the season. He had begun attending Parliament sessions, taking his place in the House of Lords. Stratford House in Grosvenor Square was undergoing a much-needed renovation, while his mother and brother were being outfitted with fashionable, new wardrobes. There was nothing left for him to do but select the woman who would become his countess.

Thus, his presence at one of the largest fetes kicking off the social season. Viscount Langford and his wife had invited everyone who was anyone to their soiree, giving Sebastian the perfect opportunity to inspect this year's crop of eligible ladies.

Shifting his weight from foot to foot, Sebastian took a slow sip of champagne. A cotillion had just ended, and his brother appeared from the throng of dispersing dancers. Felix was nearly his mirror image, only younger, slenderer, and still holding the jaunty bounce in his step of youth. His sable locks were overgrown and tousled in the style favored by the younger sort, and his eyes were a bright and vibrant green, glittering with excitement. All this was still a game to him—the chance to practice charming young ladies and flaunt his prowess before the other men.

"How goes the hunt, brother?" Felix asked with a cheeky grin. He lifted a champagne flute from a passing footman's tray and then turned to stand at Sebastian's side.

Sebastian wanted to offer some sage, big-brotherly advice about how awful it was to compare what he was doing to hunting but found he didn't have the heart. There was a reason this whole song and dance was referred to as "the Marriage Mart" in elevated circles. The young ladies wore their white gowns and paraded themselves for inspection, while the men prowled ballrooms looking for the best among them—the most beautiful and sociable and accomplished.

"Dreadfully boring," Sebastian admitted. "I'm convinced there isn't a thing to recommend a single one of them. Their parents have trained them well in the art of holding extended conversations about absolutely nothing."

Felix laughed, using a free hand to slap Sebastian's shoulder. "Come, now. They can't be all that bad. Besides, it's like you said, they've been trained to perform for polite society. If you want to know what they're really like, you have to get to know one."

Sebastian frowned into his champagne. "That would be easier if I could prod them into conversing about something other than the weather or my good health."

"My, but you've become such a stick since you inherited," Felix muttered.

Indignation sparked to life within Sebastian but was quickly snuffed out by the realization that his brother was right. "Better me than you. My becoming such a 'stick' will result in prosperity for our family and security of the title. You should be grateful to be allowed to go about life as you please."

Felix's slender, boyish face crumpled with solemn guilt. "I'm sorry. I didn't think—"

"I'm the one who is sorry. Forgive me for being such a curmudgeon."

"Think nothing of it. Now, which of these lovely ladies has what it takes to pique your interest? Oh, what about Miss Heathcote?"

Sebastian followed his brother's gaze to a young lady in a white gown covered in a gaudy spill of pink muslin flowers. "We danced a quadrille. I've had better conversations with my horse during a morning ride."

Felix snickered, ducking his head so as not to be caught. "All right, not her. What about Lady White? Her father is a duke."

"Even that isn't enough to tempt me," Sebastian replied, finding the lady in question stepping onto the dance floor with another young man. "She spent ten minutes describing her current embroidery projects to me, in full detail."

"Christ," Felix muttered, taking a long swallow of champagne. "I don't envy you."

"Is it too much to ask," Sebastian mused aloud, "that a man be able to find a wife who is both nice to look at *and* interesting to talk to?"

"When one is searching for a countess?" Felix fired back. "Yes."

Sebastian wasn't so certain. His mother was a wonderful woman whose beauty had endured the ravages of age. She was also witty and as sharp as a tack. His father hadn't deserved her, the philandering bastard.

He wasn't keen on placing his foot into the marriage trap but was prepared to do his duty. However, Sebastian didn't relish taking a woman he didn't like as his bride. If he couldn't love her, he at least hoped they could have a genial relationship. If she could participate in a stimulating conversation or laugh over a joke, all the better.

Thus far, his prospects looked absolutely dismal.

"I say," Felix said, going straight-backed and alert. "What about *her*?"

Following his brother's gaze, Sebastian found three people entering the ballroom and drawing the stares of the other guests. The ball had just reached full swing, so the timing was perfect for a fashionably late entrance. There were two women and a young man, but Sebastian's eye immediately fell to the lady wearing a white gown. He supposed the color scheme of whites and pastels for unmarried misses was an efficient way of picking marital prospects out of a crowd. Unlike many of the other debutantes, this particular lady carried off the colorless hue as if she'd been made for it.

Petite of stature and slender, she was a dark-haired beauty with a heart-shaped face and wide, doe-like eyes. She was clearly inexperienced, her expression showing none of the bored cynicism Sebastian was used to. The maiden stared at her surroundings in awe—lips parted, eyes wide, and a pink flush staining her cheeks.

"She's lovely," Felix coaxed, giving him a nudge. "If you don't ask her to dance, I will."

Sebastian hesitated only a moment. On the one hand, he didn't relish having to spend another quarter-hour on the dance floor listening to useless prattle. But then, what if this girl happened to be different from all the rest? What if she opened her mouth and something resembling sense came out of it?

What if he actually found he liked her?

There was only one way to find out.

"I believe it is my right as the eldest to approach the lady first," Sebastian quipped, thrusting his glass in Felix's direction.

He went off in search of their hostess, chuckling at the sound of annoyance Felix let out behind him. His brother couldn't have been serious about approaching the young lady. He had made it clear that he had no intention of settling down anytime soon. Unlike Sebastian, he had the luxury of remaining a bachelor for as long as he pleased.

Locating Viscountess Langford, he weaved his way through the crowd in her direction. His hostess was a society matron still clinging to decades-old fashions and powdered wigs. A heart-shaped beauty patch left a black stain above her upper lip. It danced across her face, moving with the wide smile she flashed as he approached.

"My lord," she chirped, offering him a sweeping curtsy. "I do hope you are enjoying yourself this evening."

"How could I not with such a wonderful hostess?" Sebastian replied, practiced charm rolling off him with little effort. He cleared his throat and did his best to keep from staring at her beauty patch. It was an aberration against her pale skin, and a damned distracting one at that. "I was wondering if I might trouble you to make an introduction. A young lady has just arrived whose acquaintance I haven't yet had the pleasure of making."

The viscountess's face lit up with glee at the prospect of introducing an earl to a potential match. If a courtship and marriage resulted, she would be able to brag that she'd had a hand in it. But Sebastian was getting ahead of himself.

Lady Langford took his arm and gazed about the ballroom, the plumes in her hair brushing his jaw. "Which lady is it, my lord?"

"The one who just walked in, there."

Following his discreet nod, the viscountess nodded her approval. "Ah yes, Miss Montgomery. This is her first season, and I suspect she will become this season's Incomparable, unlike that sister of hers."

Sebastian finally took stock of the other woman accompanying the young Miss Montgomery. He hadn't given her more than a passing glance but now looked his fill. The ladies were obviously sisters but appeared to be polar opposites.

While the elder sister had the same slight stature as the younger, her figure was full and rounded, with a large bosom that even the modest cut of her gown couldn't hide. Her hair wasn't quite brown, but it wasn't blonde either—falling to some shade in between. Her features were similar to the young Miss Montgomery, but the roundness of her cheeks and fuller lips gave her a different aspect altogether. There was something in her carriage that struck him as different as well. While the young debutante was poised and graceful, looking as if she had been born into this glittering world, the elder sister looked out of place in it. She hugged herself while glancing about with shuttered eyes and appeared as if she wished she were anywhere else but here.

He could certainly sympathize.

"The elder Miss Montgomery is a lovely lady," the viscountess went on, heedless to the fact that Sebastian only gave her half an ear. "But too shy to conquer the ballrooms of the *ton*, and too unfashionably shaped to be considered as beautiful as her sister."

Sebastian stiffened at the slight to the woman's appearance. He wanted to tell the old harpy that she should look in a mirror and take stock of her own faults before disparaging someone else but held his tongue. He needed an acquaintance to introduce to him and didn't want to offend his hostess during the very first ball of the season.

They neared the trio of siblings—for the young man accompanying the women looked too much like them not to be their brother—and the viscountess snapped open her painted fan, waving it about to gain their attention.

"Good evening, Mr. Montgomery, Miss Montgomery, and Miss Montgomery. I see you have just arrived and wanted to welcome you myself and also introduce you to a dear friend of mine."

Sebastian chafed at the familiar way the viscountess patted his arm but allowed it. Soon he could be rid of her. He squared his shoulders and offered a tight smile to the three Montgomery siblings.

"This is the Earl of Stratford," she went on. "My lord, I am honored to introduce you to Mr. Montgomery. He is soon to return to university, so it is good to have him as a guest this evening. He is a rare sight at such events."

Montgomery snapped to attention and gave Sebastian a stiff bow, his hands clenched at his sides. The young pup was obviously as inexperienced as his sister and nervous to boot.

Sebastian offered his hand. "Montgomery, I am glad to make your acquaintance. Tell me, are you an Oxford student or a Cambridge man?"

"C-Cambridge, my lord," the young man stammered, shaking Sebastian's hand with a trembling one.

"I am a Cambridge graduate myself," Sebastian reassured him. "You are obviously a man of good taste and superior intellect."

Montgomery blushed and grinned, then swept a graceless hand toward the women at his side. "May I introduce my sisters. Miss Harriett Montgomery and Miss Helena Montgomery."

The sisters curtsied as one and murmured "my lord" in unison. Harriett was the young sister he had crossed the ballroom to meet, while Helena was the eldest. While Harriett kept her gaze demurely lowered when Sebastian bowed to them, Helena studied him without blinking or flinching. Her eyes were an intriguing kaleidoscope in shades of brown, amber, and gold. The tawny shade of her lashes made the lighter flecks of her pupils glimmer in the candlelight.

"I am delighted to meet you both," Sebastian said. "May I fetch either of you lemonade or champagne?"

Harriett looked to her sister as if for guidance, and Helena was the one who responded.

"That would be lovely, my lord. We would both enjoy a glass of champagne."

Sebastian waited for Harriett to speak, to see if her voice would be a soft whisper like the other women he'd met tonight or a husky intonation like her sister's. Harriett merely gave him a silent, hopeful glance, leaving him with no choice but to seek out the promised champagne.

"Best of luck, my lord," the viscountess whispered before taking her leave.

Sebastian made quick work of securing two champagne flutes and returning to the Montgomery sisters. Their brother had been pulled into conversation with a group of other young men but remained within clear view. Helena and Harriett were whispering to one another but fell silent when Sebastian drew close.

They engaged in small talk while the sisters sampled their champagne, exchanging the usual pleasantries. Sebastian could almost recite the beginnings of such conversation in his sleep.

"You look very lovely this evening."

"Such fine weather we've enjoyed this week, don't you think?"

"Yes, the decorations are splendid tonight."

"Are you enjoying the start of the season?"

It was all part of the ritual leading up to the moment of truth, which Sebastian seized on once he noticed Harriett reaching the bottom of her glass.

"Miss Montgomery, I was wondering if you had yet promised the next dance to anyone? If not, I would be honored if you would allow me to claim it."

Harriett seemed surprised by his question, and the time it took her to recover left Helena filling the silence.

"You are kind to ask, my lord. We have only just arrived,

and—"

"Miss Montgomery," Sebastian injected, annoyance raising his hackles. "I do beg your pardon, but I had hoped Miss Montgomery might offer her own acceptance or rejection of my offer."

Helena's chin dropped, and a brief flicker of incredulity crossed her features. Her mouth then snapped closed, and she narrowed her eyes at him while offering no further remark. Good. How was a man to court a young lady with her older sister acting as such a distraction?

While she remained at a loss for words, Sebastian swiveled his gaze back to Harriett. "What do you say, Miss Montgomery? It would be a delight to claim your first dance of the evening."

Clearing her throat, Harriett traded glances with Helena, who gave her a nearly imperceptible nod. Sebastian gritted his teeth and resisted asking whether Harriett had a tongue and if Helena happened to be carrying it in her reticule. It seemed the chit was too timid to act without her sister's approval, something that could be easily overcome.

"I would love to dance, my lord," Harriett replied with a bright smile, accepting his extended hand.

Ignoring the blistering stare of the elder Montgomery sister, Sebastian led the younger toward the dance floor just as a minuet was beginning.

CHAPTER TWO

LESS THAN AN hour at this infernal ball, and Helena was already itching to leave. She had never cared for such affairs—even though being considered an untouchable spinster meant she was no longer forced to participate. It was enough for her to appear by Harriett's side and hover on the edge of the dance floor to ensure nothing untoward was going on. Her stomach rumbled, but she ignored it. She had another half hour at least until supper was announced and could not leave her post as Harriett's chaperone to avail herself to the finger sandwiches arranged on the refreshment table.

She had been too anxious to eat anything before departing home, though things seemed off to a good start. Helena hadn't missed the stir her sister had caused upon their entrance. Half the eyes in the room had fallen on Harriett, no small feat considering that this ball had turned into a veritable crush. Already, the young bucks who weren't yet engaged lingered on the edge of the dance floor, watching Harriett smile and chat with the Earl of Stratford as they danced their minuet. A sense of relief washed over Helena as she realized Harriett would spend the rest of her evening being partnered on the dance floor by eligible men.

A young, handsome earl paying marked attention to her so early in the evening boded well for them.

It was too bad the man was a complete bore. Helena ground her molars as she watched Stratford dance with her sister, recalling the rude way he had dressed her down when asking Harriett to dance. Did the ogre have no experience with young debutantes? Harriett was frightened witless to attend her first ball and had been tongue-tied in the face of such attentions. Helena had merely been trying to help, and the man had treated her as meddlesome and bothersome.

The back of her neck grew hot as she observed the earl, smiling and talking animatedly with Harriett. That he was devilishly handsome did him no favors. The patrician set of his facial features—the straight nose, strong jaw, and slashing cheekbones—only made him look as arrogant as he apparently was. The dark, winged eyebrows added a certain haughtiness to his appearance, and the set of his mouth was hard and stern. He was all wrong as a potential suitor for Harriett, but that didn't mean he couldn't be used for practice. Stratford and her sister seemed to be getting on well, and Harriett didn't look as pale or nervous as she had before. After this dance and some light conversation, she would be ready to begin inspecting the real prospects.

"Pompous ingrate," Helena muttered under her breath, giving in to an uncharacteristic display of annoyance. She generally got on well with everyone she met, but something about Stratford rubbed her the wrong way—like a cat whose fur was stroked in the wrong direction.

"Who's a pompous ingrate, and how can we make his life miserable?" asked a voice from Helena's side.

She flinched, her heartbeat spiking to a rapid cadence. Turning to find Cecilia grinning at her, Helena sighed with relief.

"Heavens, Cee-Cee, you frightened me!"

Cecelia's brilliant grin widened, displaying perfectly white teeth. She was a true beauty, the perfect English rose. Blonde-haired and blue-eyed, she had all the qualities of the society debutante. Unfortunately, the loss of her family's fortune had destroyed her prospects. Once word of the Finch family's misfortune had spread through London, Cecelia had gone from being declared a diamond of the first water to swimming in the shallow end of the marriage pool. Even her beauty and poise weren't enough to bring the men of the *ton* up to scratch, which was why Cecelia had joined their group of friends in the dangerous endeavor of highway robbery. If she couldn't come up with a sufficient dowry, she might be forced to make an unpleasant match for the sake of a fortune. Like Helena, she had no other choice.

"I apologize, dear," Cecelia remarked, wafting her fan and following Helena's gaze to the dance floor. "You *were* standing here talking to yourself."

Helena gave her friend a sheepish smile. "You must think me mad."

"Of course not. Now, when you begin answering yourself, that's when I'll believe you've gone mad. Well? Are you going to tell me who the pompous ingrate is?"

"That *man* dancing with Harriett," Helena grumbled, narrowing her eyes at the tall, broad-shouldered earl.

Cecelia raised delicate blonde eyebrows. "The Earl of Stratford? Harriett's going to be quite the smashing success if she managed to cultivate his interest on her first night out. Stratford might just be the catch of the season. He's newly inherited, young and handsome, and as wealthy as a sultan. His father had a rather unsavory reputation, but Stratford has always acquitted himself well. He's a gentleman."

"He is rude and obnoxious," Helena argued. "I don't like him for Harriett."

With a laugh, Cecelia looped her arm through Helena's and gave her hand a consoling pat. "They're sharing a dance, nothing more. It's hardly a marriage proposal. Although ..."

At the sly suggestion in her voice, Helena groaned. "Please, don't say it."

"It would be a spectacular match," Cecelia said, disregarding Helena's plea. "Isn't that the point of, well, you know? You needed a dowry and wardrobe for Harriett to help her catch a wealthy husband. She could hardly do better than Stratford. They do look smashing together."

For some reason, hearing those last words spoken disturbed Helena. Anyone with eyes could see that Stratford and Harriett would make a striking pair. They were both conventionally beautiful, and the earl's dark coloring complemented her sister's golden locks and fair skin. It set Helena's teeth on edge.

"I have not risked my life and the reputation of my family, *robbing carriages—*" she whispered the last bit in a low hiss, leaning close to Cecelia, "—to see her wed to someone as boorish as that man. There are other wealthy men, and this is only her first ball, her first dance even."

Cecelia patted Helena's knuckles again. "Of course, dear. The world is at her fingertips, and it is all thanks to you."

Helena's shoulders sagged, and she let out a deep sigh. "I just hope it isn't all for naught. None of it will mean anything if we are caught and exposed."

"We won't be. We've managed to go unscathed thus far, haven't we?"

Cecelia made a good point. However, Helena had begun to fear that it was only a matter of time until their luck ran out.

"You surprise me, Cee-Cee," Helena quipped, hoping to lighten the mood. "I can hardly believe I'm talking to the same woman who grew physically ill while learning how to fire a pistol. Now, you're the best shot of us all, save Mina, of course."

Plump, pink lips turned up into a sly smirk, and Cecelia shrugged. "What can I say? A lady knows how to adapt to her environment. We do what we must, don't we?"

Helena straightened as the minuet ended, and Stratford began guiding Harriett in their direction. "Indeed, we do."

She pasted a stiff smile on her face as the earl and her sister drew near, determined not to let the man upset her. They were waylaid by a young gentleman who seemed to want the next dance with Harriett. Within seconds, her sister was heading back to the dance floor for a quadrille. Meanwhile, Stratford continued on his course, his gaze fixed determinedly on *Helena*. She stiffened, her hold on Cecelia's arm tightening as it became clear he was determined to approach her. Irritation overwhelmed her anxiety as she realized that Cecelia's presence was likely the thing drawing him back. Apparently, the man was on the hunt for a beautiful bride and had forgotten all about Harriett now that he'd lain eyes upon Cecelia.

It was a completely irrational assumption to make, and the resulting reaction that made her skin feel itchy and tight was ridiculous. Yet, Helena couldn't seem to rid herself of such feelings.

"Miss Montgomery," he said once he reached them. "I had wondered—"

"Might I introduce you to one of my dearest friends?" Helena blurted, deciding they might as well get this over with. No man ever approached her at a ball unless she was standing next to one of her friends. Her lovelier, more charming, and engaging friends. "My Lord, this is Lady Cecelia Finch. Cecelia, I present you the Earl of Stratford."

The earl's jaw ticked, and something that looked like annoyance flashed in his eyes. Helena noticed for the first time that they were hazel; only, Stratford's eyes didn't hold flecks of gold like hers. In the midst of those velvety brown irises were chips of shining jade.

"It is a pleasure to make your acquaintance, my lord," Cecelia said, pulling away from Helena to offer her curtsy.

"The honor is all mine," Stratford replied, his upper body shifting in a slight bow. However, his gaze never left Helena.

"Oh, do excuse me," Cecelia chirped, staring off across the ballroom. "I see someone I simply *must* speak to. I beg your pardon."

"Of course," Stratford replied, raising one dark, imperious eyebrow.

"Helena, darling, I will look for you a bit later!"

Cecelia's tone was light, but her gaze was heavy with meaning as she gazed back over her shoulder. The next time they saw one another would be the dead of night, as they stood about the side of some dark road waiting for a vulnerable carriage to roll past.

Stratford cleared his throat, jerking Helena out of her musings. She glanced up to find he was still raising that infernal eyebrow, looking at her as if amused.

"My lord," she snapped, pursing her lips.

"Miss Montgomery," he replied with a stiff smile. "I had hoped to beg the honor of the next dance if you are not otherwise engaged."

Helena's lips parted, but no sound came forth for several seconds—the amount of time it took for her mind to grasp what he had just asked. Stratford was requesting to dance with her. Instant suspicion made her recoil, taking a step away from him.

"And just why is that, I wonder?"

Stratford gave her a puzzled look. "Well…we *are* at a ball. I was led to believe that dancing was the entire point. You *do* dance, don't you, Miss Montgomery?"

"I do," Helena replied. "But I regret to say I must decline your offer."

The earl went statue-still, his nostrils flaring and his lips compressing into a thin line. The green in his irises blazed like emerald flames. "I see."

Helena squared her shoulders, emboldened by his obvious exasperation. "I don't think you do, so allow me to elaborate. You cannot gain favor with my sister, or myself, with such patronizing gestures."

"Patronizing?"

"Yes. You've only asked me because you think it will earn my sister's approval. If you expect me to believe your motives to be anything other than what they obviously are, you would be wasting your time."

Stratford stared silently at her for so long that Helena had to fight the urge to squirm. The man's gaze was downright unnerving and rude, to add insult to injury. No true gentleman would discomfit a lady so, and Stratford was obviously doing it on purpose.

"I see," he finally said, his voice flat.

"Indeed," Helena replied, refusing to allow him the last word. "Good evening, my lord."

Inclining his head, Stratford took a step away from her and bowed. "Good evening, Miss Montgomery."

Helena found herself watching him walk away, noticing that his hair was just slightly longer than was proper—brushing the collar of his coat. The dark, waving strands were thick and lustrous, shining in the candlelight. With a blink, she tore her gaze away and clenched one gloved hand into a fist.

This was going to be a long night, and it had only just begun.

SEVERAL HOURS LATER, Helena crouched behind a tree with the hood of a black cloak pulled over her head. Her field of vision was narrowed by the mask she wore, but as it was her sole protection against exposure of her identity, Helena didn't dare lift it. The darkened road leading out of London was all but abandoned this time of night, and only Mina, Cecilia, and Selina were near enough to see her. Effie's young son, Crispin, was ill, so the fifth member of their group had been forced to remain home for the evening to tend him.

Nevertheless, one couldn't be too careful. For all Helena knew, another highwayman could be lurking nearby. A carriage or lone horseman could wander past. A moment of complacency could see her ousted and ruined, and Helena would never forgive herself for how such a mistake would affect Henry and Harriett.

From her hiding place, she watched Mina pace the width of the road, the silver flash of her flintlock showing from within the folds of her cloak. Of the five of them, Mina was the boldest and the least hesitant. This entire scheme had been her idea, and her bravery had helped bolster those of them who had been the most hesitant at first. Trading glances with Cecilia, Helena was once again reminded of the frightful girl who had wept and spewed vomit at the idea of robbing carriages by moonlight. The difference between Cee-Cee now and then was like day and night. Kneeling behind a low bush, she wore a dark, forest-green cloak and a black cap over her hair. The white-gold shade of Cecilia's tresses would give her away on sight, so she was always careful to cover them. No longer afraid of the massive blunderbuss clutched in one slender hand, she brandished the weapon with confidence and the same grace with which she did everything else.

Sharing a hiding place with Cecilia was Selina, whose inky black hair hung over one shoulder in a single braid. Selina wasn't typically a shy, mincing sort of person but still clung to some of the reluctance they'd begun this scheme with. Taking mercy on her, the other four ladies had designated her as their lookout. Selina had protested at the idea of taking on a role that required her to carry a gun or open her mouth to issue threats to their prey. And yet, her situation was perhaps the most dire of them all. Her dying father would leave behind a mountain of unpaid debt—the bulk of which was owed to an unscrupulous money-lender known for his brutish ways and violent tactics. If the funds couldn't be produced, Selina might be left to pay the price. So, like the rest of them, Selina gritted her teeth and did what she must.

"Carriage wheels!" Cecelia hissed, just loud enough for the rest of them to hear.

Helena's entire body went rigid, and she inclined her head to listen. Sure enough, the clatter of carriage wheels on the uneven road reached out to her from the darkness. Craning her neck to see beyond the trunk of the tree, she spotted a pinpoint of light in the distance—a carriage lamp.

She slowly straightened to her full height, her knees aching from her previous position. Ignoring the discomfort, Helena took deep, measured breaths and tightened her grip on the blunderbuss she hid beneath her cloak. Thus far, the only person who'd ever had to fire their weapon was Mina—who always let off a shot to spook the horses and make their presence known. Still, Helena often visited Mina's home outside the city for target practice—not wanting to lose her hold on the little skill she had developed. She had a feeling that the moment she grew lax, something awful would happen, and she would wish she had been more vigilant.

"Steady," Mina called out from where she stood in the middle of the road, legs braced wide. Like the rest of them, Mina wore a pair of form-fitting breeches, along with a shirt dyed black and a dark blue waistcoat. She wore no cloak but donned a mask and a hat with a wide brim. To anyone unfamiliar with Mina, she would appear like a slender and wiry man, her svelte figure light with curves and easily disguised by men's clothing.

Helena needed the aid of a cloak to hide the true shape of her body, as no amount of padding or binding could disguise the ample curves of her bosom and hips. Going unscathed depended mostly on them tricking their victims into thinking they were being robbed by men.

Mina waited until the carriage was close enough for them to see the outline of a darkly dressed man seated on the driver's perch. The vehicle was a coach drawn by six gray geldings, so large and ostentatiously trimmed that Helena knew their earnings would be worth the trouble. Only someone with money to spare would ride about in such a gaudy, undoubtedly expensive vehicle.

Firing a solitary shot into the air, Mina stood her ground when the carriage jerked to a swaying halt, the horses rearing and crying out their distress.

Helena and Cecilia emerged from their hiding places to surround the vehicle as Mina bellowed to be heard over the driver's exclamations, "Stand and deliver!" Her voice, already holding a low, rasping quality, sounded downright masculine with the effort she took to mimic the tones of a male.

Assuming her customary place at the back of the vehicle,

Selina raised her gun and kept an eye on the road behind them, while Mina climbed up onto the perch to incapacitate the driver. Helena strode to one door, while Cecelia took the other. They yanked the carriage open as one, producing cries of alarm from within as they thrust the noses of their guns into the openings.

Pressed against the squabs on either side of the carriage were an elderly gentleman with silver side-whiskers and a young lady who looked as if she might be his daughter. The woman was quite beautiful and wore such heavy jewels, Helena was surprised she managed to sit upright. The diamond choker, earrings, brooch, bracelet, and ring she wore smacked of a lavish lifestyle, while the opulent surroundings of the carriage confirmed Helena's suspicions. The gentleman was as gaudily turned out as his companion—flaunting a massive emerald tiepin in his cravat and holding a gold-rimmed quizzing glass over his eye.

"I say, I do believe we are being robbed," he exclaimed, peering at Helena through the single lens with a trembling chin. "Take whatever you like, just please…don't shoot."

"Out of the carriage," Cecelia commanded, dropping her voice a few octaves.

The man hurried to comply, groaning and grunting as he eased through his open door with all the grace of an overstuffed ostrich. Pressing a protective hand over her necklace, the woman gaped at her companion with bulging eyes.

"Eustace! Eustace, get back here this instance and protect me!" she screeched in a whining voice. "You coward!"

Wincing when Helena took hold of his arm and thrust her pistol at him, the man held up both hands and gave his companion a pleading look. "Come, my little crumpet. Don't be difficult. They have *weapons*! Do you want them to shoot us?"

"I don't think I would mind if they shot *you*," she muttered, giving him a venomous glare.

"Let's go," Cecelia growled, reaching into the carriage to urge the woman through the door. "Step lightly!"

"Unhand me, you cretin!" the woman howled, jerking in

Cecelia's hold but failing to free herself. "This is outrageous!"

"No," Mina said, stepping from around the front of the carriage. "Your caterwauling is outrageous. This will be all be over once you shut your trap and hand over your valuables."

Behind her, on the ground, lay the driver, who had been rendered unconscious. He lay prostrate, his face turned away from them and both hands tied behind his back. Their fearless leader had subdued him with a minimum of fuss.

Mina thrust a rough gunnysack toward their captives and motioned toward the opening with her gun. The gentleman immediately complied, hurling his quizzing glass into the sack and then using his watch chain to yank a massive, solid gold timepiece from his fob pocket. A ring from his little finger followed next, and then, from within his breast pocket, came a rather ornate snuffbox. Lastly, he retrieved a purse that jingled with coins when he dropped it into the sack.

"That's all I have," he insisted, a sheen of sweat breaking out on his upper lip. "Crumpet?"

The young lady in question jutted out her lower lip and whimpered. "I don't want to. These diamonds are mine. I *earned* them laying beneath your wrinkled, shriveled up—"

"You can take them off willingly or have them snatched off," Mina cut in, a heavy threat weighing down her words. "The choice is yours, but we are fast running out of patience."

Helena kept her pistol pointed at the gentleman—who had now been exposed as the woman's lover, not her father. Disgust and curiosity warred within her as she observed the pair. She wasn't so inexperienced that she wasn't aware of how things worked between men of means and women with beauty and limited prospects. Helena liked to think she could never be so desperate but couldn't judge this woman when she was dressed in breeches and boots, robbing carriages in the dead of night. There were so few choices for women without money and connections, and she found herself feeling a measure of pity for the girl.

"I'll buy you something else," Eustace snapped, impatience

edging into his voice. "I'll give you whatever you want if you stop being difficult and hand the jewels over. Right now!"

With a sniffle and another low, pitiful wine, "Crumpet" snatched the diamond earbobs off her lobes and hurled them into the sack. The ring followed, and then the bracelet. She glowered at her protector while unclasping the necklace, the task made slow and awkward by her satin gloves.

From the back of the carriage, Helena noticed Selina moving about. A few seconds later, a small trunk and valise hit the ground with a thud, sending up a cloud of dust. Their contents could prove to be as valuable as the jewels.

Keeping her pistol leveled at Eustace and his mistress, Mina jerked her head to indicate that they should take the luggage. Helena and Cecelia hurried over, each of them taking a handle of the trunk as Selina lifted the valise.

"Your cooperation is appreciated," Mina said, backing away from the pair without lowering her weapon. "Do try not to let this sully the remainder of your evening."

It would seem Mina's advice was too little, too late, for as they made their escape, the couple could be heard arguing—the courtesan's voice raised to a screeching pitch as she berated her lover for failing to defend her from thieves.

The four of them took off at a run, the trunk swinging between Helena and Cecelia's hands. They dashed through an opening in a copse of trees, finding the carriage they'd left hidden. Mina was the only one among them who had been able to maintain a carriage, as the vehicle had been part of her meager inheritance—one that had, sadly, not been enough to sustain her small household. They tossed their takings inside, then vaulted inside one by one. Mina came last after directing her driver—a slender, quiet man with gleaming black skin—to get them out of there.

Silence filled the interior of the carriage for the first few minutes, and Helena could hear only the sound of her thundering heartbeat. This might be their eighth carriage robbery, but she never stopped waiting for the sounds of pursuit, signaling their doom.

When it failed to come, she exchanged glances with Cecelia, who had snatched her cap off and shaken out her frazzled curls. Her lips twitched, and a sound bubbled up from her throat. What sounded like choking devolved into snorts and giggles, which Helena found contagious.

Thinking of the ridiculous pair whom they'd just fleeced of their belongings, Helena slumped against the seat beside Cecelia, shoulders shaking and her own throat itching with a laugh. Selina followed next, doubling over and letting out full-throated chuckles while Mina looked at them all as if they'd gone insane. That only made Cecelia laugh harder, which prompted Helena to follow suit.

Selina nearly fell from her seat, her eyes watering and her face going pink as she guffawed and gasped for air. A wide, mischievous smile broke out on Mina's face, and she joined them in laughter, clutching at her belly and rocking back in her seat. The laughter didn't stop until they had returned to the city.

CHAPTER THREE

"I TAKE IT things went well with Miss Montgomery last night?" Felix asked when entering the dining room the following morning.

Sebastian—who was halfway through his breakfast and second cup of tea—glanced at his brother over a fresh copy of *The London Post*. "Which Miss Montgomery would that be? The lovely young woman I shared a dance and lively conversation with last night, or her shrew of a sister?"

Sauntering to the sideboard, Felix gave him a puzzled look. "Shrew? I made a few inquiries about the family and heard no one characterized Miss Helena that way. They all described her as quiet and a bit mousy but perfectly congenial."

"Hmph," Sebastian snorted, slapping his paper onto the table and glaring into his tea. "Perhaps she has a twin because the woman I interacted with at the ball was anything but quiet and mousy."

Felix came to the table with a plate he'd managed to pile high with eggs, ham, and rolls within the span of a few seconds. Motioning for a footman to pour his tea, he then fixed Sebastian with an amused look.

"Perhaps it was the company, brother. You *do* have a way of bringing out the worst in people."

Sebastian opened his mouth to defend himself but promptly snapped it closed. Felix knew how to annoy him better than anyone else, but that didn't stop his observations from being startlingly accurate. Sebastian prided himself on being aware of his faults. He was often too serious—a symptom of a life spent trying to step out of his father's sullied shadow. He didn't always make the best impression and was often cold until a person took the time to get to know him. Realizing all this, it wasn't difficult to consider that his brother might be right.

Seeming to sense the trajectory of his thoughts, Felix winced. "You did the eyebrow thing, didn't you?"

"What eyebrow thing?"

"*This* eyebrow thing," Felix replied, sitting up straight and fixing his face into an uncanny imitation of Sebastian's somber face. Then, he lifted his eyebrow to an imperious height, his lips compressing into a line.

Sebastian cringed, feeling as if he looked into a mirror. "Christ, is that how I look when I do that?"

"You're famous for that damned eyebrow," Felix said, going back to his mountainous breakfast plate. "In the halls of Parliament or at the clubs, it makes you look distinguished and appropriately intimidating—as an earl should. But when dealing with the fair sex, a bit more finesse is required."

"I see."

Felix sighed. "That's another thing that probably rubbed her the wrong way. Those sharp, one or two-word answers. They make you seem a brutish boor."

Sebastian narrowed his eyes. "I'm starting to think you don't like me very much."

"I happen to both love *and* like you, but that is because I know and understand you like few people do. I'm certain Miss Helena will warm up to you eventually, as most people do."

Sebastian leaned his head against the back of his chair with a huff. "Miss Helena isn't the one I wish to impress, it's Miss Harriett who has my interest."

"Ah, but everyone knows the Montgomery sisters are close. As the only male, the brother could be considered the official head of the family, but he's practically an infant. Helena has assumed caring for her siblings. Any man who wants to win Harriett's hand should be prepared to impress her sister. It would seem you're off to an abominable start. What did you say to her?"

"I only asked her to dance," Sebastian countered. "The chit accused me of seeking to impress her sister and then refused me."

Felix choked on a mouthful of eggs, sputtering coughs coming out between peals of laughter. "My God, the woman is a treasure! I must meet her!"

Sebastian frowned. "Heaven forbid. The two of you would drive me quite insane."

"It's going to happen eventually," Felix said, still clearing his throat and coughing as he recovered. "At least, it will if you manage to coax Miss Harriett to the altar."

"No one's talking of marriage just yet. Such thoughts are premature."

"Of course they aren't! If you're going to court a woman, it's best to consider her family from the onset. Helena will become our sister-in-law, so the two of you will have to learn to tolerate one another at least. You're going to have to smooth things over with her."

Burying his head in his hands, Sebastian tried to fight off an impending headache. This courtship business was shaping up to be more complicated than he had anticipated. Why couldn't a man and woman simply come to know one another without all the fanfare and petty games? Not only did Sebastian have to charm a woman he wasn't allowed to be alone with until after they were married, he had to impress her relations as well.

Just then, he prayed for a beautiful, interesting, intelligent orphan to fall from the sky and into his lap. He'd marry her as soon as possible and have all this done with.

"Sebastian," Felix said, sounding serious. "Do you like Miss Harriett? Do you think she would make a good match for you?"

He glanced up, the mussed strands of his hair slipping through his fingers. "I cannot say after only a dance and a conversation, but I do know she was the only woman I spoke with last night who managed to stoke any interest. We *talked* about books and music and other things that had nothing to do with the weather or my good health. I would like to explore a further acquaintance with her."

With a resolute nod, Felix braced his hands on the table. "Then you must make an effort to charm the elder sister, as well. Miss Harriett will notice, and it will endear her to you. Miss Helena will change her opinion, and you wouldn't have to worry that she will interfere with your courtship. Simple as that."

None of it sounded simple to Sebastian. Figuring out mathematical equations was easy because arithmetic had simple rules one had to follow. Applying the practice of crop rotation was simple because of the sensible reasoning behind it. What Felix was talking about was so complicated, Sebastian nearly took a vow against marrying anyone, ever, then and there.

But he was bound to duty and the obligations of the earldom. He needed to find a woman he could tolerate to marry, and thus far, Harriett Montgomery fit his every desire. It would seem he had no choice but to play this insipid game in pursuit of his ends.

"All right," Sebastian said grudgingly. "Tell me—with clear, simple steps—how the devil I'm to accomplish such a feat?"

Leaning back in his chair, Felix smirked. "You will start where every prospective suitor begins, at the florist's shop."

HELENA ENTERED THE front door to the murmur of voices coming from the morning room. Pausing just over the threshold with her hands tangled in the ribbons of her bonnet, she cocked her head and listened. Mixed with the familiar tones of Harriett and Henry was the deep baritone of a third person. Furrowing her brow at the half-open door, she tried to place the voice. She had definitely heard it before.

"Parsons, is there a visitor?" she asked the butler, who accepted the bonnet and redingote she shed.

"Yes, Miss," the servant replied with raised eyebrows. "The calling card he presented marked him as the Earl of Stratford."

Helena's eyes widened as she held Parsons's gaze, and they seemed to share the same thought. The butler had been in service to the Montgomery family since Helena was in leading strings. He was well aware of their dire financial prospects but was one of the loyal few who remained out of affection. Like the rest of the household, Parsons understood that his future depended on Harriett's success this season.

"I see," Helena replied, darting another glance at the morning room door.

She had hoped that a single dance would be the only thing passing between the arrogant earl and her sister, but it seemed Helena wouldn't have her way. Harriett must have made quite an impression for the man to come calling the afternoon after their first meeting. On the way home from the ball, Helena inquired into Harriett and Stratford's conversation during their dance, to no avail. Harriett merely blushed and said that Stratford was charming and an interesting conversationalist, which Helena found difficult to believe.

Parsons cleared his throat, and Helena realized she had stood there silently woolgathering for an entire minute. "You might also be interested to know that several bouquets of flowers have arrived for Miss Harriett. They have all been placed in vases and arranged in the morning room."

This news was far more welcome than that of Stratford's presence in her house, causing her to smile. "Flowers?"

The butler's lips twitched in a small smile. "Dozens of bouquets, Miss. They have been arriving all day."

Relief slumped Helena's shoulders as she approached the morning room. Last night's robbery had resulted in a valuable cache of goods, and she expected to receive her share of the profits by the end of the week. If Helena were fortunate, she would only have to continue on like this for a few more months. Harriett's debut had obviously been a smashing success, and all there was left to do was allow her sister to come to know the eligible suitors and choose one.

By this time next year, all would be made right, and Helena could stop walking about feeling as if she carried the weight of the world on her back. Not that she begrudged her siblings their dependence on her. If she had made a match during her own disastrous seasons, perhaps they wouldn't be in such a position now. It might not be fair to think of the matter in such a way, but Helena couldn't help it. She had spent years watching her parents grow more and more disheartened by her failure, tension growing worse with each season that passed without an offer of marriage.

If helping Harriett succeed where she had failed would turn things around, Helena would gladly do whatever was necessary.

She paused in front of an antique, gilt mirror hanging just outside the morning room, checking her reflection before entering. The block-printed muslin walking dress she had donned for her afternoon walk wasn't her best, but at least it didn't show signs of age. Application of new lace along the bosom gave it new life, making it adequate enough for greeting an earl—even if she would rather place her foot in a bear trap.

The cloying aroma of various flowers was the first thing to assault Helena's senses as she pushed the door wide and strode in, followed by vibrant bursts of color filling her vision. Parsons hadn't exaggerated the number of bouquets Harriett received. They adorned every available surface—tables, the mantelpiece, and even a few windowsills. There were lilies and hothouse roses, tulips and crocus, and bundles of carnations. In the midst of all the flora sat Harriett, who wore a bright smile as she conversed with the man sharing the sofa with her. Under the watchful eye of Henry—who sipped tea from a quiet corner of the room—Stratford and her sister seemed to be engaged in quite a lively conversation.

Stratford looked even larger this morning—squeezed onto the delicate sofa with his long legs bent in a room crowded with flowers—than he had while standing in a spacious ballroom. His morning coat was dove gray, and combined with his stark white linen, it made his hair appear darker and called attention to a shadow of dark hair that had begun sprouting along his jaw. The man was ridiculously handsome, which only made Helena dislike him more.

Harriett and the earl fell silent upon noticing her presence in the room, both coming to their feet at once. Stratford gave another one of his stiff, formal bows, while Harriett crossed the room toward her, the slender volume of a poetry book clutched in one hand.

"Oh, Helena, I'm glad you're here!" Harriett said with a bright smile. She took hold of Helena's arm and began steering her toward the earl. "His lordship and I were just discussing poetry, and I think you will find that your views on the matter are similar to his."

The earl smiled, though it seemed forced, strained. "Good afternoon, Miss Montgomery. Your sister has expressed a deep love for the poetry of Lord Byron, which she was reading when I happened to arrive to pay my call. Unfortunately, I must confess to not being a great lover of poems in general. I was led to believe that you are of a similar mind."

Harriett urged Helena into the place on the sofa she had just occupied herself before taking her book to a matching Queen Anne chair. This left Stratford with nothing left to do but resume his seat—placing him directly next to Helena. Puzzled by her sister's actions, she looked to Harriett but found her fixing a bright smile on Stratford, who was watching Helena with an expectant look in her eyes.

Clearing her throat, she adjusted her position on the sofa. "Harriett knows how little I enjoy poetry, though I suppose it isn't very ladylike for me to admit it."

Harriett giggled. "You see, my lord? When you insisted you

must be the only person alive who didn't care for poetry, what did I say?"

"You told me that you knew one other person who felt the same way," Stratford replied with a shake of his head. "I would never have guessed that person would turn out to be your sister."

"And why is that?" Helena asked. She could hardly sit here frowning at the man when she'd been placed at the center of attention. It was a rare position to find herself in, and she wasn't entirely certain she liked it.

"Well, you're a woman," Stratford replied, shrugging as if that were explanation enough.

Helena rolled her eyes. "Of course. And as a woman, I am expected to swoon at the dramatic ramblings of flowery speech?"

Stratford's lips went tight at the corners, the motion so slight one had to be close to witness it. Because Helena was nearly pressed against him—heavens!—she noticed the sign of his displeasure. When had this sofa become so small? The man was taking up nearly half the space with his wide shoulders and Corinthian bulk, leaving Helena feeling rather twitchy. Her left foot bounced beneath the fall of her skirts with restless energy that seemed to have come over her out of nowhere.

"Forgive me," Stratford said, a thread of acerbity vibrating through each word. "I did not mean to offend. It's only that I've always been led to believe that ladies enjoy such sentimentality."

Helena repressed an annoyed sigh. The earl seemed sincere, even if his notion was misguided. He could hardly be blamed when most men shared his mindset.

"Poetry and sentiment are not mutually exclusive," she said. "Instead of wasting words comparing someone's eyes to lakes or jewels or the sky, one could simply be straightforward. I find such posturing disingenuous. Sentiment feels so much more genuine when expressed in simple, straightforward terms."

Harriett pressed a hand to her chest, her eyes going wide. "Why, my lord, did you not say almost those exact same words to me not a moment ago?"

Helena found Stratford watching her with a slack jaw, seeming momentarily stunned. "I…well, yes," he stammered with a shake of his head. "Well said, Miss Montgomery. I could not agree more."

"Helena much prefers philosophy over poetry, my lord," Harriett chimed in. "She has always been the smarter of our siblings."

"Honestly," Helena chided, her cheeks growing warm. "That isn't true at all. We each have our strengths. Harriett has a mind for math that I envy, my lord. It really is quite astounding."

She followed her effusive compliment with a pointed look in Harriett's direction. What was her sister doing, thrusting her into the center of this little meeting? The entire point was for the visiting suitor to come to know her better, not her spinster sister.

Stratford, however, took it all in stride. "While I did well enough in mathematics at university, I took a first in philosophy. I would rather read Locke than Byron any day."

"While Locke's *Two Treatises* are certainly illuminating reads, I much prefer the philosophy of Astell," Helena replied without thinking. "I find it shameful that her status as a woman hinders her work from being mentioned in the same breath as such men as Hobbes and Locke."

Stratford smiled again, only this time there was nothing stiff or strained about it. The expression was as startling as it was magnetic—wide and unrestrained and riveting. "Miss Astell was a brilliant mind, and I agree that she is unfairly overlooked. I am particularly fond of her philosophy on the reasoning power of the mind. Unlike Descartes, she was willing to accept and acknowledge that not all minds have the same abilities and that—"

"—God created the human mind with intrinsic differences," Helena finished, unable to contain the sudden excitement overtaking her. It was rare for her to be able to discuss philosophy with anyone, let alone find a common mind in regard to the works of Mary Astell. "Isn't it so interesting how she shows that relationships between human beings are only possible *because* of those differences? How boring would the world be if we were all created from the same blueprint!"

A heavy silence fell over the room as she and Stratford locked gazes, and Helena realized that the earl was no longer the only one smiling. Enthusiasm had her grinning like a fool.

"Indeed, Miss Montgomery," Stratford murmured, his smile fading away as his face took on a more serious expression. "Yet again, I cannot help but agree."

Helena pulled her lips closed and sat up straighter, hoping that the barest half-inch of additional space between them would diffuse the sudden unease. His presence had gone from being annoying to disconcerting—taking up too much space and making him impossible to ignore. Why had she allowed Harriett to draw her into this? Why hadn't she retreated to the corner with Henry to have a nice, quiet cup of tea? She suddenly felt like an intruder between the earl and her sister, taking up a share of the attention that didn't belong to her and distracting from the matter at hand.

Tearing her eyes away from Stratford, Helena shot to her feet and approached the nearest bouquet of flowers. "So many arrangements you've received today, Harriett," she said, feeling like a right idiot but desperately needing to change course. Perhaps if she pointed out how many other men had shown an interest in Harriett, the earl might be warded off. The man was all wrong for Harriett, and besides, Helena didn't think she could bear him as a brother-in-law. She couldn't control the tumultuous emotions his presence caused. Harriett should marry someone more jovial and light-hearted—someone more akin to her in personality. The earl was too serious, too old, and too...something. There were a number of adjectives floating in her head to describe Stratford, but she had the devil of a time choosing from among them.

"Not all of them are for me," Harriett said, drawing Helena out of her muddled reverie. "This one is for you!"

Helena nearly knocked over the vase of white and blue roses

she inspected when she whirled to find the bouquet her sister indicated. It sat on a console against the wall, the centerpiece among a cluster of other arrangements.

"For me?" she repeated, slowly making her way to the table and taking in the sight of the first gift of flowers she had ever received from anyone. No one ever sent bouquets for Helena. She had never made enough of an impression to garner flowers.

The bouquet in question was a simple cluster of golden daffodils, purple crocuses, and sprays of pure white daphnes. They weren't as spectacular or expensive as the roses and lilies littering the room, but Helena liked them all the more because of that. She preferred flowers that could be picked in open fields over those grown in hothouses. They felt more real to her—more earthy.

"They're from Stratford," Harriett called out, barely contained glee in her voice. "Aren't they lovely? He brought the arrangement of roses and tulips beside it for me."

Helena's hand froze in midair, just short of touching the delicate petals of a crocus blossom. Glancing over her shoulder, she found Stratford watching her. His face had become a blank slate once again—stern and unreadable. But there was a clear challenge in his eyes, pointed and direct. She had taken him to task for patronizing her, but he had not heeded her warning. Seeing Harriett sighing and smiling over the flowers was exactly what the earl's intentions had been. How better to gain Harriett's favor than by pretending to care about her wallflower of a sister?

"They are lovely," Helena said, her voice clipped. "Thank you, my lord."

Stratford's cheek twitched, his eyes narrowing slightly as he held her stare. She hoped he could hear every drop of disdain in her voice. She hoped he choked on it.

"It was my pleasure," he replied, better than Helena at smothering his annoyance under a polite veneer. "And now to the purpose of my visit. Miss Montgomery, I had hoped to invite you to join me for a ride in Hyde Park. With your brother or sister along as a chaperone, of course. The day is so fine, it would be a shame to waste it indoors."

Harriett's face lit up, and she set her book of poems aside. "That sounds lovely. Helena, would you like to accompany us?"

Helena's stomach quivered at the thought of being forced into close proximity with Stratford for an extended period of time. Sitting beside him on the sofa had been difficult enough. "I…I would, but…well, perhaps Henry would prefer—"

"Henry has plans and will be unavailable," their brother interjected, glancing up from the plate of biscuits he'd been silently devouring for the past five minutes. "Would you mind terribly, Helena?"

It would seem she had no other choice. Harriett was giving her that irresistible, pleading look—the one proved enough to make Helena willing to do anything. Her sister clearly liked Stratford, which meant Helena would be selfish to come between them. The season had only just begun, and the display of flowers indicated that other suitors would come to call. Stratford might be a front-runner now, but that was only because Harriett had yet to explore other options.

"Of course I'll accompany you," she relented.

"Perfect!" Harriett chirped, turning to rush from the room. "I just need a moment to fetch a hat and coat."

CHAPTER FOUR

"I FEAR I have offended you."

The words were out of Sebastian's mouth before he could stop them, but once spoken, they brought him a modicum of relief. Now that Harriett Montgomery had left the morning room, he was relatively alone with Helena—notwithstanding Henry, but Sebastian had murmured the words in low tones, and the young man was engrossed in his biscuits.

She had stood facing a window overlooking the street, presenting him her profile. Now, she whipped about to face him, a sudden change overtaking her. Before Sebastian had spoken, Helena had seemed softer, vulnerable. Upon meeting his gaze, she transformed into the prickly rosebush he'd first encountered last night. He could imagine a brick wall rising up between them out of thin air—invisible but still hard and impenetrable.

"Whatever gave you that idea?" she asked, hands folded neatly before her.

Sebastian rested a hand on the back of a nearby armchair. "Just a feeling. Oh, and the fact that you refused to dance with me last night, looked at the flowers I brought you as if they were weeds, and wouldn't be accompanying your sister and me on this drive if your brother had been available. I saw you dance with two men last night. I've never met a woman who didn't like flowers, and of the two of us, I assume my company is what you find odious rather than that of Miss Harriett. Thusly, I have deduced that you have taken offense to my interest in your sister. Does that about sum it up?"

She wrinkled her nose as if taking in a noxious odor, then let out a labored sigh. "You are mistaken. Harriett only met you last night. She hasn't known you long enough to form an opinion, and thus neither have I."

Sebastian's throat simmered with a low growl. He had been as cordial as possible and thought he'd done a damn fine job attempting to thaw her icy demeanor. She was being difficult on purpose.

"Then I suppose you intend to give all your sister's suitors the cold shoulder," he snapped. "At this rate, she'll end up—"

"An unwanted spinster like me?" she interjected, raising her chin. Her hands curled into fists, and a becoming pink flush colored her cheeks.

He was taken aback and struck dumb for two very different reasons. Firstly, her outburst had struck true, riddling him with guilt that she had verbalized what he'd nearly implied. Secondly—and most striking of all—Helena Montgomery was ravishing when she was angry. Her eyes simmered like hot coals, and her bosom heaved with every breath, calling his attention to what might be her most noticeable asset. How this woman had been relegated to the wallflower corner of the ballroom was beyond him.

"That isn't what I meant," he protested, albeit feebly.

"Isn't it?" she pressed, her voice remaining low, but her tone hardened with a steely edge. "Of course it would be *my* fault for Harriett not to secure a match when I was unable to make one of my own. I am certain you think you have me all figured out, which is why you've gone out of your way to court my favor as well as Harriett's, thinking that showering her unwanted, untouched, undesirable sister with flowers and attention will earn her favor. I can assure you, my lord, that I have no intention of interfering with Harriett's courtship of anyone, even if I do think you are a pompous, arrogant brute. The choice of whom to wed will be left entirely up to her, and what you may have perceived as meddling last night was my attempt at smoothing the way for a debutante at her first ball, who was clearly nervous at being introduced to such a person as yourself. There is no need for you to ask me to dance, or buy me flowers, or pretend as if you actually care about my good opinion."

In the time it took for Sebastian to recover from such a lambasting, she turned and strode toward the door. It didn't occur to him to wonder where she might be going, only to impede her escape because he would be damned if she had the final word.

She stiffened when he took hold of her arm, firmly but gently. But Sebastian felt the shiver that roiled through her, and the beat of her pulse where his thumb pressed against tendons and veins.

Helena parted her lips as if to deliver a set-down, but Sebastian took hold of years' worth of practice throwing his weight around as a peer of the realm.

"Miss Montgomery," he ground out between clenched teeth. "You seem to have made a lot of assumptions for someone whose acquaintance with me is no older than twelve hours. Perhaps I asked you to dance because I *like* dancing and had hoped for a partner. Maybe I purchased you flowers because I did not think it right or gentlemanly to purchase them for one lady of the house and not the other. And lastly, it might have escaped your notice that when courting a lady, a gentleman should show an interest in her family if he ever thinks to have a chance at becoming part of it. And at the risk of sounding like even more of a *pompous, arrogant brute*…if you have a propensity for treating every person of the male gender with such suspicion and disdain, it is no wonder you are unwed."

He had released her arm a few words into his tirade, and she backed away a few steps once he fell silent. Sebastian didn't think he would ever forget the look on her face at that moment— bewildered and shocked and furious all at once. She made a spectacular sight.

The flush in her cheeks deepened, and she took a deep breath as if to argue but was rendered silent at the sound of footsteps. Sebastian placed more distance between them with a swift step when Harriett appeared in the doorway.

"I'm ready!" she announced, her voice raised a bit too high in volume and pitch.

Sebastian forced a smile and gave Helena a wide birth, crossing toward Harriett. He felt as if he navigated a bog filled with sinkholes but managed to arrive unscathed.

His brother had been wrong about everything. Sebastian didn't need to flatter both Harriett and her sister into accepting him. He didn't need to give Helena Montgomery an iota of his attention.

He was in for one hell of a long season.

CHAPTER FIVE

WHEN SEBASTIAN ENTERED White's, he was confronted with the sound of excited voices and the flurry of men moving back and forth between tables. Dinners and drinks sat forgotten, and card games had been abandoned as copies of various newspapers were passed from hand to hand.

With a furrowed brow, he weaved his way toward his favorite table, finding one of his usual companions already occupying it. Derek Thorne was one of the few men he considered a true friend. They had connected at university when Sebastian had defended him against a group of young men who'd cornered him with their hands clenched. He had only succeeded in taking part of the beating upon his own person, yet from that day forward, he and Derek had been close. In the months following that first meeting amid flurries of kicks and punches, the two of them had exacted their revenge on their assailants, thereby cementing their status as men who were not to be trifled with.

Derek sprawled in a high-backed chair with one leg crossed over the other, a copy of the *Post* clutched in his hands. He was impeccably dressed, as always, the cut of his clothes and quality of his fabrics giving off the aura of a man swimming in wealth. The pristine white of his starched linen proved a sharp contrast to the mahogany brown of his skin and the black shade of close-cropped hair.

Unlike most of the other men crowding this club, Derek had

earned everything that was his by the sweat of his own brow. There had been no inheritance, and he would never hold a title. His father had been a merchant, whose success afforded him a spot in the finest schools in England. His mother came from landed gentry, giving him access to the lowest rungs of high society—though he stood much higher than others of his class and background.

"Has something happened?" Sebastian asked, taking the chair across from his friend.

Lowering the paper, Derek fixed dark brown eyes on Sebastian. They were often wary and closed-off, but when in the company of people he knew and trusted, they softened considerably.

"Apparently, there have been some rather distressing reports of highway robbery occurring on the roads leading out of London," he replied, offering Sebastian the paper. "Seven in all over the past few months."

Sebastian frowned. "That's hardly unusual. Highwaymen run rampant throughout England."

"That might be true," Derek said. "But a *group* of them working together? I daresay no one's ever heard of such a thing."

While Derek returned to the half-eaten dinner sat before him, Sebastian found the story that had sent the gentleman's club into chaos. He was taken aback at the accounts of robberies occurring in the middle of the night and the attacks carried out by a band of thieves. Even odder was the varying tales of just how many of these rogues took part in the scheme. One victim had reported only three, while others had mentioned as many as four or five. However many there were on any given night, they dressed in dark clothing, half-masks, and hooded cloaks to conceal their identities. Coachmen and the male occupants of carriages were subdued before the passengers were stripped of their money and possessions. Among the items reported stolen were gilt snuffboxes, jeweled rings and hair combs, pouches of coins and pound notes, pocket watches, and an array of other costly baubles.

It was, as Derek had mentioned, unheard of for highwaymen to work in groups. Highway robbery was a dangerous occupation, one fraught with the danger of death and capture, with the punishment being public hanging. Along with the perils came a great deal of notoriety. It wasn't uncommon to find illustrations and romanticized accounts of lone highwaymen in the papers, and executions were often attended by women weeping into their handkerchiefs and swooning. For as few as three or as many as five of the brigands to join ranks was certainly odd. Judging by the reactions of the men around him, it was also wildly entertaining.

"It's all anyone is talking about," Derek remarked once Sebastian had set the paper aside. "Everywhere I've gone today, people are speculating over why highway robbery seems to have become a group effort. Can you imagine if this becomes a trend? Traveling the roads after dark will become impossible."

Sebastian ticked his eyebrow upward and pursed his lips. "Not for me. My coachman is always armed, and when traveling at night, so am I."

Derek grinned, swirling a deep burgundy claret about his glass. "Good man. Here's hoping neither of us is ever so unfortunate to have to defend ourselves against these criminals."

He raised his glass, but Sebastian had not one of his own to return the gesture. This was quickly remedied when he waved down a passing attendant and requested a brandy.

"How goes the start of the season for you, Seb?" Derek asked.

Sebastian made a face. "Tedious. You are fortunate not to have to participate in it."

Coming from anyone else, that comment might have caused offense. Derek faced no end of scorn due to the "low" manner of his birth and the fact that his father had been of African descent. The clear stamp of his father's linage was written into the shade of his skin and the full, plush features of his face—something that some could overlook but that others took as a sign that he did not belong among them.

However, Derek might have clawed his way into high society

by expanding his late father's merchant enterprise into a grand, money-making empire, but he had no desire to cement his place there in the same manner as others in his position. It was fast coming quite the thing for gentlemen of means but no title to marry the daughters of peers, thereby ensuring that the next generation would enjoy the benefits and privileges that the world had to offer. But Sebastian knew very well that after the souring of a betrothal, Derek was opposed to the idea of marriage altogether—let alone taking someone's spoiled, debutante daughter to wife.

Derek issued an ungentlemanly snort. "You and I both. Is it really so awful? I spoke with Felix briefly at one of the hells last night, and he mentioned a young woman who seems to have snared your attention."

Sebastian had stopped talking at Derek's account of his brother visiting gaming hells. It was within those dens of iniquity that the previous earl had fallen into a pit of debauchery he'd never been able to crawl his way out of. The last thing he wanted was for Felix to follow in their father's footsteps.

"You saw Felix in a gaming hell? Which one? Was he still there when you left?"

Derek grimaced. "He's a young man, Seb. His behaviors are no different than other gentlemen of his age."

"Those other gentlemen didn't have our father as such a shining example," Sebastian spat, aware of how bitter he sounded. "If Felix falls into those same patterns—"

"You don't know that he will," Derek argued. "Your father made choices of his own and went about life relatively unchecked. Felix has you to guide him."

"Precisely. And I intend to discuss his gambling habits with him at the first opportunity."

Derek looked as if he wished to say more but swiftly changed the subject instead. "You aren't going to get out telling me about this lady you've begun courting, so you may as well tell me everything. What's her name? Is she pretty? Are you honestly thinking of marrying her?"

Sebastian was saved from having to give an immediate answer while his brandy was delivered. He took a slow sip and tried to determine where to begin. Should he tell Derek that he had met a perfectly lovely young woman—one who would make him a fine countess—but that he found it difficult to think of her or be in her company without the specter of Helena intruding? Should he mention that he'd stuck his foot in his mouth when speaking to her, not once, but twice?

"Her name is Harriett Montgomery," he began. "Do you know of her family?"

Derek furrowed his brow. "Montgomery...I knew of the father. He and his wife died together in a terrible carriage accident a couple of years ago. There wasn't much of an inheritance, and their son is little more than a boy. Two daughters, yes?"

"That's correct. It's the youngest who I've begun courting. Though, I cannot pretend not to have competition. She's shaping up to become this season's Incomparable. Every eligible man with a pulse has begun sniffing around her skirts."

"I see," Derek chuckled. "And is the lady worth the trouble? Last we spoke, you weren't too keen on this season's prospects."

Thinking back to their carriage ride through Hyde Park, Sebastian smiled. "She's not just pretty, she's witty and smart. A bit young, but not girlish."

The image of Helena seated across from them in the landau filled his mind, unbidden. She was just as witty as her sister, just as smart. And she was certainly not a little girl. Even the plain, unfashionable cut of her clothing couldn't hide the bountiful curves of her lush body. Sebastian was hard-pressed to forget the way that magnificent bosom had heaved with every enraged breath she took after the things he had said to her. That he found her so bloody appealing when she was angry only made him feel guiltier. The woman didn't even like him, and he doubted she would appreciate knowing he had ogled her breasts like an overeager boy.

"Competition is irrelevant when a man holds your rank," Derek said, shrugging one shoulder. "If you bide your time, the others will fall away in the face of your grand presence and fortune."

Sebastian wrinkled his nose at the thought. While he held out no hope for a love match, he had hoped to find a bride who might choose him for reasons other than his wealth and title. However, Derek made a good point. If a man had to compete for the attention of a woman, it helped to have an advantage. Thus far, Harriett Montgomery was the only woman he actually wanted to spend an extended length of time with. While he couldn't say he was yet enamored with her, Sebastian knew she was his best prospect. She was certainly more than he had hoped for at the onset of the season.

"Perhaps you are right, but it might be wise to explore other options, which is why I'm spending my evening at Almack's."

Derek looked as if he'd just been forced to swallow a cup of rancid milk. "Dear God. You must be truly desperate."

Sebastian snorted. "Hardly. Apparently, it's where all the unwed debutantes gather for inspection. I suppose it's as good a place as any to continue my search."

"I wish you well with it. I, for one, wouldn't be caught dead in such a place. Not that I'd have a need to attend the assemblies. I've decided that being wed to my work is the perfect situation for a man like me."

"Is that so?"

"Quite so."

Sebastian smirked and inclined his head toward the betting book—erected in its proper place for all members of the club to see and use. "Care to wager on it?"

Returning Sebastian's smile with a cocky tilt of his lips, Derek waved a dismissive hand. "It's your money to waste, my friend. When wild boars sprout wings and fly over London, I will settle down with a wife. Until then, I'm afraid your wager would be in vain."

Now caught up in the distraction of such a frivolous bet, Sebastian came to his feet and began sidling toward the betting book. Other members perked up to watch, none of them able to resist a spectacle or a bet.

"If you believe I stand no chance of winning, you will have no problem agreeing to a wager of...oh, let's say … three hundred pounds?"

Derek stood and followed him to the betting book, where a cluster of men had gathered around to watch. A quill was dipped into ink and promptly placed in Sebastian's hand.

"Three hundred pounds," Derek repeated.

"If you aren't married within the next year, I will gladly hand over every pence," Sebastian challenged. "If you lose, then on the day of your wedding, I expect to be chosen to stand up with you as your best man and receive my three hundred pounds in exchange."

"Done," Derek replied, arms crossed over his chest.

Low murmurs rippled throughout the club, and Sebastian found several smirking faces turned his way, many of them filled with doubts. Even those who didn't know Derek were aware of his status as a confirmed bachelor. However, what none of them knew—because they didn't know Derek the way Sebastian did—was that the man would eventually grow bored of an endless pursuit of wealth. Like Sebastian, Derek was loyal to his family first, though there wasn't much of it left. The need for more would overcome his past heartache, and the man's resistance to marriage would crumble once he encountered the right woman. Sebastian was more than confident that he would be the one to win this wager.

He signed his initials after writing out the terms of the bet, and Derek followed immediately after. With half the gentlemen crowding the club looking on, the two clasped hands.

"Best of luck with the wife hunt," Derek teased. "Do try not to shower your prospective bride with too many gifts. You will need the money to retain your honor once this bet has been won."

Releasing his hand, Sebastian returned toward their table, hurling his parting shot over one shoulder. "I think I'll spend it on the suit I will wear to your wedding instead."

"AND SO I told him, 'that's no more than you deserve after you glued my bottom to a chair and forced me to ruin it when standing up!'"

Sebastian pinched his lips to muffle the deep-throated chuckle that erupted from him as Harriett finished the most amusing story. He had sought her out once arriving at Almack's and now accompanied her through a quadrille. Whenever the figures brought them back to one another's sides, Harriett had been relating a childhood tale of a war of pranks that had broken out between herself and Henry.

He was reminded of Harriett's young age as she told him the stories, and that realization made him feel ancient. It wasn't only that he was eight years her senior, but that the experiences of his life made him *feel* old. However, he had laughed more in the past ten minutes than he had in ten months, and he would have Harriett to thank for that. She was bright and sunny, sweet and always smiling—his opposite in every way. He was positively charmed by her, making the chore of attending the assembly fade by comparison.

"That is positively diabolical," he replied, guiding her through a graceful turn. "But I agree with you, wholeheartedly. After what Henry did, he deserved for you to glue his head to his pillow. How did he get free?"

Sebastian had to wait for his answer as Harriett spun away from him to join hands with three other women and skip in a circle. He waited his turn to execute the next steps, watching heads turn, and eyes light up at Harriett's bright smile. She was the envy of the entire ballroom, and he wasn't arrogant enough to think that his attentions had anything to do with it. Talk might have begun circulating of their acquaintance, but Harriett had pushed herself to the forefront of the marriage race all on her own. She was fast becoming a favorite amongst the *ton*.

"Our nurse had to cut him free," Harriett replied with a breathless giggle once they were paired again. "The hair on the back of his head was shorter than that on the top for months. He looked like a cockatoo!"

They nearly tripped over their next step as they fell into each other, shoulders shaking with laughter. Sebastian corrected the misstep with a swift turn, hopefully disguising the faux pas from anyone watching. While it wasn't a secret that he was about the search for a wife, Sebastian would never want to smudge Harriett's reputation by seeming to become too familiar too soon. The ease with which they conversed was a happy whim of circumstance, but others might see it as a sign that something improper was going on.

"And where did your sister's loyalty lie during all this?" he asked. From the corner of his eye, he spotted the sister in question, standing within a group of ladies on the edge of the dance floor. "Did she involve herself in this little war?"

"Oh, God no. Helena was always so serious, even as a child. As our eldest sister, she was always pulling us apart and chiding us for our follies. Neither of us was ever brave enough to pull a prank on *her*."

Sebastian could well imagine it as he had stood on the other end of her chiding. He had never been forced to face a firing squad, but he imagined it felt a lot like being stared down by an irritated Helena Montgomery.

"That does not surprise me at all," he said aloud once the next change had passed and she came to him for another set of figures. "She strikes me as the motherly sort, especially when it comes to you."

Harriett's smile grew wistful, and he followed her gaze back to Helena—who was smiling at something one of her female companions had said. She had beautiful teeth—white and straight and sparkling in the candlelight. The expression of humor enlivened her entire face, transforming her into something soft and approachable.

"Helena is the best elder sister one could ask for," she said, voice filled with affection. "She is wise and steadfast and so selfless. I do not know how I would have survived our parents' death and the start of this season without her."

Harriett's eyes grew wide as she danced away from him, and she avoided his gaze until their hands were joined for the final promenade. "Oh, I do apologize. I don't suppose you wish to hear about such a thing during a dance. We're supposed to be enjoying ourselves."

"Not at all," he soothed with a soft smile. "You obviously think very highly of your sister."

Her sweet smile was back, and the moment of maudlin contemplation passed. "I admire her more than anyone else in the world."

"I don't think she likes me very much," he admitted. It wasn't the most polite thing to say, but the camaraderie that grew between them made it easy to forget such social niceties. "I'm certain that must be entirely my fault."

"Not at all," Harriett replied. "It isn't that she doesn't like you, my lord, only that it is difficult for her to like anyone until she's come to know them better. Helena can come across as aloof and icy, but that is only to those who do not take the time to discover what lies deeper. She is truly a warm and kind person and very accomplished. She plays the pianoforte better than anyone I've ever heard, and she's an excellent horsewoman, as well as a fabulous dancer."

The final steps of the dance brought an end to the music, so Sebastian laid her hand on his arm and slowly guided her back toward her sister. "I thought I asked you to call me Stratford," he chided. "And I will keep that in mind while trying to win over your sister. If we are to be friends, I could not stand for her to dislike me."

"And you will insist I call you Stratford," she teased, her elbow discreetly nudging his side. "Very well, I will, thank you. And I would like for you to call me Harriett, but I have a feeling you will not do it."

"It is difficult for a gentleman to let go of years' worth of training in such protocols. Propriety suggests that it is entirely too soon for me to call you by your Christian name where others might overhear. But, if ever I am able to speak it without drawing attention, I shall do so, and you will call me Sebastian."

"Agreed."

They were waylaid by a young gentleman with heavily pomaded hair and bristling side-whiskers, who begged the pleasure of taking a turn about the room with her. Harriett accepted the invitation but turned back to Sebastian before allowing herself to be led away.

"Helena's favor might not come easy, but it is worth the effort," she murmured. "I hope you aren't the sort to give up easily."

"Never," he quipped, giving her a bow before she wandered off with her other suitor.

He found his gaze drawn back to Helena as if controlled by some unseen force. She was still standing where he'd seen her last, though she seemed distracted despite the conversation taking place around her. Harriett's words lingered in his mind as he observed Helena. She was like a fortress, completely unreadable and closed off from this distance. However, as he made his way toward her, Sebastian began to notice the small details he had previously overlooked.

The tension in her jaw and the tiny lines between her eyebrows, which were pressed together as she watched Harriett promenade about the room with the blond suitor. The way her lips softened with just the hint of a smile at the evidence that her sister was having a good time. The way she seemed to fold in on herself when in public, somehow making herself nearly invisible.

Had Sebastian not been seeking her, his eyes might have passed her over entirely. Not because she was plain or unremarkable, but because she seemed to go out of her way to pass herself off as both those things.

Their eyes locked when he drew closer, close enough to see the way her widening pupils darkened her eyes to a riveting shade of cognac. Her expression remained neutral, but her eyes darted away from him once he paused before her, his body dipping in a bow.

"Good evening, Miss Montgomery," he murmured.

"My lord," she replied with a curtsy.

"I would be honored if you would call me Stratford," he corrected, tilting his head to try to catch her wandering gaze. Unlike their last encounter, when her eyes had burned straight through him, she seemed unable to look at him. "I would also be honored if you would allow me to partner you for the next dance. A waltz, I think."

Sure enough, the beginning swells of a romantic melody filled the air, and the energy in the room eased into a languid calm. There were few debutantes here old enough to be permitted to waltz, and while Sebastian only ever danced out of necessity, he found himself wanting this particular dance with this particular woman. Perhaps because he had unwittingly insulted her on the night they'd met or because he'd added insult to injury the afternoon of his visit. Or, perhaps it was the fact that this was the second time he'd attended a function and witnessed her being passed over as a dance partner by the majority of the men.

Whatever it was, Sebastian boldly offered his hand as if expecting her to take it. Helena might have interpreted such a move as arrogant, but she didn't say so as she lifted her eyes and placed her palm against his.

"I would like that, thank you…Stratford."

The heaviness in the pit of his stomach lessened as they

walked toward the dance floor, where other couples were already swept up in the lilting steps of the waltz. Sebastian held his breath as they moved into the proper position—his hand clutching one of hers and his other braced between her shoulder blades. Because of her buxom figure, there was little if any space between their bodies, and the inches of height between them allowed Sebastian the most spectacular view. From here, he could see how smooth her skin was and how the golden strands of her hair were shown to their advantage beneath the lighting of crystal chandeliers. He could see the swell of her cleavage against a cream-colored gown and the graceful arches of her collarbone below the stretch of her lovely neck.

Sebastian let his breath out on a low sigh as they began to move, her skirts brushing his legs and her bosom skimming his lower chest with every step. Helena was boldly returning his stare, though her lips were slightly parted and her eyes unfocused. She was soft in his hold and smelled like a bed of spring flowers. He needed to speak, to dispel this tension between them that had been made worse by such close proximity. Sebastian felt his body beginning to stir in response to her nearness and the perfume that made him want to lower his head into the crook of her neck.

Clearing his throat, he spat out the first words he could conjure. "I must apologize—"

"I'm sorry," she blurted at the exact same time, then pressed her mouth shut as she realized what Sebastian had just said.

They fell silent for a few seconds, their eyes fixed on one another now that the ice had been cracked between them. It wasn't enough. Sebastian was determined to change her opinion of him, even though he had previously told himself he didn't care. Because the truth was, he *did* care—enough that having her think him a complete cad was completely inconceivable.

"You first," he said.

She pursed her lips, and Sebastian was struck with the realization that it wasn't rouge that made them appear so pink. The color was completely natural and undeniably alluring. "In matters of apologies, I think the concept of 'ladies first' is to be forgone. I will allow *you* to speak first, Stratford."

For the umpteenth time tonight, Sebastian barked a laugh, surprising both Helena and himself. There must be something special about the Montgomery sisters, as he always found himself either smiling like a fool, laughing until his belly ached, or feeling as if his head might explode when in their company. That last feeling applied only to Helena, but it was just as potent as the comfort and camaraderie Harriett made him feel, if not more so.

"I understand if you do not wish to forgive me for the horrid things I said to you when last we met, but I cannot allow my apology to go unsaid or unheard. It was ungentlemanly of me, and as hard as it might be for you to believe, completely out of character for me. I sincerely apologize for the offense I have caused you."

Her eyes glittered with humor as he twirled her across the marble floors. "Which offense would that be?"

"All of them," he answered quickly. "And might I also apologize in advance for any other egregious faux pas I might commit. I wish I could promise not to slip my own foot into my mouth again, but I dare not, for the risk of disappointing you."

Her lips quivered with a smile, one she was clearly trying to fight. She truly was lovely, even if she couldn't be called a beauty by conventional standards. The longer Sebastian spent closely studying the parameters of convention, the more annoying and irrelevant they became. Helena was easily lovelier than many of the debutantes receiving the most attention this season. Convention be damned.

"I am the one who should apologize," Helena replied, suddenly serious. "I was rude and confrontational, and as you, I acted almost entirely out of character."

"Almost?" he prodded.

One of her shoulders rolled in a shrug, calling attention to the gold trim along her bodice and the plump flesh it cradled. It took every ounce of his will to keep from staring.

"I will never apologize for being protective of my sister," she stated. "The death of our parents made me responsible for her, but in a way, I've always felt a duty to see to her happiness."

"She is grateful for your efforts. When we danced, she could not praise you enough. Your sister thinks very highly of you, and I think it is well-deserved."

She inclined her head graciously, her lashes lowering as if she didn't know how to accept such a compliment other than a nearly whispered, "thank you."

"But what of you?"

She frowned. "What about me?"

Sebastian lifted her hand and used the momentum of their steps to lead her through a turn. She went up onto her toes, skirts flaring about her, then surrendered to the pull of his arm as he drew her back into his hold.

"Your devotion to your sister is admirable, but what do you want out of life? I'm an elder sibling, too, you know. My mother is still living, but as the head of the family, it has become my duty to care for her as well as my brother. But the day will come when Mother leaves this world, and Felix grows into a man who no longer needs my guidance. At that time, I would hope to have a life of my own, something to apply my energies toward."

"That is a highly personal question, Stratford."

Sebastian grinned. "It is, but I have decided that we are friends."

"*You* have decided?"

"Yes," he insisted. "After all, we have already had our first row and traded insults. In this situation, between men, we would be considered friends."

"But I am not a man."

"Ah, but I think you would agree with Francois Poullain de la Barre, who wrote that men and women have equal intellectual capacities and argued that women ought to be afforded the same rights and opportunities as men."

"But, of course," she replied, a lightness creeping into her tone. Her face had lost all of its severity, and her body relaxed in his arms.

"Very well, then we are friends, and I must beg your indulgence. I asked because I am genuinely curious."

Her lower lip disappeared between her teeth and then reappeared. Sebastian's gut clenched in reaction, and he tightened the grasp of the hand at her back. Helena sucked in a swift breath but didn't protest.

"I suppose I haven't thought of it. At least, not for a very long time. Once a woman reaches my age and remains unmarried, there are few options left to her. You mentioned wanting something of your own on which to expend your energies. As a man, you have a world of opportunity before you, and as a peer, your position affords you even more such chances. Once the option of marriage has eluded a woman, she must find some other way to be of use to those around her for the risk of becoming a burden. For me, that means supporting my brother and sister in whatever way I can. Henry has nearly reached the age of his majority, but Harriett still relies on me, as she might have our mother were she still living. The task of guiding a young lady through her first season is a most serious one, as it can set the tone for her entire future."

"If you care to hear my opinion, you've done exceptionally well. Her season is off to a good start."

Helena craned her neck this way and that, as if searching for her sister. Sebastian spotted Henry in the crowd seconds before Helena did, noticing that he remained near while Harriett talked with a group of young people near the lemonade table.

"I think so, too," Helena replied. "I was worried, but perhaps that was unwarranted. Just look at her, doing so well on her own. She hardly needs me at all."

Sebastian squeezed Helena's knuckles, drawing her gaze away from her sister and back to him. It was improper for them to stare at one another for so long during a waltz, but he couldn't seem to look away.

"She told me herself that she didn't think she could survive this without you," he murmured. "I'd say that sounds like a woman who very much needs her elder sister."

For the first time, Sebastian was privileged to have her smile bestowed upon him. He had witnessed it from a distance, had seen her direct it on someone else. None of it had prepared him for what he witnessed now—an unrestrained flash of teeth and parting of those rose-petal pink lips. Helena Montgomery was downright enchanting when she smiled.

"I suppose you are right. As for myself, seeing Harriett settled and happy will be more than enough."

Will it? The question echoed through Sebastian's mind, though he dared not voice it aloud. He had only just managed to tiptoe his way into her good graces. He wouldn't risk upsetting this new and fragile peace between them.

The dance ended far too quickly for his satisfaction. Why was it that the dullest dances at a ball took up what felt like hours, while the sensual and romantic waltz ended as quickly as it began. Maybe, Sebastian mused, it had something to do with the way one was affected by a waltz. He'd never understood why it was considered scandalous among elevated circles and only grudgingly accepted out of a desire to appear worldly and fashionable.

But now... He could understand why the youngest ladies of the *beau monde* were barred from participating. His heart galloped, and his pulse thumped hard in his throat. Every muscle in Sebastian's body had gone tense, including the organ between his legs. He tingled from head to toe, longing to take that soft, supple body back into his arms.

Bloody hell, he was losing his mind.

Regaining a tenuous hold on his senses, he led Helena from the dance floor, then lifted her hand to kiss her knuckles. "There, you see? Dancing with me wasn't such anathema after all."

Instead of walking away as he expected, she gave him a con-templative look. Something mysterious flashed in her irises for a breath of a moment, but before Sebastian could determine what that was all about, she was composed once more, eyes shuttered.

"It was lovely," she replied. Her voice was so low that Sebastian had to lean closer to hear her. "I love to dance. It's only…"

She bit her lip again, just as she had on the dance floor. Sebastian suspected Helena didn't realize she did this right before divulging something about herself—something personal he doubted she might share with many others.

"Only what?" he pressed, leaning in and finding that he truly wanted to hear the rest of what she had to say.

She sighed, and her shoulders sagged. "No one who asks me to dance ever actually wants to dance with *me*."

At his bewildered look, she gave a shake of her head and let out a rough snort.

"I have the honor of being friends with some truly exceptional women, and I am not the only one who notices it. In their quest to earn the attention of my sister or my friends, gentlemen often see me as a means to an end. I am only ever asked to dance in an attempt to impress other, more desirable ladies. Harriett has barely been out for a fortnight, and already I've noticed an increase in the number of men who have asked me to dance, and they are nearly three times as many as usual. Every one of them has angled for an introduction to Harriett either immediately after or within the same breath as their invitations to me. So, you see, while I love to dance, I do not indulge very often in public because I do not relish being used. I might not be a diamond of the first water, but I deserve better than that all the same."

Sebastian wrestled with a plethora of reactions to the revelations Helena had just made. He was insulted on her behalf and annoyed with the men of his world for their treatment of her. At the same time, he couldn't deny the guilt it brought him to realize that he was guilty of overlooking women just like her. How many wallflowers had he walked past when first spotting Harriett from across that ballroom? How many languishing spinsters had he inadvertently wounded by failing to pay attention, notice their presence, and concern himself with whether anyone had asked them to dance or brought them a glass of champagne? In that moment, he felt like every inch the arrogant, pompous brute Helena had accused him of being.

There was nothing he could say to soothe the hurts of the past, nor would an apology toward her for his slights against several faceless women be enough. It wouldn't solve anything, and it wouldn't come out of his mouth in a way that conveyed the depth of his feelings on the matter. So, he simply reached for the first words that came to his mind before parting ways with Helena.

"You're right. You do deserve better," he said. "But not just from others, from yourself as well. Miss Montgomery, your first mistake was in thinking yourself anything less than exceptional."

"Helena, are you all right?"

Glancing up from the cup of tepid tea cradled in her hands, Helena found Effie giving her a concerned glance from across the bed where her young son lay resting. Crispin's complexion was sallow and pale, and a sheen of sweat dampened his brow and made tendrils of dark sable hair cling to his temples. However, Effie had reported that her son's fever had finally abated this morning. Effie's concern was now focused on Helena, her eyebrows knit and her pale blue eyes probing.

Helena cleared her throat and sat up straight, setting her tea on the bedside table. "Perfectly well. Why do you ask?"

Effie smiled, and it brightened her face, drawing attention away from the dark smudges of exhaustion beneath her eyes. "Only because I've been talking to you for the past three minutes, and I don't think you've heard a word I have said. You look as if you're a hundred miles away."

She might as well have been, as Helena couldn't recall the

topic of their conversation. "I'm sorry, Effie," she murmured, pressing two fingertips against her aching temple. "I suppose I've been a bit distracted lately."

Effie gave her a sympathetic look while lifting a cloth from a bowl of water and ringing it out before laying it over Crispin's brow. "It's quite all right. I know you have been under a tremendous strain lately."

That was putting it mildly, though Effie was referring to her money troubles and Harriett's season. While those issues were still as pressing as ever, Helena found herself ruminating over another problem altogether—that of Lord Sebastian Radcliffe, Earl of Stratford.

She had remained frustratingly aware of him no matter what she did, which only made Helena annoyed with herself.

Why should she give him a second thought? She ought to expend her energies observing other suitable gentlemen for Harriett. After Stratford's visit, Harriett had received half a dozen other callers and another string of bouquets. Invitations to various events had begun arriving in droves, and Harriett seemed to be enjoying all the attention. Truly, there was nothing for Helena to worry over. Harriett hadn't yet indicated that she favored Stratford over any of the others. They weren't officially attached in any way.

Helena realized too late that the snort she'd only intended to echo through her mind had slipped free, alerting Effie. She glanced up from her task of bathing Crispin's face and raised her eyebrows.

"Is it something you want to talk about?" Effie prodded. "Are things not going well with Harriett?"

Helena hesitated only a moment before caving in. Of all her friends, Euphemia Green was the most levelheaded and the most experienced. Despite being only twenty-five years of age, she had already married, become a mother, and then a widow, all within the span of a few years. Helena often thought Effie was too serious for someone so young, but life had made such staunchness a necessity.

With the loss of Stephen Green to pneumonia, Effie and Crispin had also lost their means of maintaining a comfortable life. His work as a tutor for the children of titled lords had given them a home in a nice neighborhood and enough income to keep the family in warm clothes and adequately fed. With his loss, Effie had been forced to take work as a seamstress—which did not pay nearly as well as her husband's profession had. Along with a son to care for, Effie also sheltered a spinster aunt who helped look after Crispin while she worked in exchange for a place to live and companionship.

In her friend's eager eyes, Helena found Effie's need to escape her own problems for a time. If nothing else, Helena could offer a brief moment of distraction.

"One of Harriett's suitors," Helena admitted. "Harriett thinks him charming and handsome. I think him ill-suited for her. He's an infuriating sort of person." How could she openly admit how well they had got on together? There were moments of clarity between them, when they could have been friends, and then times she wanted to call him a brute.

Effie's lips twitched with amusement. "I notice you did disagree with Harriett's characterization of him as charming and *handsome*."

"Well, I do still have eyes," Helena said grudgingly. "The Earl of Stratford isn't exactly hard to look at."

"It is only his personality you find odious. And I suppose he is a dullard to boot."

Helena bit her lip, finding it difficult to besmirch the earl when Effie put it that way. "He isn't exactly dimwitted. He took a first at university in philosophy."

"Your favorite subject," Effie murmured. Her tone was light and unassuming, but Helena stiffened in the face of that fact.

"He might be intelligent, but he is a gentleman in name only. The night of Harriett's ball, he took her onto the dance floor, then returned immediately afterward to ask *me* to dance."

Effie went still in the midst of tidying up—one of Crispin's nightshirts hanging from one hand and a pair of little stockings in the other. "The horror," she muttered sarcastically. "How dare he?"

"Effie—"

"If you say he's an ogre, I believe you," Effie soothed. "Now, I might not have as much experience with high society as you, and I have never attended an actual ball, but I've been led to believe that dancing is rather the point."

Helena wrinkled her nose. "No one ever asks me to dance without ulterior motives."

Effie added Crispin's discarded nightclothes to a basket and then perched on the edge of the bed. "What do you mean?"

Helena squirmed in her seat, suddenly discomfited. What they were about to discuss was a simple fact of her life—one she had learned to accept years ago. Still, it didn't feel good to go poking about at the hurts of her past.

"Do you know what it's like to be friends with Cecelia or to have a sister who looks like Harriett?" When Effie didn't respond, Helena pressed on. "I've attended ball after ball, dinner party after dinner party, and it's always been the same. I'm invisible until I am seen standing next to someone who draws notice. No gentleman ever engages me in conversation or asks me to dance unless he sees a way to the woman he really wants through me. I might be a spinster, and I might not be very popular amongst the *ton*, but I don't believe that means I deserve to be used."

"Of course not," Effie replied, taking Helena's hand and giving it a gentle squeeze. "And anyone who thinks that doesn't deserve your good favor. But…"

Helena heaved a sigh. "Effie…"

Her friend held up defensive hands. "Hear me out, Helena. I understand that the man asked Harriett first, but that doesn't mean anything. A bachelor attending such events to find a wife *should* converse and dance with multiple ladies. Perhaps the earl asked you to dance because he actually wanted to dance with *you."*

"And the flowers he gave me on the day he called upon Harriett?"

Helena didn't add that she had separated her bouquet from the dozens clogging the morning room. Having never received flowers before, she couldn't deny the urge to have them nearby so she could admire the arrangement and the sweet perfume of the blossoms—no matter who had given them to her.

"It sounds like a perfectly nice gesture," Effie said with a shrug.

Frustrated, Helena held up her hands. "Oh? And would you say it was *nice* of him to point out that my state of spinsterhood is my own fault?"

Effie scowled. "He said that?"

"He didn't say that precisely. But he implied it. Of course, this was after I told him that Harriett's choice of groom wouldn't depend upon him securing my good opinion, so he might as well not even bother."

"Oh, heavens!" Effie exclaimed before clapping a hand over her mouth to stifle a giggle. "I'm sorry. I don't mean to laugh, it's just, this man sounds absolutely riveting!"

Helena folded her arms over her chest. "I'm glad you find my discomfort so amusing."

Taking a deep breath, Effie went still, and her face became serious. "Forgive me. I only meant that it sounds as if you and this earl are a lot alike. You have always been one to speak your mind freely, and it seems he is of a similar set."

Helena bristled at the insinuation but didn't voice her denial aloud. Effie went to the teapot resting on a tray at the foot of the bed and poured herself a cup before refreshing Helena's.

"Helena, I understand that others have treated you abominably, and you have every right to be protective of both yourself and your sister. However, I cannot help but think you haven't given this gentleman much of a chance."

Effie was right, and Helena felt even more wretched being

confronted with the truth. While Stratford's words had certainly hurt, she had drawn first blood. As well, she could admit to having arrived to a snap judgment.

"I don't mean to be this way," she whispered, staring down at her hands. "It's just that I know the people of this world, Effie. I've stood on the fringes of it my entire life. My parents didn't hold the loftiest titles, and we weren't the wealthiest among our peers. Because of that, I have learned what to expect from the people I rub elbows with daily."

Offering the bowl of sugar cubes, Effie gave Helena a sympathetic look. "Yes, but at times we must learn to change our expectations, mustn't we? Perhaps the earl isn't as bad as you suppose."

"Perhaps," Helena allowed. "Still, I don't think he's quite right for Harriett. He's significantly older than her, for one thing. For another, he's entirely too brooding, serious. Harriett is young and has such a sunny personality. She should be with someone with a similar temperament. Like you and Stephen. The two of you seemed made for each other."

Effie's eyes darkened with wistful sadness as she gazed at the small, framed portrait of her late husband hanging from a nearby wall. Stephen Green had been plain in looks, but the painter had captured the twinkle in his eyes hinting at a good sense of humor. He had been the quiet, studious sort but often quipped witty jokes to those closest to him when others weren't listening. It had always warmed Helena's heart to see him and Effie leaning into one another to share a private joke. It was something she had wanted for herself, but Helena had now set her sights on such a future for Harriett. She certainly couldn't have such a life with a man as rigid as Stratford.

"Perhaps some people are more suited to one another than others," Effie replied. "But the courtship is the easiest part. It is only after marriage that the real trials begin, and even people as compatible as Stephen and I fail to see eye to eye now and then."

Helena returned Effie's soft smile. "How have you come to

be so wise?"

Lifting the pair of spectacles hanging about her neck, Effie slipped them on. "The glasses have a bit to do with it. The rest is simple experience, my friend."

Helena stood and pulled Effie into an embrace. "You're a gem, and I am fortunate to have you as a friend."

When Helena moved to separate from her, Effie only clung tighter, her slender arms constricting around Helena's shoulders. "I am the one who is fortunate to have such wonderful friends. I appreciate you all so much."

"Well, it seems I have arrived just in time. Is there room for one more?"

Still holding on to one another, Helena and Effie turned to face the doorway—where Mina stood beaming at them.

"Mina!" Effie exclaimed, separating from Helena and rounding the bed. "What are you doing here? I thought you would have returned to Kent by now."

The skirts of a pink and white muslin walking dressed swished about Mina's long legs as she approached, holding up two heavy-looking purses. "Mother and I decided to remain for a few days. Besides, I wanted to see the look on your face when you caught sight of this."

With a wide grin and a dramatic flair, Mina loosened the mouth of one of the purses and upended it on the bed at Crispin's feet. Effie muffled a gasp behind one hand, her eyes flaring wide as she took in the pile of gleaming coins and pound notes that spilled onto the counterpane.

Swinging the second purse by its drawstring, Mina then turned to Helena. "And I had planned to stop in to visit you after I left Effie, but here you are."

Helena marveled at the weight of the sack in her hands, her eyes stinging with tears as she realized it was more than enough to pay her staff, purchase Harriett a few new dresses, and perhaps have something other than roast chicken for dinner.

Effie sobbed and laughed at the same time while picking up

each coin and counting under her breath. "There's so much here. I hardly feel right taking a share when I wasn't with you all to earn it."

Mina gathered up a handful of the pound notes and pressed them into Effie's already overflowing hands. Her expression was fierce with devotion and conviction. "You will accept every pence. Staying at home to care for your ailing son doesn't negate the agreement we made as a group. I know how much this is needed."

Effie sniffled, coins falling back onto the bed as she used the back of one hand to mop at her damp eyes. "I've patched Crispin's good trousers so many times they're falling apart, and he needs new shoes. He's growing like a weed, you know. Oh, and Aunt Agnes is nearly out of the liniment for her joints, and—"

"And," Mina interjected, gathering Effie's hands and the crumpled pounds into her grasp. "I hope that you will allow yourself a treat, Effie. You take such good care of your family, and you are always here when we need you. Do something nice for yourself for once."

"I agree," Helena chimed in, leaving her unopened purse on her abandoned chair. "You deserve to have something for yourself."

Effie began placing her earnings back into the purse. "Oh, I suppose I might purchase some new fabric or some ribbon or such. It has been easier to maintain my own clothes than it has Crispin's. But really, I don't need new things to make me happy. Knowing Agnes and Crispin are cared for is enough."

Mina and Helena traded silent glances that spoke volumes. Effie's most endearing quality was the concern and care she showed for others. However, it was also her most debilitating flaw. She spent so much time tending to the people she loved that she often forgot to take time of herself.

Effie finished collecting her earnings and tucked the purse into the pocket of her gown. "Mina, will you have tea? Helena and I have finished a pot between us already, but I had planned to make another."

Mina removed her hat with a sigh, finding a place to sit on the cushioned bench at the foot of the bed. "Tea would be lovely, thank you. And while I'm here, we must talk. I have already reported the news to Selina and Cecelia, so I'm glad I found the two of you together."

Sensing the dire note in Mina's tone, Helena sat, pushing her purse onto the bedside table and folding her hands. Mina was—by nature—a very serious and severe sort of person. Such a personality had been cultivated out of necessity. Being the illegitimate daughter of a duke came with its share of notoriety and scorn, and most women would wither away from the shame of it. But Mina was made of sterner stuff, meeting the world with her head held high and her eyes flashing defiance. Anyone who knew her was used to the hardened veneer that concealed a vulnerable nature. Just now, though, Mina looked more stoic than usual. Something was wrong.

"Has something happened?" Helena asked.

Effie stood with the teapot in hand, reluctant to leave the room just yet. "Mina?"

Their friend took a deep breath, then reached into the reticule hanging from her wrist. Uncurling a wrinkled slip of paper, she held it up for their inspection.

"Ladies, we've made the papers."

CHAPTER SIX

A FEW NIGHTS after attending Almack's with her siblings, Helena visited the suite of rooms Mina and her mother had occupied during their stay in London. The accommodations were sparse, but the suite was clean and warm, and a light nuncheon had been served at Mina's request. She had sent for Helena, along with the other three members of their circle, to discuss the circulating stories of their nighttime escapades.

They assembled in Mina's room, closed off from the separate chamber where her mother took an afternoon nap. Conversation had been stilted as they helped themselves to tea and finger sandwiches, the true nature of their meeting creating palpable tension. For her part, Helena's mind was occupied with other matters, the most pertinent of which concerned the Earl of Stratford. The man was as puzzling as he was infuriating, as alluring as he was obnoxious. Only, the more she tried to lean on the most unflattering of those terms in her thoughts of him, the harder it became to maintain her dislike of the man.

It had been easier to think of him as a being like all the other men who had used her as a path toward the women they really wanted. However, he had spent what was left of the evening at Almack's tearing down every one of her preconceived notions. He hadn't even had to return to her company to do it. Helena had spent more time on the dance floor than she had at any ball or assembly, and she imagined it had much to do with being singled out by one of London's most coveted eligible bachelors.

Helena wasn't the only woman who had benefited from such regard. Following his waltz with her, Stratford had spent the rest of the evening partnering various ladies on the dance floor. Every one of them had been plucked from the fringes of the assembly room—the shy spinsters, the unwanted wallflowers, and the forgotten widows. He moved about the room like a man on a mission, being introduced to this woman or that, then shocking them into wide-eyed expressions of awe and infatuation with nothing more than a few words and the offer of a gloved hand.

Tuesday evening had been a night for the discarded ladies of the *ton*, and Helena hadn't been the only one to receive multiple requests for a dance following Stratford. The ballroom had been ablaze with questions of what made the recipients of the earl's regard so special, and it seemed every eligible gentleman had been determined to find out for himself.

How could she go on hating a man who, when hearing of the plight of Helena and others like her, not only showed compassion and care but actively made an effort to do more than offer empty platitudes? Whether because he had been convicted by her words, or because dancing with ladies he had not yet been introduced to offered relief from the tedium, Stratford had brought hope to those who had likely lost hold of it long ago. The night would be memorable for them all, Helena especially.

"Now then," Mina said, the clink of her cup in the saucer jolting Helena back to the present. The world of white columns, marble floors, and the intriguing hazel eyes of a certain gentleman faded in the face of Mina's regimented determination. "We must discuss the reports in the papers and the resulting gossip. I hope it hasn't been enough to frighten any of you into backing out. The stories are mostly inaccurate and vary so much from person to person that I assert we haven't much to worry over."

Cecelia lifted one of the papers from the haphazard pile littering the space between the teapot and various platters. "I find it all highly amusing. They've taken to calling us the Band of Brigands.

Has a nice ring to it, if you ask me."

"I'm certain it will still be just as amusing while we're dancing at the end of a set of nooses," Selina grumbled with a shake of her head. "We shall go down in history as the first women to be hanged for highway robbery."

"I would rather hang than see Crispin starve," Effie argued. "I agree with Mina. The reports aren't enough to concern me just yet."

"That's just the thing," Selina fired back. "*Yet*. How long before the stories begin revealing the truth—namely, that the Band of Brigands is comprised of five women?"

"Your questions have merit," Mina soothed. "But at the moment, I say it is best to make a few adjustments and carry on rather than retreat and hide. Having a fearsome reputation is a *good* thing. It means people will be less likely to try rebelling when they are forced to hand over their effects."

"Indeed," Cecelia chimed in, raising her teacup to her lips. "Selina, darling, I understand your worries, but we've come this far together. None of us is yet in a position to give up now. I am still saving every shilling I can spare toward the fund for my dowry. Without one ..."

She scowled down into her tea, her upper lip curling in revulsion. No one needed to hear her say aloud that her parents had become desperate enough to take any man who would offer for her. Heiresses were in high demand this season, which boded well for Cecelia for the time being. However, there were still unscrupulous men who desired a young and beautiful wife to flaunt on their arms, and they weren't above throwing their titles and money around to secure one. To be able to choose her own groom was one of the few freedoms women of their world were afforded, but even that much would be lost to Cecelia if she couldn't replace her lost dowry.

"This is the first time in weeks we have been able to afford meat at supper," Effie admitted, eyes lowered as if in shame. "Crispin was so happy, and now that he is recovered from his sickness, his appetite has returned. He ate every bite and asked for seconds."

Helena had remained silent thus far but spoke up now as she helped herself to a small sampling of the tiny lemon tartlets sitting on a platter before her. "I'm having some new gowns commissioned for Harriett and was finally able to pay our staff. I feared we would lose them all before that happened. I cannot pretend to be happy that we've made the papers, but that was the risk we took when agreeing to do this."

In the fleeting moment of silence that followed Helena's declaration, Selina lowered her head and burst into tears. Glossy locks of thick, black hair fell into her eyes, fighting the constriction of her hairpins. Her slender shoulders shook with sobs that broke Helena's heart.

As Selina pressed both hands over her face, Effie stood and leaned over the back of Selina's chair to embrace her. Cecelia fished in her reticule for a handkerchief, which she promptly placed into Selina's hand. Helena braced a supportive hand upon Selina's knee, years of caring for her siblings, bringing crooning words of comfort to her lips.

Mina went to her knees before Selina, trying to catch her gaze, both hands braced on the arms of the chair. "What's wrong, Selina? Has something happened?"

Sniffling into Cecelia's handkerchief, Selina lifted watery blue eyes and hiccuped around another sob. "Papa's condition is worsening. The physician predicts he may have only months left. And now, now a man has visited on multiple occasions, insisting on having an audience with Papa. He refuses to tell me what he wants, but talk among our neighbors has made its way to me. The man is a moneylender, one who is known for doing bodily harm to those who do not meet his demands. I do not know what to do!"

"Shh," Mina soothed, taking hold of one hand as Helena grasped the other. Selina clung tight to them both, tremors rocking her slight body and making her chin quiver. "It's going to be all right. When was the last time this man called upon you?"

"Three days ago," Selina replied. "He warned me that he wouldn't be put off much longer. He will have his audience with Papa, or there will be consequences. But how can I expose my father to that bounder without causing more injury to his poor heart? I fear he cannot take the strain."

"Have you written to Julian?" Helena asked. Julian Russell, Selina's elder brother, was currently on a campaign aboard a royal navy ship. The delivery of letters to seamen stopping in at various ports was irregular at best, but the occasional missive made its way to the correct recipient.

"I have," Selina said while dabbing at her leaking eyes. "There has been no word, and he isn't due to return for another five months, at least."

"We will think of something," Mina declared, those fierce eyes of hers flashing with defiance and conviction. "In the meantime, perhaps we ought to move you and Mr. Russell to new living quarters. The moneylender won't be thrown off the scent forever, but moving someplace new without disclosing where your lodgings are will buy you a few weeks, at least."

"She can stay with Crispin, Aunt Agnes, and me," Effie offered. "My aunt prefers to sleep in her favorite chair near the parlor hearth these days, so I am certain she will not mind if we use her chamber for Mr. Russell's comfort. You can share a bed with me."

Selina smiled through her tears, her cheeks blotchy and flushed. "You are the very best friends a woman could ask for. Thank you all."

"There is no need to thank us," Mina replied. "This is what friends are for. We stick together, and when one of us needs help, the rest do their part."

"So we are agreed, then?" Helena asked. "We act as one or not at all."

"Agreed," Mina said. She was echoed by the others, and they remained near Selina until she had calmed.

They had just begun steering the conversation toward arranging their next escapade when the door leading to the adjoining suite swung open to reveal Mina's mother. Abigail Barrington had become a withered, frail ghost of her former self over the past few years. The once vital spitfire of a woman suffered a debilitating illness of the mind that often made her forget what year it was or who the people around her were. Such a spell seemed to have fallen over her now as she clutched at the neckline of her dressing gown and stared warily at them, eyes darting from face to face.

"Who the devil are you?" she demanded, a quaver in her voice underlying the imperious tilt of her chin. "What are you doing in my house?"

Mina approached her mother, hands outstretched. "Mama, we aren't at home. Remember? We're in a hotel. I let these rooms for us."

Abigail recoiled from her daughter's touch as if avoiding the strike of a serpent. "London? I haven't been to London in ages, and I think I would remember arriving at a hotel. And why are you calling me Mama? I don't even know who you are?"

Horror made Helena's chest ache as she realized that Abigail didn't even recognize her own daughter. She couldn't imagine how much that must hurt Mina.

"Of course you know me," Mina replied, her voice steady and calm. "It's me, Mama, Wilhelmina, your daughter."

Abigail wrinkled her nose and looked Mina over from head to toe. "Is this supposed to be some kind of joke? My Mina is only a little girl, no more than five years old! I demand you tell me who you are and what I'm doing here this instant!"

Tense silence filled the room, and Helena traded concerned glances with Effie, Selina, and Cecelia. They had only ever heard Mina's descriptions of her mother's spells but had never witnessed the phenomenon in person.

Mina took it all in stride, executing a graceful curtsy and lowering her head. "I apologize, ma'am, for the tactlessness of my jest. I am Poppy, the new lady's maid His Grace hired for you."

Abigail inspected Mina with a critical eye. "You're rather finely dressed for a servant."

Amusement made the corner of Mina's mouth twitch, but she maintained her facade. "My mother always told me I should dress my best when I travel, ma'am."

"Hmm," Abigail murmured, narrowing her eyes. "Your mother sounds like a wise woman. Where is the duke? I certainly hope he doesn't intend to keep me waiting all day!"

For the first time, Helena witnessed the slightest fissure in Mina's composure. Her nostrils flared, and her lips compressed at the mention of her late father—who had kept Abigail as a mistress for years yet failed to provide for them in the event of his untimely death. It was *His Grace's* fault that Mina had to rob carriages by moonlight to keep her mother sheltered and cared for.

"He has sent word that his carriage will arrive for you at six in the evening," Mina said with a tight smile. "You asked me not to wake you because you wished to look your best for the opera tonight."

"Yes, yes, I remember," Abigail muttered, waving one bony hand through the air. "I suppose I ought to rest a while longer."

"That sounds like a fine idea, ma'am."

Once Abigail had retreated into her chamber, Mina shut the door behind her, then turned and leaned against it with a sigh. She stared up at the ceiling for a moment before squeezing her eyes shut in the expression of one carrying the weight of the world on her shoulders.

"Mina?" Helena ventured. "Are you all right?"

Mina's eyes snapped open, and she pushed away from the door, her features fixed into a mask of nonchalance and her eyes inscrutable. "Of course."

Four pairs of eyes bored into her as she resumed her place at the table, fiddling with the teapot and a cup that didn't need refilling.

"How often does it happen?" Effie asked, her voice low.

Mina shrugged one shoulder. "Oh, every now and then…but it isn't anything I cannot manage."

Despite the forced lightness of her tone, Helena couldn't shake off the mournful heaviness that had fallen over her. Her parents had been taken from her tragically and unexpectedly, and it had been the most devastating event of her life. However, she couldn't fathom what it might be like to watch one's parent waste away before their very eyes—slowly and painfully while being impotent to do anything about it.

Before anyone else could speak, Mina raised her chin. "Now then, let us return to our planning. The Band of Brigands has a reputation to uphold."

SEBASTIAN GLANCED UP from the book lying open in his lap. He had read and re-read the same page four times but hadn't truly absorbed a single word. He had opted to spend a quiet evening at home, and Felix had seemed content to follow suit. They had shared a companionable dinner with their mother and now occupied the drawing room at Stratford house.

The dowager countess had taken to playing the pianoforte their father had purchased as a gift for her fiftieth birthday. It was one of the few things she hadn't allowed him to sell to pay off his debts.

Felix sat in an armchair near the fire, pretending to read a treatise on government while oblivious to the fact that Sebastian had clearly seen him hide a copy of an erotic novel between the pages so their mother could not see.

There was no reason at all to break the silence, except for the fact that Sebastian had been wrestling with an idea in his mind all day. It wasn't in his nature to be indecisive, so struggling to make a decision made him annoyed with himself. There was only one remedy, and it was allowing his mother to take charge. Once he voiced his thoughts aloud, the decision would be taken out of his hands, and he could pretend to have never made a choice at all.

"I've been thinking," he murmured, thumbing to the next page of his book. "Perhaps we ought to host a dinner party."

Felix jerked his head up to give Sebastian a stunned look, and the naughty tome he'd been hiding within his treatise fell to the floor. The dowager was too distracted by Sebastian's announcement to notice, so Felix was able to snatch his contraband off the rug and hide it away without attracting attention to himself.

"Truly, Sebastian?" their mother asked, eyebrows raised. "You've never wished to host parties here before. In fact, you have always been adamantly *against* entertaining. What has brought on such a change?"

Felix cut in before Sebastian could answer. "Perhaps it has something to do with Miss Harriett Montgomery. She and Sebastian have caused quite a stir amongst the *ton*."

Sebastian glared at his brother, who returned his frigid stare with a boyish, mocking grin. The dowager, who rarely left the house these days due to arthritic joints, wasn't as ignorant to the goings-on of society as they might assume.

"I had heard the rumors but assumed they had been exaggerated," she said, her thin, wrinkled face lighting up with a bright smile. "Then it is true, you've begun seriously courting this young lady."

Sebastian fought not to squirm in his chair, wrestling with how to respond. Should he tell his mother that he had begun pursuing Harriett but now found his waking thoughts consumed by Helena? It was a hell of a conundrum for a man to find himself in. Sebastian could hardly make sense of it himself, let alone broach the subject with his family.

"Miss Montgomery and I have formed a connection of sorts, yes," he managed. "I think a dinner party would provide a good opportunity for more time spent in her company and for you to meet her, of course."

The dowager used her silver-handled walking stick to ease herself to her feet. Sebastian caught Felix's eye and shook his head, discouraging his brother from rising to help her move faster across the room. While very much aware of her age and limitations, the dowager couldn't abide pity and didn't care to be coddled. As long as she could stand on her own two feet, she wouldn't stand for her sons to make a fuss over her.

She pulled the bell cord to summon a servant, then sank into the nearest armchair rather than return to her previous seat. When the butler, Simmons, arrived in the entryway, the dowager set determined eyes on him.

"Simmons, we are to host a dinner party this coming Friday."

"Dear God," Felix groaned, pressing his thumb and forefinger to the bridge of his nose.

Sebastian didn't echo the sentiment aloud but felt his brother's exasperation. Leave it to their mother to act swiftly and efficiently with very little direction. Hosting the dinner this coming Friday only gave the staff three days to prepare.

Simmons took it all in stride, giving the dowager a placating smile. "Very good, my lady."

"I will want to send word to Lady Abbott that I simply *must* hire the talents of her chef for the evening. He is French, you know. When last I supped at her home, we enjoyed the most sumptuous *coq au vin*. The occasion is a special one—we are to be introduced to His Lordship's future bride."

"Mother," Sebastian cut in. "She is hardly that, not yet, anyway."

"She will be once you have asked her, for no woman would be mad enough to refuse you," she countered with a delicate sniff. "Simmons, I want the best china and silver prepared for the occasion and towering arrangements of whatever flowers are in season for the table. Oh, perhaps we ought to arrange entertainment for after the meal, a stringed quartet, perhaps?"

Simmons didn't bat an eyelash at the hurried string of directives, and Sebastian knew the man well enough to know he wouldn't forget a single detail. As his mother went on planning the affair, Sebastian's mind began to wander, caring little for the details. He only knew that he needed more time in Helena's company. He needed to discover if what had passed between them at Almack's had been a fleeting distraction or something worth exploring deeper.

Harriett Montgomery was the consummate debutante—beautiful, poised, and well-mannered. Helena, while not fitting to all the conventions dictated by society, was something else altogether. Something intriguing and beguiling. She had caught him quite off guard, upending his notions of just what it was he wanted in a wife.

For a man who didn't truly wish to marry, it had seemed enough to find someone he might be friends with—someone he could grow to like, for tolerance didn't seem quite enough to build a marriage on. Beauty and charm came secondary to someone who would take well to the duties of a countess and who would make a good mother to his future children.

But Helena, she challenged him; she infuriated him; she aroused parts of him other than his body. Oh, she most certainly appealed to him in a physical manner. Sebastian would be deluding himself by denying that his eye had been drawn, on several occasions, to the curves of her lush mouth and the swell of her magnificent bosom. The sway of hips that would overflow in his hands tempted Sebastian from beneath her swishing skirts.

There was more to what he felt than that, however, and it was that *something more* that made him want to get to know her. Her love of philosophy had engaged him. The sharpness of her tongue had annoyed at him first but now made him want to spar verbally with her. He could imagine spirited conversations with her over politics and books and art. She would never defer to him because he was a man or say what she thought he would want to hear. So many of the ladies of high society had been trained to do just that, and it was why he'd been so dashed disinterested in them all. While Harriett was certainly unique, Sebastian felt they had developed a cordial friendship rather than a romance. She was funny and sweet, and he enjoyed talking to her. If they married, he didn't think he would have any aversion to consummating the union and sharing a bed with her.

But Harriett didn't make him feel as if he'd been kicked in the gut at the mere sight of her. She didn't make him fantasize about silencing her sarcastic mouth with a searing kiss. Helena did all that, and then some. Sebastian would be a fool to ignore what his instincts were trying to tell him.

Helena Montgomery might possibly be the woman he was meant to marry.

He nearly laughed aloud at the realization. He had never been one for romanticism or flights of fancy. Because of the troubles his father had caused the family, Sebastian had lived a very sensible and pragmatic life. Logic guided his every action, and duty drove his ambitions.

These new emotions were completely foreign to him, leaving him no idea how to act on them. But then, he was getting ahead of himself. He had only just smoothed things over with Helena and was only fairly certain she didn't hate him completely. If he could coax her into actually liking him, well, it would be a start.

Felix appeared at his side, sinking onto the sofa. "By God, Seb, what have you done?"

Sebastian followed his brother's gaze to where the dowager sat, still giving very pointed orders to Simmons. A slight smile softened his lips at the sight of her, glowing with the thrill of doing what she loved best—planning an event to rival any other. "I've made her happy. We will indulge her and make certain she knows we appreciate her efforts."

"Very well," Felix sighed. "I suppose I cannot be too miffed with you. After all, if she busies herself playing matchmaker for you, she will be too busy to pester me to take a wife."

"I wouldn't grow too comfortable if I were you. Until I'm wed and have produced an heir and a spare, *you* are next in line for the earldom."

Felix made a great, dramatic show of snatching at his shirt collar and giving a noisy gulp. "God preserve me. Do you happen to know if there are any properties for let in Cornwall? Beautiful countryside, I've heard."

"You'd be bored to tears in Cornwall," Sebastian fired back. "Besides, I want you right here in London where I can keep an eye on you. Thorne tells me he happened upon you in a gaming hell recently."

Felix heaved a heavy breath, his body going stiff at Sebastian's side. "Don't lecture me, Seb."

"I will lecture you whenever I please, and you will listen. Our father—"

"Was his own man," Felix argued, his voice a low hiss to keep their mother from overhearing. "One who made his share of mistakes and allowed his passions to get the best of him. I'm not Father, and I hardly think his inclinations were genetic, otherwise, you would be as much a reprobate as he was."

Sebastian gritted his teeth, annoyed at Felix for arguing with him but also for making such a valid point. "I never meant to accuse you of following in his footsteps, but I hope you know what you are doing. I'm certain Father thought of his habits as nothing to worry over, just a few hands of cards, or a dalliance with one lady, or one drink too many. It wasn't until it was too late that he realized a few hands of cards had become a gambling problem, and that one dalliance had grown into a string of mistresses, and that one drink too many had led to him becoming a raving drunk."

Felix avoided his gaze, jaw flexing tight as he ground his teeth. "You must not think very highly of me if you think I would travel down the same path."

"No," Sebastian countered. "It's *because* I think so highly of you that I say these things. You're my brother, and there isn't much family left. I'd like us both to live long enough to marry and have children and grow the Radcliffe progeny and, you know, perhaps leave behind a legacy other than a widow and children who hate us."

"I suppose I understand. You have always led by example, though. So, I think I will enjoy the final follies of my youth while watching you trip over yourself trying to win Miss Montgomery. The day your heir is born is the day I begin to take my future seriously."

Sebastian chuckled, reaching for the decanter of port resting on the table before him. He poured a finger's worth each into two cut-crystal glasses and handed one to Felix. They indulged in a toast, the crystal clinking as their mother sent Simmons off to carry out her instructions.

"Brother, I will hold you to that."

CHAPTER SEVEN

HELENA LOWERED HER head against the stiff, chilly breeze whipping through the afternoon air. Her daily walk had seemed like a good idea this morning, as the sky looked no grayer or drearier than usual. However, within a half-hour, she had found herself in serious danger of being soaked by a coming rain shower. The sky had darkened since she ventured from the house, and she was wearing a light, worn walking dress and a scrap of a spencer. Her hat wasn't enough to block the stray raindrops that slapped against her cheeks.

Wrapping her arms around herself, she quickened her pace, hoping to return home before being soaked to the bone and contracting a fever. Perhaps she might have been more cautious had her mind not been so preoccupied. Weeks into the season, Harriett was still no closer to settling on a single suitor. It shouldn't worry Helena, but she knew very well how fickle the men of the *ton* could be. If Harriett didn't narrow the field soon, many would lose interest and move on to their other available choices. That path of thinking only led Helena down a slippery slope of guilt. Harriett was young and unattached and ought to be able to enjoy her season without the burdens of her impoverished family hanging over her head.

However, that simply wasn't possible. Even if Henry left university and set out to find work of some kind, he would never make enough money to keep them all afloat. When it came to skills that might earn one a living, Helena was woefully lacking. Marriage was the only thing that would save them, and unfortunately, the men of their world had proven over and over that they didn't see her as marriage material. Harriett was their only hope.

As if that weren't enough to fret over, the Band of Brigands had planned another excursion for next week in hopes that another haul like their last would tide them over for a few weeks before they were forced to strike again. Helena never stopped worrying that they might be caught, but now that the beginnings of notoriety had begun surrounding them in the press, the danger was all the more potent. Yet, it wasn't enough to prompt her to back out of the scheme.

One thought of her siblings, Effie and Crispin, Selina and her father, Cecelia, or Mina and her poor mother was all it took to strengthen Helena's resolve. The world seemed to be working actively against them all, determined to destroy their lives. If a cache of weapons, a few masks, and hooded cloaks were what it took to keep all their heads above water, then Helena was willing to do what was necessary. Besides, they had never robbed anyone who didn't have more wealth than they knew what to do with.

Telling herself that often, combined with having coal for fires and food to warm her belly, was enough to assuage the guilt that often kept her awake at night. They weren't hurting anyone, and the things they took were replaceable. But nothing could compensate for the loss of their livelihoods.

As if responding to the despondent trajectory of her thoughts, the sky opened completely, and a light patter of rain turned into a shower. Helena sucked in a shocked breath as the cold water battered her skin, soaking through the thin layers of her daytime garments and wilting the cloth flowers lining the brim of her hat. The air had felt mild upon leaving home but now left her shivering, the previously gentle breeze stabbing through her pores like tiny icicles.

"Bloody hell," he muttered under her breath, breaking into a trot. If she didn't get home soon, catching a cold would soon accompany the other troubles on her list of woes.

The street was all but abandoned, proving that she was one of the only idiots who had ventured out of doors without anticipating the coming storm. She paused before crossing an intersection between streets, noting that a carriage was turning right into her path. However, the vehicle didn't move out of her way—rather slowing to a stop as its occupant whipped the curtains apart to gape at her.

A low, frustrated growl simmered in Helena's throat as she moved to walk around the carriage and the bounder inside it—who, apparently, had never seen a lone woman soaked to her skin, trying to make a swift path home. How rude to sit and stare from the comfort of one's dry, warm carriage. Unfortunately, even if the Montgomery family still owned an equipage, Helena would never have taken it out in such horrid weather. No one ever thought of how dangerous rolling wheels could be over slick roads and how reckless driving could imperil those inside. Helena herself had never pondered it until news of her parents had been delivered, and then it had become all she could think of at the merest hint of a rain shower.

She had nearly moved past the massive carriage, which was adorned with a large and rather gaudy family crest on its doors when the bellow of a man's voice hurtled at her through the pounding of rain against cobblestones.

"Helena, wait! Helena! By Jupiter, you walk fast!"

Helena turned abruptly to meet whoever had accosted her, causing her boots to skid over the uneven stones. Arms wheeling, she experienced the nauseating sensation of her heart dropping into her belly. However, the viselike grip of a hand around her upper arm saved her from falling onto her rump, and she grew dizzy as, with a single tug, her world was tipped back onto its axis. A dark shadow fell over her, and Helena found herself standing under the shelter of an oiled umbrella, a few bare inches away from…*him*. The other persistent thought distracting her and making her absent-minded and foolish.

The one person whose company she should eschew for fear that she might ruin Hariett's chance at making the best possible match.

Stratford.

He was annoyingly dry beneath the shelter of his umbrella, the open door of the carriage behind him revealing just who had halted their vehicle in the middle of the street to block her path. Stratford was also ridiculously handsome, a black greatcoat swathing him from shoulders to ankles, offering the slightest peek at a bottle-green coat, black waistcoat, and frothy white cravat. His eyes appeared a dark green in the shadows of the umbrella, and their close proximity made her more aware than ever of the sheer height and breadth of him. He towered over her, his figure large enough to blot out the meager light of the afternoon. Helena suddenly felt as if the entire world had fallen away as Stratford filled the whole of her vision.

"My lord," she ground out, through teeth clenched to keep them from chattering.

"What are you doing out here?" he bellowed to be heard over a rumble of thunder in the distance. The sound caused Helena to flinch, making her feel more foolish than she already did. "You'll catch your death in this weather."

Helena shuddered as the chill of her skin began to permeate deeper, making her feel frozen stiff. "I...it wasn't raining when I..."

Still holding steady to her arm, Stratford began gently prodding her toward the carriage. "Come, I will take you home."

Irrational fear overtook Helena, prompting her to dig her heels in and resist. The looming carriage suddenly appeared like the open maw of Hell, and her limbs refused to move her in its direction. Rain splattered her boots and soaked her hem as Stratford turned back, giving her a bewildered look.

"What's wrong?"

"I cannot get in the carriage with you."

When she failed to elaborate, the earl sighed and rolled his eyes. "Miss Montgomery, no one is about to see you in my company. Besides that, I doubt anyone would blame you for accepting shelter and transportation from me in such ghastly weather. Your reputation will remain intact, and perhaps we can save you from developing pneumonia or some such."

Helena pulled her arm out of his hold, stumbling back a few steps and out of the shelter he provided from the rain. Stratford gave chase, thrusting the umbrella out so that she was covered but risking his own person. In the few seconds it took for him to duck and join her beneath the covering, his hair became soaked, the strands inky black and clinging in coiled tendrils to his forehead and neck.

He parted his lips, but Helena spoke before he could utter the question she knew sat on the tip of his tongue.

"It isn't my reputation I'm worried about," she blurted, lowering her eyes to avoid his penetrating gaze. "You might think me foolish, but my parents perished in a carriage accident during a rainstorm. Ever since then, getting into a carriage when it is raining terrifies me."

For a moment, Stratford didn't speak. He didn't even move, save for the rhythmic rise and fall of his chest with every breath. She stared at the buttons of his waistcoat, realizing how improper it was to fix her eyes on this part of his anatomy. Helena had never paid much attention to the structure of a man's torso, but something about Stratford's struck her as decidedly sensual, even when covered in layers of fabric. Perhaps it was the broad width of his chest tapering to his waist or the coiled power and strength concealed by the finery of silk and linen. Whatever it was, Helena was held captive by each of his breaths and the way they made his chest expand and the fabric of his waistcoat shift and stretch.

He lifted his hand and used two fingers to brace her chin, lifting it so that she looked into his eyes. There was no confusion or mockery in Stratford's stare, only compassion and understanding. "That isn't foolish at all," he murmured, his voice low and deep, stroking along her chilled skin like a warm caress. "I'm sorry to hear of your parents. I knew they had died, but I didn't know how."

Helena knew she should put some distance between them, even if it would move her from beneath the shelter of the umbrella, even if no one was nearby to witness them standing so close while staring into one another's eyes. Knowing this didn't make it any easier to do what was right or proper. She was swimming in the greenish-brown pools of his eyes, losing herself to a moment of camaraderie and empathy from another person. Helena hadn't realized how badly she'd wanted to feel those things until Stratford offered them to her, and now she couldn't force herself to step away.

"It doesn't make any sense," she said with a harsh laugh. "It isn't as if I was in the carriage with them when it happened. I was at home, tucked away in my bed and oblivious to the fact that along their way home, Mama and Papa were...they were..."

Stratford stroked her cheek and whispered a soft, "Shh."

Helena choked back a sob, embarrassed by the sudden emotion welling up from deep inside her. She had been despondent for months following her parents' death, even finding it impossible to leave her bed some days. With time, it had become easier to push her grief down and carry on, though nothing could ever fill the emptiness left inside her by their loss. Yet, Helena often found herself facing moments like this—when she could pretend to have forgotten that her parents were lost to her forever, only to have the reality come crashing down upon her at the slightest provocation. Whenever that happened, the blow felt fresh, and the trauma was renewed. She would find herself feeling as if they had died yesterday instead of nearly two years ago.

"We don't have to go anywhere," Stratford said, his large palm gently cradling her jaw and his thumb caressing a tear away from her cheek. "If you want, we can simply sit inside the carriage until there's a break in the weather. We will not budge an inch until you are ready."

Helena darted a glance at the carriage, a longing for warmth and shelter beginning to overcome her irrational fear. "I wouldn't want to inconvenience you. I am certain you were on your way to someplace important."

"Nothing awaits me that is more important than making certain you are all right. Will you come and sit in the carriage with me?"

Helena bit her lip and glanced about, finding herself left with no other recourse. She was still several blocks away from home, and a flash of lightning overhead reminded her of the dangers of remaining outdoors.

"Of course," she relented. "Thank you."

Stratford took one arm in his firm grasp, then braced his other hand at her back as they picked their way around puddles toward the carriage. Helena wanted to lean into him and absorb some of the heat radiating from him but resisted the urge. This encounter was improper enough as it was; there was no need to knowingly compound the situation.

Helena allowed herself to be handed up into the carriage, then settled, shivering and hugging herself, onto the squabs. Stratford exchanged a word with his coachman before closing the umbrella and handing it off, then hauling himself in after her. The spacious vehicle was large enough to seat four people yet seemed to shrink when the earl closed the door and then slid the curtains closed over the windows. The dim interior and close confines made Helena aware of how close the toes of his boots came to touching hers and how close the occupants of a carriage were actually forced to sit. There was nothing decent about it.

"You're shivering," Stratford remarked while shrugging out of his greatcoat. "Here, let me."

"Oh, no, I shouldn't. It isn't necessary."

Despite her protests, he leaned across the carriage to sweep the coat over her shoulders, efficiently pulling the lapels together over her chest. "It isn't much, but hopefully, it helps."

At the questioning note in his voice, Helena looked at Stratford and discovered him watching her with concern furrowing his brow. Clutching at the lining of the coat, she held it tighter to her body, suppressing a sigh of relief at the warmth his body had left on the garment. She wouldn't want him to think she was reacting to the intoxicating scent of him still clinging to the worsted fibers. That would be even more improper than the press of his knees against hers when he had shifted to the edge of his seat.

Helena swallowed past the knot in her throat and forced words to pass from between her lips. "Th-thank you. I'm so sorry to inconvenience you this way."

"Stop apologizing," he commanded with a decisive wave of one hand. "I'm glad I happened upon you. Actually, I had planned to pay a call later today to deliver this in person, but…"

He reached into the breast pocket of his tailcoat and retrieved a thick, embossed card.

Helena's fingers had thawed just enough for her to accept it, and she turned it over to read the scrawling words spelling out an invitation. "You're hosting a dinner party?"

Stratford smiled and gave a shake of his head. "Actually, my mother is hosting the event, though it is being arranged at my behest. I wanted her to meet the woman I…"

Helena's gaze snapped up from the invitation when he trailed off, surprised to find that he looked rather shy just now, as if embarrassed at what he'd nearly voiced aloud. She could hardly believe her eyes. "Harriett will be so excited," she said lightly. "Thank you for inviting us, my lord."

That infernal eyebrow of his lifted toward his hairline, its effect no less striking with his hair wet and limp. "I thought I asked you to call me Stratford."

"And I thought I had made it clear that despite that…the *thing* you do with your eyebrow. You look downright villainous when you do it. No, actually, you look very much the rake."

"Was that supposed to be an insult?" he teased, his lips parting in a smile. A fluttering sensation erupted low in Helena's belly at the sight. With his hair soaked and dripping, he looked younger, and that smile gave her a glimpse of what he might have been like as a boy. He couldn't possibly have always been so stoic and rigid. "I was led to believe that rakes are all the rage amongst society ladies."

Helena wrinkled her nose in disgust. "Hardly."

His grin widened, and he leaned forward, elbows braced on his knees. "Do you know what I think?"

She pressed her back against the squabs, suddenly robbed of breath. Was she imagining it, or had it suddenly become stifling hot inside this carriage? Stratford was leaning too close—so close that she detected the masculine scents of shaving balm and cologne—sandalwood, peppermint, and bergamot.

"What?" she croaked, starved of air and sanity.

His smile turned devilish. "I think you are jealous. Most people who cannot raise one eyebrow at a time feel the same way."

Helena scoffed to cover the giggle simmering in her throat. "What a ridiculous accusation! I'm certain raising one eyebrow cannot be very difficult at all, especially if *you* can do it."

Stratford pressed a hand against his chest and groaned as if in pain. "You wound me, madam. I assure you, it isn't as simple as it looks. It took me years to perfect the left eyebrow, and months more to isolate the movement of the right. If you don't believe me, try for yourself. Go on, I'm waiting."

Her lips quivered with laughter that became increasingly harder to keep stifled. She screwed up her forehead, the muscles in her brow twitching and straining as she attempted to rise to his challenge.

"Am I doing it?" she asked. "Do I look intimidating and lord-ly?"

Stratford barked a laugh and shook his head. "You look as if you have a stomachache. You must learn the proper technique. First, you have to stop smiling—that only increases the difficulty. Like this."

The way he pinched his lips and jutted his jaw only tickled Helena more, making it impossible to control her quivering mouth and convulsing chest. She feared she might actually faint for want of air as she tried and failed to choke down a spurt of giggles.

"Then, you simply focus your thoughts on the eyebrow you wish to lift. One will come more naturally than the other, so the trick is figuring out which that is. For me, it is the left, and now I can manage it without much thought. It helps if you stare imperiously down your nose as if everyone in the vicinity is beneath you. Like so."

One dark eyebrow arched upward, combining with the set of his mouth to make him look diabolical. Helena offered him a round of teasing applause.

"Bravo! That was quite impressive, and I stand corrected. Apparently, there is an art to it that I had not previously considered."

"It isn't too difficult for you to learn. Come on, try it. First, set your mouth correctly."

Helena did her best to pinch her lips but feared she wasn't achieving the same effect. She felt so ridiculous that she began to laugh again and helplessly shrugged her shoulders.

"I suppose I am hopeless," she said.

"Not at all," Stratford said, reaching out to grasp her chin between his thumb and forefinger. "You just have to concentrate. Here, like this."

Helena went deathly still at the touch of his hand on her face, warmth flaring in her chest and spreading rapidly throughout the rest of her body. Her breath hitched as she noticed he wore no gloves and that the sensation of his bare skin against hers was disconcertingly electrifying. She certainly wasn't laughing now. There was nothing amusing about the way Stratford was looking at her, his eyes growing heavy-lidded and his lips parting as they sat locked in each other's gazes.

"Your mouth," he murmured, his thumb lightly coasting along the edge of her lower lip. "It…"

His throat convulsed with a swallow, and the hand at her chin trembled. Helena clenched her hands in his greatcoat, torn between knowing she needed to pull away and wanting to know how his hands might feel on other parts of her body. Her face flushed hot at such unladylike thoughts. It was no wonder unmarried women were warned not to be alone with men at the risk of their virtue. Just now, she experienced sensations previously foreign to her, and they were too thrilling to be overcome by a simple act of will. She felt as if she'd been craving something her entire life and had only just now discovered what that was.

A touch on her face, a longing glance. It was nothing at all, yet somehow it was everything at the same time.

She lowered her eyes, grappling for words—any words to dispel the unnerving tension winding between them. "I've been told that my mouth presents a bit of a problem. I am too free and uninhibited with my opinions and often speak without thinking."

Stratford's expression softened, his lips quirking in a hint of a smile. "The only problem with your mouth is that I've become captivated with it beyond good discretion. It is a wonder. *You* are a wonder."

Her belly clenched and quivered, and her palms broke out into an anxious sweat. Had she slipped on the cobblestones in the rain and bumped her head? Perhaps she lay in the street, abandoned, dreaming things that weren't happening, because, surely, the most frustrating, mysterious, incomprehensible, beautiful man she had ever seen wasn't actually drawing closer by the second, his gaze fixed on her lips as if ready to consume them with his own.

"Stratford," she whispered, uncertain whether there was an actual warning in her voice or if she only imagined it.

He hesitated only for a moment, his eyes flicking up to meet hers. "I've changed my mind. I think I'd rather you called me Sebastian."

His mouth was on hers before she could offer a response, though all she could have managed with a whimper of surrender as she found herself caught up in his magnetic pull. The hand on her face was gently insistent, angling her head and stroking along the line of her jaw as his lips brushed hers in a tentative overture. Helena knew she ought to put a stop to this, pull away and castigate him for taking liberties with her person. But, dear God, his lips were soft and insistent, and Helena had never been kissed. She had wondered how it might feel and worried that a kiss with the wrong man might put her off the act for the rest of her life.

She had been woefully unprepared for what the kiss of the right man could do to her. Helena became boneless, leaning into Stratford—no, *Sebastian*—to accept the offering of his lips and give her own in return. She had no idea what she was doing, but he gently coaxed her along, tilting his head and tutoring her with firm but gentle presses of his lips. His thumb pressed her chin, easing her lips open and exposing her to the slick feel of the inside of his mouth and the wild, heady taste of him.

It shouldn't feel so exceptional, the tender, silken flesh just within someone else's mouth, but Helena longed for more of it, needing to know what her lack of experience had deprived her of. Another foreign sound escaped her throat, desperate and high-pitched, as he stroked his tongue along the seam of her mouth. Deepening the kiss, he swallowed her moan of capitulation, his grip shifting to the nape of her neck and holding her captive to his whims. Helena scrambled for purchase, feeling as if she were about to fall. Her hands found the sturdy beams of his thighs, the muscles taut and warm and forbidden against her palms. A low hum echoed through his chest, and she realized that she was doing something right. He proved her right by deepening the kiss, his tongue now pushing against her own and seeking deeper entrance into her mouth.

Helena threw herself shamelessly into the intimacy, thrusting her tongue back at him and marveling at the satiny velvet feel of such an intimate part of someone else's anatomy. A kiss was nothing like she had expected and everything she had ever longed for. Years of telling herself she was content to be alone melted away, and she discovered within herself a deep need for something more, something, it seemed, that Sebastian was willing and able to offer her. If this man could look upon her and feel desire, then express it in such a poignant, unmistakable way, perhaps she wasn't hopeless after all. Maybe her sister didn't have to be the savior of their family.

Dear God. Harriett!

The sudden recollection that this man was actively courting her sister broke the spell overcoming Helena's good sense. She reared away from Sebastian, holding up one hand to ward him off as he seemed ready to pursue. Her chest heaved as she caught her breath, and the remnants of his kiss lingered on her palate. She could still taste him, still feel the tingling warmth of his mouth on hers though they were physically separated.

Sebastian licked his lip, staring at her with eyes gone muddled with confusion and desire and a dozen other things Helena couldn't put a name to. "Helena—"

"Stratford," she interjected, conjuring what little resistance she could muster. "We shouldn't have done that."

He leaned back in his seat and stared at her, all humor wiped from his face. No twitching eyebrow. No imperious stare. "Perhaps not, but I cannot deny that I've wanted to do that from the moment I met you. I might not have realized it then, but that doesn't change how I feel, how I've felt all this time without wanting to acknowledge it."

Helena blinked, stunned by the words coming from his mouth. The short time of their acquaintance filled her mind in a series of short encounters, terse words, and one waltz that had haunted her dreams in the days since.

"I think it is time we stopped dancing around what we've been trying to avoid," he added. "What we mistook as animosity has been attraction all along. Can you look me in the eyes and tell me you don't feel something, anything?"

No, no, she could not. Even in the beginning, when she had been determined to dislike him, Helena had found him handsome and intriguing. Even when he had annoyed her to no end, she had been unable to pretend he wasn't the very picture of what she had wanted for herself in her youthful days of foolish fantasy.

But this wasn't a fantasy. It wasn't a dream or some frivolous scene plucked out of her imagination. This was reality—and in reality, none of this was a simple as succumbing to attraction or admiration. There was more than Harriett to consider, though the involvement of her sister proved an insurmountable complication. Helena couldn't allow herself to forget the commitment she had made to the other important people in her life. Effie, Mina, Selina, and Cecelia weren't her sisters by blood, but they were bonded by their experiences and their woes. The kinship that had brought them together had been strengthened by the secrecy of their activities—the truth of which could never be shared with another.

If she allowed herself to want Sebastian, to care and long for him, she would want to give him parts of herself that could never be given. Besides, she couldn't fathom ever letting him get close enough to discover the truth. He wouldn't think so highly of her if he knew that Harriett's season and her eventual trousseau had been financed by highway robbery.

"What I might feel is irrelevant given the circumstances," she stated, straightening her back and folding her hands neatly in her lap. "You have been pursuing my sister for marriage."

"I have made no promises to Harriett, and she has made none to me," he countered. "I admire your sister, and we have become friends, but I haven't found myself plagued with thoughts of kissing her. I haven't been near her and been forced to fight the urge to take her into my arms."

"Stratford, please—"

"Sebastian," he pressed. "I don't want to be only 'Stratford' to you. I understand that this is complicated, but certainly it isn't hopeless or completely out of the question. I care for you, Helena. I want you."

His words struck as intended, penetrating her resistance and making her want to throw herself across the carriage to pick up where they had left off. But it wasn't possible. Even if Harriett had nothing to do with this, Helena had to protect herself—and him—from the potential consequences of choices she had made.

"Do you love your brother, my lord?"

Agitation made a muscle in his cheek spasm, and he narrowed his eyes at her. "What has that to do with—"

"Answer the question. Do you love your brother? Do you want what is best for him?"

"Of course I do."

Helena raised her chin. "Then you will understand why I cannot allow this, whatever this is...to go on. Harriett must marry, and you are one of the suitors she is considering as a potential match. You say that you do not feel passion toward her, but I cannot ignore the possibility that *she* feels amorously toward *you*. I've seen the way you smile at each other, the ease with which you converse. If she thought I wanted you, she would stand aside because she is loving and selfless. All the while, any heartbreak she might feel at letting you go would be hidden away, and perhaps, it would even keep her from considering anyone else, ruining her chances of ever making a good match. Were our roles reversed, and it was you who had your sibling to consider, would you ever purposely hurt your brother that way?"

Sebastian's jaw flexed and ground stubbornly as he glared at her, clearly unable to deny her, though Helena could see he wanted to. "No," he ground out after a while.

"Then do not ask me to do that to Harriett," she said, shrugging his coat off her shoulders. Pushing the curtains aside, she noted that the storm had calmed for now, and the sun had begun to peek out from behind receding clouds. And not a moment too soon. If Sebastian continued looking at her with such heat in his eyes, Helena didn't know how much longer her will could hold up. "I must go."

Sebastian caught her hand just as she threw open the carriage door, halting her from making a quick escape. "What if you could be assured that Harriett has no feelings toward me other than friendship?"

Helena gazed at him mournfully over one shoulder, her eyes stinging with coming tears. "I'm afraid that even then, anything more than cordiality would be impossible between us. I apologize if it hurts you to hear it."

"I see," he murmured, releasing her hand.

When he didn't say anything more, Helena stepped down from the carriage and turned to look at him through the opening. He was delectably mussed and ruffled, his cravat loosened, and his hair beginning to curl. Something deep within her lurched toward him, but Helena restrained it, knowing that this was for the best. If he knew what she was hiding, he would thank her.

"Thank you for weathering the storm with me," she said, unable to help expressing her gratitude. "I shall never forget your act of kindness."

Without waiting for him to reply, Helena turned and walked away as fast as her legs would carry her, blinking to keep the tears from slipping down her cheeks.

CHAPTER EIGHT

B Y THE STANDARDS of those in his level of society, Sebastian's dinner party turned out to be a smashing success. Every invitation had been answered with confirmation of attendance—though he shouldn't have expected any less. The notoriety of his family had always made him an intriguing public figure, even when he didn't wish to be. For this occasion, the Radcliffe reputation worked to attract a dining room full of illustrious guests. His mother's plans had come together without a wrinkle, and by the time their guests began arriving, every polished piece of silver and washed dish of china had been arranged to her specifications on the table.

Candles were lit, while fresh flowers offered bursts of color and perfumed fragrances. The anteroom buzzed with conversation and the soft notes of music provided by the hired stringed quartet. Wine, Madeira, and brandy flowed, and the borrowed French chef had promised seven courses of fine cuisine.

Despite all that, Sebastian couldn't seem to throw himself into enjoying the evening. He wouldn't delude himself into pretending his displeasure had nothing to do with Helena. It had *everything* to do with her. Since the day he had encountered her walking in the rain and the resulting kiss in his carriage, Sebastian had made every possible attempt to make contact with the woman who had unexpectedly become the center of his waking thoughts. Her rejection oughtn't have hurt as much as it had.

Sebastian liked to think he wasn't so arrogant that he couldn't handle learning that the object of his affection was indifferent toward him.

But there was the rub. Helena *wasn't* indifferent to him. A woman with no regard for a man wouldn't have kissed him the way Helena had kissed Sebastian. As he came to understand her better, he realized that she kept her guard up to protect herself—whether from hurt or from the discovery of deep vulnerability, Sebastian wasn't entirely certain. But he had come to recognize those small moments when she allowed the mask of her aloofness to fall. She had shown him parts of her true self that day—her fear and her grief, her smiles and her laughter, her sense of humor.

Sebastian wasn't blind, and he didn't think he was mistaken. Their kiss hadn't been a fleeting mistake or a sordid tryst. It hadn't even been at the forefront of his mind when inviting her to sit in the carriage with him. He'd simply seen her alone in the rain and gave in to the urge to have her in his company. Approaching the subject of his tendre for her hadn't even occurred to him until the words were coming out of his mouth.

He had spent his entire life being so careful with his actions, doing his best not to become his idiot of a father. On the rare occasion that he indulged in an affair with a woman, he met her on honest terms. He never dallied with ladies whose reputations could be damaged by association with him, and he had never laid a hand on an innocent. He didn't pay for mistresses, either, finding the practice repugnant. Widows and the occasional actress or opera singer did well enough when he grew weary of his solitude, and all connections were broken amicably. He behaved as a gentleman in every way possible, always aware that a single misstep would affect not only his family but the lives of those who crossed his path.

But Helena Montgomery made him want to forget caution and decorum. As she sat at his dining room table, avoiding his gaze and pointedly making conversation with everyone around her except for him, Sebastian was overcome with the urge to drag her from the room to steal another kiss. He wanted to convince her to reconsider an offer he'd never quite come around to making before she'd bolted from the carriage as if her backside were on fire. He wanted to show her that her reasons for resistance were meaningless in the face of what they could have together.

However, they were surrounded by some of the most influential people of the *ton*—including some of the worst gossips. He didn't think he would ever be desperate enough to embarrass her and himself by behaving in such a way.

There was nothing left for him to do but wait for a convenient, discreet opportunity. Sebastian bade his time through all seven courses of rich, sauced French foods and a selection of delectable desserts. He watched Helena like a hawk, grinding his teeth every time she smiled or laughed at something that was said. Whenever he spoke, she stared down at her plate and pretended as if he were invisible. She seemed less reticent tonight than she typically was while in the company of others, perhaps because of the intimacy of the setting or the presence of both her siblings, as well as her friend, Lady Cecelia Finch. Whatever the case, Sebastian would find it a welcome change if not for the fact that she seemed determined to ignore him entirely.

On the one hand, he supposed he had no one to blame for himself. This was what impulsive behavior resulted in. The effort he had made at making friends with Helena had been undone with a kiss, and now he was left with no idea what to do. On the other hand, he wasn't willing to let their last conversation be the end of it. There was too much that had gone unsaid for Sebastian to leave it there.

By the time dinner ended and the men excused themselves from the women's company for their port and cigars, Sebastian had nearly lost his hold on patience. He could hardly keep up with the conversation taking place around him as he wondered what the ladies were up to and how he might maneuver Helena into a quiet corner of the drawing room for a private conversation.

After what felt like hours, the gentlemen finally returned to the anteroom to the dining chamber, where the ladies sat about talking, enjoying the talents of the musicians, and indulging in after-dinner drinks. He found Helena standing near the pianoforte with her friend, Cecelia; their heads bent close. Felix took up with one of his university friends, while his mother sat playing cards with a group of matrons. Before he could make his way toward Helena, Harriett stepped into his path wearing a bright smile.

"Stratford," she said, reaching for his arm and leaving him with no choice but to politely extend it to her. "I cannot thank you enough for inviting us into your home. Your mother is a lovely woman and has been so kind."

"It has been my pleasure," he replied, grudgingly allowing her to guide him away from the bulk of his guests. "I was just about to—"

"We must talk," she interrupted, turning to face him. Humor danced in her eyes, juxtaposed to her serious expression—which he suspected she wore as a thin veneer. *What the devil was going on?* "It is important."

Sebastian's gaze darted to Helena for the umpteenth time. She wore navy blue silk tonight, and a silvery gauze over the skirt made her look like some kind of heavenly vision. He ached at the sight of her standing so near, yet so withdrawn from him. When had she gained this power over him? Had it been when she'd cut him with the sharp side of her tongue the first night they'd met? Or had it been when they had danced, and Sebastian had realized he could dance with her forever if she'd let him?

"My lord," Harriett said sharply, drawing his attention back to her. "I am afraid I must inform you that I am no longer interested in your attention as a romantic suitor."

Sebastian's mouth gaped open, then pulled shut several times as he searched for a response. She had caught him off guard, as he hadn't given his farce of a courtship with her a second thought since that night at Almack's. "I beg your pardon?"

She gave him a sympathetic look and inclined her head in Helena's direction. "I have become aware that your affections have turned in the direction of another. Because of this, I think it is best for us to be honest with one another. I like you, Stratford. We get on well, and I have come to think of you as a dear friend. However, though it is necessary for me to marry by the end of this season for the sake of my family's future, I simply cannot countenance marrying a man who is so clearly in love with my sister. If I have no choice but to marry, I'd like to choose someone who I might come to love. It is clear that would be impossible between us, and marriage would only make you miserable."

Sebastian worked to keep his expression neutral as he stared at Harriett, taken aback and momentarily speechless. While he had alluded to her assertion when talking to Helena, it was still surprising to have it so bluntly laid out. Apparently, he hadn't done a very good job hiding his true feelings from Harriett, whose assessment was so accurate it was eerie.

"How did you know?" he asked for lack of anything better to say.

Harriett snorted and shook her head. "I've noticed from the beginning, Stratford. The two of you practically give off sparks whenever you're in the same room with one another."

A sudden thought occurred to Sebastian, and he narrowed his eyes accusingly at Harriett. "The day we went riding in Hyde Park, you started that conversation about philosophy because you knew we were both lovers of the genre. You left us alone to go fetch your things instead of sending a servant for them on purpose."

She shrugged one shoulder and gave him a coy smile. "Henry was there, so you weren't entirely alone. But, yes, it was done on purpose."

"And the things you said at Vauxhall."

"All to convince you to set your attention on her. Did it work?"

Sebastian sighed. "Yes, for my part, at least. But I don't think

Helena is interested."

"Nonsense. Helena is very good at hiding her emotions. She is also selfless to a fault, which means if she thinks I am considering you for a husband, she will push her own feelings aside. So, I have decided to make it clear that I will not stand in your way. You are free to pursue her without worrying that you have insulted me. Besides, I think Lord Amberly and I have formed a connection of sorts. I...I like him very much."

Sebastian followed her gaze to the young viscount who had recently come into his title. He was slender and blond, with boyish features and an uninhibited grin. He didn't know the young man well, but Amberly shared Harriett's sunny nature and was known for his amiability. They would make a splendid match.

"I am glad for you," he said.

"And I will be glad when you and my sister stop being so obstinate and admit that you are perfect for one another."

Sebastian chuckled. "In the matter of obstinacy, your sister certainly has me beat. However, I am known for my stubbornness. Wish me luck?"

"The very best of luck," Harriet said before turning away to approach her viscount.

Sebastian watched her go with a feeling like brotherly affection welling up in his chest. Had he not been so determined to marry any lady who met a set list of his qualifications, he might have recognized that from the beginning. Harriett would make some man a wonderful wife, but she was not the one for him.

Swiveling his determined gaze back to Helena, he told himself he'd already found the perfect woman. Now, all he had to do was convince her to give him a chance.

He waited until there appeared to be a break in the conversation between Helena and Cecelia, then approached with surety in every step. Sebastian paused only long enough to procure two glasses of Madeira from a footman, then approached the ladies with them.

"Miss Montgomery, Lady Cecelia, may I offer you some Madeira?"

Cecelia took the proffered glass with a smile. "You are a godsend, my lord. And what a lovely time we've been having. Helena, weren't we just discussing how wonderful dinner was?"

"Indeed," Helena murmured, staring somewhere over Sebastian's shoulder while accepting the wine he offered. "Thank you."

"It is my pleasure. Lady Cecelia, I do beg your pardon, but I had hoped to have a word with Miss Montgomery."

The lady exchanged a pointed glance with her friend. "But of course, my lord. Excuse me while I go thank your mother for her hospitality. Good evening."

Helena looked as if she wished to protest, but Cecelia was gone before she could, leaving her in Sebastian's sights. She took a sip of her wine and went on staring past him. "My lord."

"Helena," he whispered, stirred to his very depths at the way her name sounded on his lips. He couldn't deny a little thrill at the impropriety of speaking it in the company of others.

It satisfied Sebastian even more when the utterance of Helena's name drew her eyes to him at last, and he didn't even mind that she looked as if she wished to upend her wineglass over his head.

"Please, I thought I made myself perfectly clear when last we spoke."

"You did," he relented. "But I wasn't given the chance to plead my case. Besides, if nothing else, I feel compelled to tell you how wounded I am that my foolish blunder has resulted in the end of our friendship—especially as it was so newly forged."

"I never said we could not continue as friends."

"Hmm," he murmured, rubbing his chin. "Well, you have yet to speak a single word to me all night. You will not even look at me. Is this some new way of expressing friendship that I am ignorant to? I must admit to not always being the most fashionable of men."

From the corner of his eye, he saw her lips twitch as they

often did when she was trying to hold back a laugh—progress, at last.

"I have never been kissed by a friend," she replied, her voice so low he had to strain to hear her over the music. "So, forgive me if I am at a loss as to how to proceed."

Some of the rigidity eased from his shoulders as they reentered familiar territory. If he could coax her into conversation and jesting, then all was not lost.

"Why didn't you say so?" he teased. "I have two solutions, each of which has their advantages. Would you like to hear them?"

"I suppose."

He folded his hands behind his back because he needed to do *something* with them. He was more aware of her than ever before, now that he knew the taste and feel of her in his hands. The bare few inches of skin between her sleeve and the edge of her glove tempted his fingertips. The slope of her neck beckoned to his lips. Every inch of him was seized with desire—powerful and all-consuming. It was as if he had been walking about robbed of his senses, and Helena had engaged them all in one fell swoop. He couldn't stop drinking her in with his gaze. He couldn't turn his mind away from the phantom memory of her taste or the need to discover if she was as soft and yielding to the touch as she looked.

"The way I see it," he said, "we can either pretend it never happened and go on with a cordial friendship. This first option seems the easiest and most efficient, though it isn't my favorite."

"Of course," she said, sarcasm edging her voice. "You *would* prefer the more difficult path, you obstinate boor."

"Quiet, you churlish shrew. I haven't finished. What you call the more difficult path, I choose to see as the most rewarding." He waited until Helena had finished feigning a coughing fit to disguise her laughter before going on. "Our second option is for you to excuse yourself to the retiring room in ten minutes and instead meet me in the morning room at the front of the house— first door before you reach the entrance."

"Sebastian," she hissed, her cheeks flushed and her eyes wide with shock. "To suggest such a thing—"

"Oh, come now," he prodded. "Be daring with me for a little while. No one will notice we are gone, and I just think we need a moment to reassess the situation."

To his surprise, she raised her right eyebrow in perfect imitation of his own imperious expression. "I'm on to you, my lord."

Sebastian grinned. "By God, you're doing it. You've been practicing, haven't you?"

"Maybe," she hedged. "But that isn't the point. You're trying to convince me to sneak away so you can kiss me again. It is indecent. Even being overheard speaking of it could ruin me."

"I will not deny having ulterior motives," he admitted. "But I think we owe it to ourselves to ensure we wouldn't be making a mistake by choosing the first option."

Helena fell silent for so long Sebastian feared she wouldn't answer him. Finally, she sighed and used her wineglass to motion in Harriett's direction. "My family means more to me than anything. You know I could never hurt Harriett that way."

Thinking of the conversation he'd just had with the youngest Montgomery sister, Sebastian smirked. "Helena, look at her. Does she appear even the slightest bit concerned with me right now?"

He watched Helena observe Harriett, who was in an animated discussion with Viscount Amberly and Lady Cecelia. The viscount seemed taken with Harriett, not bothering to hide the admiration written all over his young face.

"No," Helena relented. "But—"

"No buts," Sebastian said firmly. "If you were to ask your sister, I'd be willing to wager she would tell you she doesn't give a fig about me in a romantic sense. If you can honestly tell me that you don't, either, I will let the matter lie for good. If you cannot, then I would be a fool not to ensure you know exactly where I stand. Please, Helena. I just need a moment. We'll be discreet, I promise."

Helena's lower lip disappeared between her teeth as she glanced about, as if worried they were being watched. The relaxing atmosphere of post-dinner card games and conversation had taken hold, and they had escaped the notice of everyone.

"Very well," she relented. "But only a moment and no longer."

"Upon my honor," he replied. "Ten minutes, Helena."

Despite wishing to linger at her side, Sebastian sauntered off and waited for a convenient moment for him to precede Helena in slipping from the room. He felt her eyes following him and took comfort in knowing that he hadn't ruined his chances entirely. Helena had done well building up her defenses, but now that she'd allowed him to see that it was possible to break through them, there was no stopping.

He wouldn't rest until Helena Montgomery had agreed to become his wife.

BY THE TIME Helena joined him in the morning room, Sebastian had nearly gone out of his mind wondering if she would cry off. Or—God forbid—worrying that she had been caught trying to sneak away. But that was ridiculous. Even if someone noticed her slipping away, they would have no reason to think anything was untoward. Sebastian had made a great show of pausing to whisper back and forth with a footman, to appear as if there was a matter of importance for him to attend to. In reality, he had merely told the man to ensure the servants kept the wine and spirits flowing. The more his guests enjoyed themselves, the less likely they were to notice that both he and Helena had gone missing at the same time.

He would adhere to his plan—a conversation of a few minutes and perhaps another kiss because he wouldn't be able to help himself. Then, he would send her back to the party and hang back long enough that his return wouldn't fall too close to hers. In that short of a time, he hoped to convince her to at least set aside her reservations and allow him to court her properly. Secrecy and slinking about weren't his usual method of operating, but desperate times called for desperate measures.

Sebastian's mind went quiet when the door opened just wide enough for Helena to slip through before swiftly pushing it closed. She looked frightened out of her wits as she leaned against it.

"Well, that was more than mildly terrifying," she murmured, letting out a relieved breath. "But I believe I managed to arrive unseen."

"Good," Sebastian said, closing the distance between them with swift steps.

She pressed herself against the door at his approach, eyes widening and lips parting on a helpless sigh. With a teasing grin, he pulled up just short of kissing her, his lips hovering over hers as he reached past Helena to turn the key in the lock and slip it into the breast pocket of his coat.

Glaring at him, she held one hand out, palm up. "I'll hold on to that, thank you."

Sebastian put on his most innocent face. "Don't you trust me, Helena?"

Her right eyebrow winged upward with what appeared to be very little effort, and Sebastian was seized with the urge to press a kiss right against the lovely, blond arch.

"Not farther than I could throw you," she said dryly. "The key, if you please."

Sebastian retrieved the key and set it in her hand, then leaned a hand against the door just above her shoulder. "I'm still going to kiss you," he teased.

She braced a hand against his chest to hold him at bay. "I thought you wanted to *talk*."

"I do," he insisted. "Kissing is one of my favorite things to talk about. Just now, I would like to talk about that kiss in the carriage. It was magical, perfect. You taste like strawberries and peppermint."

Her lips parted on a gasp, and the delectable swell of her bosom rose on the sharp intake of breath. "Sebastian," she whispered, her voice hoarse and strained.

"You're right," he said, leaning in until the forelock of his hair brushed against the fringe of curls kissing her brow. "Why dwell on the past? I'd much rather talk about the future kisses we will share and how badly I want to kiss you right now. And not just your lips. I've had very vivid daydreams about kissing you just here…" She whimpered when he stroked a finger down the side of her neck, caressing just where her pulse hummed through a blue-green vein. "And here," he whispered, trailing that same finger down to her collarbone and tracing the delicate line.

Her eyes slid closed, and she let her head fall against the door. "Sebastian."

"I do like the sound of my name on your lips," he said, pressing his lips to her cheek, then kissing his way down to the contour of her jaw. "But perhaps you want to say something else?"

She trembled against him, and Sebastian used one hand at her lower back to steady her. All his good intentions fled in the face of her acquiescence, and now all he could think of was being close to her, touching and kissing her. One taste hadn't been nearly enough.

"I…don't know what to say," she managed between soft, strained breaths. He nuzzled the smooth patch of skin just below her ear, noticing the way it made her squirm. He'd have to remember that.

"Say yes," he whispered, tugging at the lobe of her ear with his teeth.

"What am I saying yes to?"

"Whatever you want. Let me court you. Let me kiss you senseless. Marry me."

"I think we might be getting ahead of ourselves," she managed between the short, soft kisses he pressed to her mouth.

"We've only recently decided to be...friends."

"Fine then," he sighed, drawing back to look her in the eyes. "A friendly courtship that can last as long as you want it to. But I will insist on a short engagement and a small wedding."

She gave him an incredulous look, pressing his chest to put more distance between them. "My sister—"

"Doesn't want me. She told me so herself."

Helena sighed. "That isn't the only reason this might not be the best idea. There are things you do not know about my family, about me."

"That's what the courtship is for," he said, tapping the edge of her nose.

"And if you come to know things about me that you find repugnant?"

Sebastian straightened, realizing that it had come time for him to stop being frivolous. It was rare for him to show this side of himself to anyone outside his family, but Helena made feel free to speak as he chose, to laugh, and to give in to moments of lightheartedness. But she was making it clear that she needed him to be serious just now.

"Helena, I am not a fickle man. Finding out that you dislike hot chocolate or snore like an elephant isn't going to make me cry off."

She pursed her lips. "I don't mean things that are so easily dismissed."

For a brief moment, Sebastian wondered what secrets she might be keeping, but then decided it didn't matter. Their attachment was still very new, and there was time for him to get to know Helena and for her to become more at ease with him. He was far from perfect and would hope she could accept any unpleasant facets of his personality.

"Look at me," he urged, noticing that her gaze had begun to stray. "And hear me. I have spent my entire life striving to become the antithesis of everything my father was. If you are unaware of his reputation, the short of it is that he was a drunk who didn't know when to quit the gaming tables and changed mistresses as often as he did his clothes. If a string of women turned up on my doorstep claiming that their half a dozen squalling brats were his by-blows, I wouldn't even bat an eyelash or question their integrity. That's how much of a lecher he was."

"Heavens," she breathed. "That's awful."

"It is, and not only because he made my mother miserable or because he was the worst model of a gentleman that two boys could have had. It was awful because it placed the burden of restoring the family name squarely on my shoulders. So, I have spent every year of my life building an image and trying to live up to it. I thought that marriage to the perfect society debutante would be the final achievement cementing my legacy. I wasn't keen to marry but held out hope that I might find someone I actually liked, someone respectable and of a good family, but someone I could talk to and laugh with. Someone I could come to admire."

"I see nothing wrong with those aspirations," Helena remarked. "Some of us haven't gained even that much."

Sebastian cupped her face and tipped it up so he could stare down into the pools of her fathomless eyes. The honeyed tones in their depths leapt out at him in the sparse glow of the candles he'd lit before her arrival. "That's just it, Helena. I thought it would be enough until I met you. Now I want *more*. I want a wife who will argue philosophy with me, or anything in general, really, because I'm arrogant and need someone to remind me that I'm not always right. I want someone who makes me laugh and smile and actually enjoys dancing at those infernal balls. I want *you*, and I don't care if you come with a dozen filthy orphans or a gaggle of cats—which I detest, you should know. So, it doesn't matter if there are things you worry I might not like about you. None of it matters in the grand scheme of things."

Helena placed her hand over one of his, bracing it against her cheek. "Oh, you are very good at this. It's a wonder you've gone unwed this long."

"Shocking, considering how little practice I've had."

"It's all very wonderful. You've said all the right things."

Sebastian frowned. "I sense a 'but' coming."

"But," she said with a meaningful look, "it hardly seems right. My family is all but destitute, while you—"

"Are ridiculously wealthy," he interposed. "Honestly, it's sickening."

"Sebastian, be serious, please."

He pressed a longer, firmer kiss to her lips. "I'm completely serious. I want to marry you, but I understand that you are a more cautious person than I and need some time to consider my offer. Thus, I will give you all the time you need to come to trust me enough to let down your guard. The things you confided in me at Almack's, I understand, Helena. It infuriates me to know that you've been made to feel invisible or that other men have seen you as nothing more than an avenue through which to connect with the women you are attached to." He paused, letting out a rushed, heavy breath. "I am even ashamed for having overlooked you in the beginning because Harriett matched up to an ideal that never really appealed to me to begin with. But I need you to understand that I see you. I see you, and I want you, and if you give me a chance, I'll prove you have no reason to be afraid."

Helena still looked uncertain, yet he witnessed a gradual change in her demeanor. The rigid hold of the arm holding him back eased, and her eyelids grew heavy over eyes gone dreamlike. She released a soft, beckoning sigh, trailing her hand up his neck and into the hair at the nape of his neck.

"Yes," she whispered. "God help me. Yes, to courtship, to this…you."

Sebastian fell into her with a barely contained groan, seeking her lips with an urgent need that surprised even him. He hadn't realized until this moment how her refusal might have affected him. In the face of outright rejection, he would have had no choice but to accept her decision graciously. But, what then?

It didn't matter, and he had no need to think of what might have been because she was his. Helena was in his arms and rising up on tiptoe to return his kiss with an inexperienced fervor he found as endearing as it was arousing. She wasn't reticent or skittish, as he might expect from a woman who held herself so closed off from others. It was as if she'd held a lifetime's worth of passion locked away, and now it was his to experience, to enjoy.

Sebastian bent his legs to meet her height, gripping her waist and hauling her against him. He couldn't seem to get close enough, the barriers of clothing becoming a stifling nuisance. He reminded himself that she was a lady and an innocent and that frightening her away from him was the last thing he wanted. But Helena gripped at his shoulders and pressed into him eagerly, her tongue tentatively stroking against his own. He lifted her off her feet, her back braced by the wall and her front caged in by the width of his body. She clung to him and sucked in panting breaths, her lips reddened from the pressure of his, and her eyes unfocused.

"You're perfect," he declared, determined for her to not only hear it but believe it. "You're beautiful. Never let anyone make you feel as if you aren't."

She only had time to offer a swift nod in response before he was on her again, sucking at her bottom lip, kissing her chin, nuzzling into the curve of her neck.

"Oh," she murmured when he lapped his tongue at her beating pulse. "Oh, I, Sebastian!"

"Shh," he muttered, kissing along the exposed stretch of her shoulder toward the sleeve of her gown. "We haven't much time left, and I want you to enjoy this. Let me cherish you."

She relented with a moan muffled behind her lips as Sebastian put her back on her feet, then slid the sleeve of her gown off her shoulder. Smooth, peaches-and-cream skin filled his view, and her bodice sagged enough to tease him with the top of one glorious breast.

He pressed his nose to her bare skin and took in the intoxicating scent of her, then trailed his lips over satin-soft flesh. Her head fell back to allow him access, and Sebastian took advantage, kissing and nipping and trying to get his fill of Helena before he was forced to let her go. He was going out of his mind, feeling drunk on the sensations of desire and infatuation, and—dare he even think it—love. Now that Helena was in his arms, open and free of reticence, Sebastian couldn't imagine being without this, without *her*.

He allowed himself another moment of indulgence, taking her lips in a final, fiery kiss while cradling the weight of her breast in his hand. Helena clung to him, her fingers threaded through his hair and her back arching in reaction to the squeeze of his fingers around her soft, vulnerable flesh.

Sebastian tore himself away before he lost himself completely to such madness. She made him feel reckless and daring, but not enough to flirt with the chances of ruining her reputation.

"Go," he rasped, taking a step away from her, then another. "You'll be missed by now."

Helena stared at him as if in a daze, the color high in her cheeks and her eyes glassy. "Yes, I should go."

Sebastian snatched the sleeve of her gown back into place and smoothed a few stray strands of her. "Now might be good."

She blinked as if waking from a dream, then opened her palm to find that the key was no longer there. "Oh, bother," she muttered, turning in circles and searching the floor. Moving her skirts aside, she revealed the key, then crouched to retrieve it. "I suppose we shall see one another soon? In private, I mean?"

Sebastian's chest lurched at the longing in her voice, while an organ south of his waistline throbbed at the promise of being alone with Helena again. "As soon as can be managed. Now go, sweet. We cannot linger much longer."

Having come fully back to herself, Helena slipped the key into the lock and disappeared from the room as quickly as she had arrived. Sebastian leaned against the door, pressing his forehead into the wood, while willing his sudden and persistent erection to die a swift death. Helena was turning out to be more of a temptation than he was certain he could bear. If he were lucky, she would come to a decision about marrying him sooner rather than later.

CHAPTER NINE

T HAT EVENING, HELENA undressed for bed in the company of both Harriett and Cecelia. Her friend had requested to spend the next several nights in their company, as her parents were away in the country for the next fortnight, and she detested sleeping alone in an empty house. The reminder that there were servants at her beck and call did nothing to soothe her, but Helena didn't mind. She was grateful for the company, and Cecelia's talkativeness would distract Harriett from the fact that Helena was too diverted to talk.

While the pair helped one another out of their stays, Helena sat at her vanity in a dressing gown and clean nightrail, plucking pins from her coiffure. Meeting her own gaze in the mirror, she blushed and pinched her quivering lips to hide the smile threatening to split her face. The rational part of her mind told her she was being ridiculous and that acquiescence to Sebastian had been a dire mistake.

The matter of Harriett aside, there was still the issue of her nocturnal escapades to consider. What would happen with her friends if she told them she must bow out of their agreement in order to marry an earl? They wouldn't begrudge her, and she knew that well enough.

Each of them sought another path out of their respective conundrums, and their band of highway robbers had only ever been meant as a temporary solution. More concerning was the chance of Sebastian learning how she had financed the maintenance of her household and Harriett's season. He claimed not to care about any secrets she might be hiding, but Helena suspected that Sebastian had been thinking of something a little more benign—like an irritating laugh or a hidden physical deformity. Finding out that one's sweetheart was a criminal who pilfered the belongings of others at gunpoint was the sort of secret any suitor would flinch away from.

And yet, the previously smothered young girl in her—the one filled with romantic dreams and flights of whimsy—was just so bloody happy. Keeping her smile at bay became harder as she sat brushing her hair and reliving the passionate moments between her and Sebastian. The man had a way with words, tearing away her resolve and stoking to life all the hope Helena had thought dead and buried within her darkest depths.

It was difficult to remain so cynical with him looking at her the way he had, with his heart in his eyes. And the way he'd kissed her. Her skin flushed hot beneath the layers of her robe and nightgown as she thought of the liberties she had allowed him. Not just his lips on hers, but upon her neck and shoulder. His hand had cupped her breast, and for that brief moment, she'd become a bundle of nerves, experiencing only pure sensation.

The man was going to be the death of her. How was Helena to be rational about his offer with him seducing her with his smiles and his charming wit? How was she to consider all the factors involved when all she could think of was how badly she wanted to be in his arms again and perhaps find out how his hands might feel touching other parts of his body.

"Helena," Harriett said, drawing Helena away from her improper thoughts. "You have been awfully quiet this evening."

Helena flinched as her brush snagged a tangle but straightened on her stool and spun to face her sister and her friend. Cecelia had slipped into a robe over her chemise, while Harriett sat on the bed to untie her garters and roll down her stockings.

"Have I?" she hedged, avoiding both their gazes.

"Yes, and you seem distracted," Cecelia chimed in. "Are you all right? I noticed you hardly ate at Stratford's dinner party. Do you feel ill?"

Helena forced a smile. "I'm perfectly all right. A bit tired, I think. A good night's sleep will be just the thing."

Harriett's lips quirked into a coy smirk. "Did you hear what I just told Cecelia?"

"Erm, no," she admitted sheepishly. She had been in a world all her own, deep in her mind where Sebastian dominated her thoughts. "I'm so sorry."

"Well, it's just that I have decided to narrow the field of my potential suitors. We are already a month into the season, and Henry is set to return to university in a few days. I've been introduced to so many eligible gentlemen, and I think I have decided which one I like best."

The hairbrush slipped from Helena's hand and thumped to the floor. "Oh?" she murmured while bending to pick it up. "Who have you settled on?"

Despite his insistence that Harriett wasn't interested in him, Helena was terrified that she would name Sebastian. How horrible would it be to hear such a thing after having just decided to succumb to her feelings for him?

To her relief, Harriett announced the name of a different suitor while unwinding strands of her chignon loose around her shoulders. "The Viscount Amberly. He is such a lovely man, don't you think?"

Helena couldn't help the relief tinging the words that came out on a rush. "Oh, yes, he is very handsome and cordial. I've noticed he seems quite taken with you."

Harriett sighed, wistfully staring off across the room. "And I with him. It is early yet, but I do think he could be the one. I cannot risk discouraging him by courting the attentions of my other suitors."

"I think you have made a wise decision," Helena said, falling back into her role as the practical elder sister. "Amberly is an old, distinguished name, and his title came with a rather sizable fortune. He will make you a wonderful husband."

"Indeed," Cecelia agreed, flopping onto her belly across the bed. "Much better than that odious Stratford."

Helena went still, halfway through braiding her hair for bed. "What's wrong with Stratford? I found him a perfectly acceptable gentleman."

Harriett made a rough sound from the back of her throat. "He would have done well enough, but now that I've had time to meet other gentlemen, I realize he and I would never have suited. I suppose he is handsome in his own way for a man of such advanced age."

"Advanced, he's barely thirty!" Helena exclaimed.

Harriett shrugged, collecting her hairpins and walking to the vanity to store them in a ceramic jar. "Perhaps not so old, but, well, he is rather *stuffy,* isn't he? So sober all the time. I didn't laugh a single time when I was in his company."

"Hmm, that isn't good," Cecelia said. "I find a good sense of humor very attractive in a man."

"He isn't so very stuffy," Helena protested, turning her back on them both. Irritation made her pull harder on her hair than necessary as she finished off her braid. "He is quite witty when he wishes to be."

Harriett perched on the edge of the vanity and stared down at her. Ignoring the discerning gaze of her sister, Helena tied off her braid with a scrap of muslin.

"Goodness," Harriett said. "I thought you didn't like the man, Helena."

"I didn't," she snapped, "but that was before I opened my mind and decided to get to know him. Stratford didn't make the best first impression, but he is gallant and polite and quite *young* for a man of his status. Any lady would be fortunate to have him as a husband."

"What you mean," Cecelia called out, "is that *you* will be very fortunate to have him as a husband."

Helena stood and swept across the room, busying herself with putting out the tapers near the window to keep from having to look into the accusing eyes of her sister and her friend. "Of course, that isn't what I meant. What a silly thing for you to suggest."

Her hands shook as she snuffed the candles, and she feared she might never be able to turn around and face them. How ever would she tell the truth? She didn't have much time to do so, as Sebastian had made it clear he intended to begin their courtship immediately.

"Helena," Harriet said, her soft voice coming from directly behind her.

Helena flinched and turned to face her sister. "Yes?"

"Why don't you just admit that you love him? He loves you, you know. He all but told me himself. I'm the one who convinced him not to give up his pursuit of you after I assured him I had no interest in marrying him, of course."

Helena's shoulders sagged as she stared from her sister to Cecelia, who had left the bed and stood near, wearing a knowing grin. "Is it that obvious?"

Cecelia snorted. "About as obvious as the fact that you have a magnificent set of dugs."

Harriett burst out laughing, while Helena snatched her robe closed over her bosom. "Cee-Cee, honestly!"

Cecelia shrugged. "What? It's true. I have always been jealous of what you've been blessed with by nature. Anyway, yes, it is obvious that you and Stratford have developed a tendre for one another. It has been from the beginning."

Helena turned back to Harriett, taking hold of both her hands. "And you do not mind? Please, you must tell me if you do, because I will tell him sod off without another thought."

Harriett squeezed her hands tight. "That is nonsense. No, I do not mind in the least. Stratford is a wonderful man, and I adore him, but in the way I adore our brother. He isn't the man for me, but I suspect he might be the one for you."

Helena smiled, overcome with emotion. "Oh, Harriett, I think you may be right. He is so dashing and romantic, and he wants to court and marry me. I never thought this would happen!"

Cecelia placed a hand on her shoulder. "You have always been so unaware of how extraordinary you are. We have always known it, and now Stratford does, too. Mark my words, the Montgomery sisters will both be wed by summer!"

Harriett pulled Helena into her arms with a girlish squeal, squeezing her tight. Helena clutched her sister, allowing herself to feel all the things she'd never hoped to experience—excitement, hope, expectation, love. It was ridiculous to think she loved Sebastian after so short a time, but there was no other word for the giddy happiness that had seized her or the sensual awareness and longing he had stoked to life within her. She was still determined to take her time and allow the ritual of proper wooing to take place. After all, it was what she deserved after years of being set on a shelf and ignored.

When they pulled apart, Helena turned to find Cecelia watching them with watery eyes, her hands folded over her chest. Her heart sank for her friend as she realized that while her own situation would soon improve, Cecelia was still in danger of a miserable future.

"Cee-Cee," she rasped, reaching a hand out for her friend.

Cecelia clasped it and shook her head. "Don't think about me. I forbid it. This is your moment, Helena, and you deserve it. Be happy. I am certainly happy *for* you."

"Thank you," Helena whispered, tugging Cecelia close so she and Harriett could wrap her in their embrace.

They held on to each other, united by joy and sisterhood. Helena closed her eyes and prayed that their present course of good luck held out. If there was hope for her, then surely fate would shine upon Cecelia, who was no less deserving than she was.

"I CANNOT BELIEVE Helena is getting married. This is so exciting!"

From where Helena hid behind a cluster of shrubs along the road leading out of London, Selina's excited squeal reached her through the dark. It was quickly followed by a sharp reprimand from Effie.

"Shh! Do you *want* us to be caught? Someone might hear!"

"The irony," Mina groused from where she stooped at Helena's side, the folds of a frock coat fanned out around her bent legs. "As if anyone within a ten-mile range cannot also hear *her*."

Helena muffled a giggle behind one hand while peering past Mina to where their other friends hid in their vantage points. It was well past one o'clock in the morning, and they had been waiting for a carriage to pass for the past quarter of an hour. A fortnight had passed since the official beginning of Sebastian's courtship of her, and there was no hiding their attachment from anyone. The rest of her friends had reacted with the same excitement and encouragement that Cecelia had, making it easier for Helena to begin looking forward.

Sebastian had announced his intention of doing things properly and proposing to her when he felt the time was right—which meant her life would change, more than it already had, with little to no notice. Helena only had so much time before she must prepare to step into the new phase of her life. While becoming Sebastian's wife would bring her happiness and an end to the trials of caring for her family with little to no means, it was also an intimidating prospect. She would become a countess, a substantial thrust up the social ladder and into the spotlight. For someone who had spent her entire adult life clinging to the periphery of the sphere of the *beau monde*, it was a daunting prospect.

"I am glad for you," Mina whispered, though she kept her eyes glued to the open road before them. "I'm also at a loss as to what you're doing here. I will not fault you for abandoning us to allow your earl to carry you off into the sunset. May we all be so fortunate."

Helena shook her head. "As a friend, I would never abandon any of you, no matter how much my circumstances have improved. On the matter of my setting down my pistol and leaving the Band of Brigands, I am not married yet. I'm not even engaged. Anything could happen, and until any marriage is finalized, I still have a duty to care for Harriett and Henry."

Mina tore her gaze from the road and glanced at Helena with a strained smile. "You know, I have always admired that about you—unflinchingly doing what needs to be done."

"You're the one who always takes the lead," Helena protested. "Without you, none of us would have had the courage to go through with this."

"There are different kinds of courage, and none of them is any greater than the other. I wouldn't have been bold enough to suggest it if I didn't think the four of you didn't have what it took to pull it off. For what it's worth, it won't be the same without you."

"That's because once I am gone, someone else is going to have to keep an eye on Selina and ensure she remains calm."

Mina let out a low chuckle. "I nominate Cecelia."

Helena's quipped response was drowned out by Effie's bellow from the other side of the road.

"Carriage!"

Mina's aspect changed from one of supportive friend to stalwart general. She straightened, drawing her pistol from the waistband of her breeches, and resolutely marched to her place in the middle of the road. Helena wiped sweating hands on her thighs and then palmed her own weapon, reminding herself that they operated like a well-oiled machine at this point. There was nothing for her to be anxious about.

All went as usual, with Mina firing her warning shot and bringing the carriage to a halt. With all five of them along for the undertaking, Effie was able to leap onto the driver's perch rather than wait for Mina to manage the feat. Grunts and muttered epithets rang out through the air as the man raised his whip to strike out at Effie but missing by a long shot. Effie promptly kicked the man's hand to send the whip flying, then leveled her gun at his chest.

Helena darted out of her place in the shadows toward the carriage door facing her side of the road but was drawn up short when she realized it was already hanging open to show the shadowed interior. It was a cloudy night with little moonlight, and one of the carriage lamps had been doused in Effie's struggle with the driver.

Panic gripped her as she lifted her pistol and waited for movement from within the carriage. The sounds of a struggle emitted from the other side of the conveyance, leaving Helena torn between investigating and remaining at her post in case there was more trouble to be faced. Her heart thundered, and her stomach heaved at the realization that none of this was going as planned. What the devil was happening on the other side of the carriage? Had the occupant exited the other side and gone on the offensive? Where were the others?

Helena didn't have a chance to puzzle it out because the sound of footsteps alerted her to a presence behind her. An arm wrapped around her neck, and she was hauled back against a male body.

"I've got you!" growled a deep voice near her ear.

Terror drove Helena to thrash in the stranger's hold, her legs kicking and arms flailing. The man grunted and wrestled with her, trying to take her to the ground. She parted her lips to call for the help of her friends but found her airway constricted by a strong, solid arm.

A sudden calm fell over her as she told herself no one would save her. Calling upon the hours of training she had endured alongside her friends, she dropped all her weight downward, throwing her assailant off balance. Then, she sent an elbow flying back into the man's belly. The arm loosened enough for her to fall free, pain radiating from her rump up her back and rattling her teeth.

Panting for breath and driven by the rush of blood in her veins, Helena rolled and sprang to her feet, raising her pistol at the exact moment the man stood.

"Halt!" she rasped, not having to work very hard to deepen her voice. Her throat was on fire from being choked, and trying to draw air made her chest burn. "Stand and deliver!"

In the shadowy light, she saw the flaring of the man's eyes, the white around his pupils flashing as his mouth fell open. He held both hands up in surrender but never took his gaze off her, clearly in shock. Helena's arm trembled as he went on staring in silence—a bizarre occurrence, as most couldn't take their eyes off the gun thrust into their face to pay much attention to the person holding it.

And then, the unthinkable happened. The man staggered toward her a step, and the smallest beam of moonlight revealed the whole of his face. The familiarity of those features struck Helena like a kick to the chest, leaving her paralyzed with dread.

Felix Radcliffe stared back at her, seeming just as dismayed as she. "*Helena?*" he whispered, shaking his head in disbelief. "But how?"

Keeping her gun level, Helena used her free hand to feel about her face. Horror washed over her as she realized her mask had slipped up to her brow in the struggle. She had been too busy freeing herself from Felix's clutches to notice.

She quickly slipped it back down, despite knowing it was no use. Felix had recognized her! He knew she was one of the highwaymen filling the papers with exaggerated stories of harrowing deeds and nefarious aims. Everything was ruined, and there was nothing she could do to change that.

Her throat burned with coming hysteria, her eyes blurring and stinging with tears that threatened to spill any moment. This wasn't how things were supposed to happen. She was supposed to have her happy ending, which would enable her to leave behind this double life of secrets and danger. But her sinful deeds had come full circle in a twist of fate that would be funny if it weren't so absolutely devastating.

She blinked, and Felix parted his lips as if to say something else, though he never had the chance. He was jolted from behind, following a heavy thud, then his eyes rolled up into his head as he pitched forward and landed face down in the dirt. Effie stood over him, eyes wide and wild as she held her blunderbuss up like a cudgel.

"Are you all right?" she asked, using one foot to nudge Felix's prone form. He was unmoving though his back rose and fell with deep, steady breaths. Effie had rendered him unconscious."

"Y-yes," Helena stammered, lowering her pistol with a shaking hand. Her knees trembled, and she feared she might faint. Being saved from this confrontation with Felix made her feel no better, for it was only a matter of time before her entire world came crashing down around her.

She choked down the bile rising up in her throat and took a few deep breaths. There was no stopping what would happen next, so she had no choice but to move forward and weather the storm. At the moment, getting away from this blasted carriage was her first order of business.

"What happened?" she asked, tearing her gaze away from Felix.

Effie scowled. "There was a footman, and we didn't see him until he rounded the carriage and attacked. While I subdued the driver, Mina, Cecelia, and Selina took him down. What about him?"

She jerked her head in Felix's direction, but Helena refused to look at him. Just knowing he lay at her feet made her belly quiver with nausea. How much would Sebastian come to hate her once he was informed that the woman he wanted to marry had taken part in robbing and assaulting his brother?

"I am not certain," Helena replied. "I took my eyes off the

carriage long enough to ensure you had the driver in hand, and he must have sneaked out and circled around to surprise me. I…I fought him off, but…"

Effie took her hand and steered her around the back of the carriage. "You poor thing. Thank God you weren't hurt."

Helena winced at the twinge that radiated up her spine with every step. She had hit the ground harder than she'd thought. "Is everyone all right?"

"Better than all right," Effie declared. She came to a stop and swept her arm out to indicate their friends, who crouched over a gunny sack. Mina was rifling through its contents while Cecelia hoisted a heavy-looking valise in one hand. "Whoever he is, he's more than well-off. He must have been on his way to the country, because we found a treasure trove of goods."

Helena noticed Felix's trunk for the first time—a massive thing of leather and hand-tooled gilt—and her heart sank. For the first time, their good fortune didn't make her feel hopeful. Guilt welled in her as she wondered how many of the stolen items were family heirlooms. How many of the baubles inside had been passed down from one brother to the other? In the past, it had been easy to distance herself from the people attached to the things they stole. Material things could be replaced, and most were willing enough to hand them over without much of a fight. But those people hadn't been of the family she hoped to one day become a part of. No one had ever been seriously hurt by their crimes.

She pressed a hand to her stomach, fearing she might become ill. Effie tugged on her arm, alerting her that they were on the move.

"Let's get out of here," Mina muttered, helping Selina lift Felix's trunk. "That was entirely too close for comfort."

Helena nearly laughed at that statement. For the others, the event had been harrowing, but for her, it had been something else entirely. Her back and hips ached as they dashed for the trees and Mina's hidden carriage, but that was nothing compared to the pain that flared from deep in her chest as the full weight of what had just occurred fell over her.

She had been such a fool. Years of cautious practicality had been shoved aside in the face of her desire for love and a future that didn't relegate her to the dust heap of unwanted spinsters. It had seemed silly, in the face of Sebastian's romantic declarations, to worry about her secret actions intersecting with her bright future. Yet, she had known deep down that it was always a possibility and had ignored her instincts. Her worst fear had come to fruition, and she must now accept the consequences.

CHAPTER TEN

SEBASTIAN LEANED BACK onto his elbow and stretched his legs across the blanket spread over the grass. From where he sat, enjoying the fine spring weather, he could see the rest of his guests in the spacious garden off the back of Stratford House, blankets and hampers of food dotting the landscape. Helena and her friends, along with Harriett, were engaged in a spirited game of battledore and shuttlecock, their skirts flaring and their laughter floating through the air as they batted the birdie back and forth between them.

He had coaxed Helena into inviting her friends to his home for the afternoon, not just because he would want her to become comfortable having them about once they were married. Sebastian also wished to know everything there was to learn about Helena, and that included the details of a life that had only just recently included him.

He valued their time together—the walks they took in Hyde Park, the trips to Gunter's where they sampled the strangest flavors of ice they could find, and nights at the theater. He hardly went a day without laying eyes on her and found himself increasingly coveting her time and attention, wanting to be near her every waking moment. His feelings were intense and frightening, but Sebastian had chosen to embrace them. A man could certainly do worse than falling ridiculously, head-over-heels in love with a woman like Helena Montgomery.

On the other side of the central courtyard of the garden, the young son of Helena's friend, Effie, kicked a ball about with one of the scullery maids. When Sebastian had mentioned to his mother that one of Helena's friends came with a child, the dowager had immediately sent for the girl, excusing her from her duties for the day to make a playmate for Crispin.

Everything was as near to perfect as could be, but a few problems clouded the back of Sebastian's mind. Three nights ago, his brother had set out to travel to Yorkshire for a house party being hosted by a friend, only to be waylaid just outside London by the notorious Band of Brigands. Sebastian had been awakened out of a sound sleep when a servant pounded on his door to deliver the news. He had sat outside Felix's bedchamber, consoling his weeping mother as a physician examined his brother.

According to the report of the coachman, they had been ambushed by at least five assailants, all armed with pistols. The driver had been subdued, his hands and feet bound. While he was left face down in the dirt, the footman had attempted to prevent the highwaymen from overtaking Felix. Unfortunately, the sheer number of the criminals had won out in the end. The footman had met a similar fate as the coachman, while Felix had exited the carriage and attempted to fight back. From there, the details were hazy. Felix hadn't told him much the morning after the incident, claiming that it had been dark, and he wasn't certain just how many attackers there had been. He could only recall grappling with one before another had bashed him over the back of the head.

Fortunately, his injury was minor—no more than a concussed head and a heavy dose of wounded pride. However, Sebastian was unwilling to let matters lie. He had been infuriated to find his brother lying abed, pale and drowsy. The loss of his personal effects was nothing compared to the indignity of being terrorized and robbed by a ring of violent thieves.

Witnessing his mother's upset had only added insult to injury. He was determined to do his part in bringing the vigilantes to justice. The morning following Felix's attack, Sebastian had visited the magistrate's office at No. 4 Bow Street to report the crime. He had been assured that an investigation had already commenced into the activities of the so-called Band of Brigands and that an investigator would be sent to question Felix over the details of the incident.

In the meantime, there was little Sebastian could do other than wait for the magistrate to do his job and hope that Felix wouldn't suffer any ill-effects of his concussion.

As he reached into the hamper near his elbow to retrieve a cluster of grapes, Sebastian allowed his gaze to linger on Helena. She was lovely today in a sprigged-muslin day gown of powder blue with embroidered white flowers. In the privacy of his garden, she had removed her hat, and the beams of sunlight shining from above brought the golden tones of her hair to life.

They had attended the opera together last night, and while she had claimed to enjoy herself, she had been unusually quiet and reserved. The phenomenon continued on today, baffling Sebastian to no end. She had arrived a few minutes before her friends, taking tea with him and the dowager while they waited. His mother had carried the bulk of the conversation, probing into Helena's background to learn more about her. She had been surprised at Sebastian's announcement that his true affections lay with the elder Montgomery sister rather than the younger but had taken it all in stride. Once she had interviewed Helena and seen how well she got on with Sebastian, the dowager had approved of the match.

While Helena was polite and gave the dowager her full attention, her answers to various questions were sparse, and when she wasn't speaking, she was staring into her tea or down at her hands with a worried look on her face. Sebastian wanted to ask about what might be troubling her but didn't want to cast a shadow over the afternoon. He had hoped that being in the company of her friends would improve her mood, and as he watched her stumble, laughing as she swung her racket and missed the hurtling birdie, he was pleased to note he had been right. She was enjoying herself, and it was all he could want.

Still, he couldn't help but wonder what put the tiny lines of distress between her eyebrows. Sebastian couldn't imagine it had anything to do with him, specifically, because he knew Helena well enough to realize if he had upset her, she would simply say so. She wasn't one to hold back, and it was one of the things he liked most about her. There must be something else she didn't wish to speak of.

As she bent to pick up the birdie she had missed, her skirts raised enough for Sebastian to get a peek at her feet—and the roughly aged slippers she wore on them. His mouth went tight at the corners as she shifted to adjust the heel of one of them— which was so worn, it sagged pitifully. The soles were beyond repair, and it was a wonder she didn't feel the jab of every pebble in the yard. She showed no sign of discomfort; however, her smile as wide and as bright as ever.

Perhaps financial woes were the reason for her previous mood. It couldn't be easy for Helena to push aside the burdens she carried, though she often did so without an outward show of despondence. Sebastian's hands were tied by the distance she had created around this particular problem. She had told him more than once that she wanted *him*, not his money, and while that was a lovely sentiment, Sebastian hated that it barred him from doing anything to help her.

During a light conversation, Helena had let it slip that she and Harriett hired hackneys when the distance to some place or another was too far to walk. When he'd questioned further, she had flushed, seeming embarrassed to confide that they'd had to sell their carriage and horses months ago due to the expense of maintaining them. Sebastian had offered them the use of one of his vehicles, as there were five stored in the row of mews behind the street his townhouse was situated upon, but Helena had refused, stating that she and Harriett were happy to make do.

Sebastian had pressed the issue, only to come up against

Helena's stubborn resistance. In an effort to keep the peace between them, he let the matter drop, though he wasn't happy about it.

The Montgomery sisters should have a coach of their own, with a dependable driver and a duo of footmen to keep them safe. They would have all those things once Helena was his wife, along with all the other comforts his money could afford. However, Helena seemed determined not to accept any such gestures from him in the meantime. While he respected her wishes and understood her reasons, Sebastian abhorred seeing the evidence of her hardships. The deaths of her parents had left her shouldering the burden. She might have the love and companionship of her siblings, but for all intents and purposes, Helena was completely on her own.

Sebastian finished off his grapes and stood, deciding that the answer to this conundrum was simple enough. He would simply have to speed along the process of their courtship and coax her to the altar sooner than planned. It would take time for the banns to be read and even the smallest of ceremonies to be planned. Sebastian didn't think he could wait much longer than that to make Helena his, nor did he wish to watch her go on struggling to hide the truth of her situation from the world.

As he approached and Helena glanced up to meet his gaze, his insides went warm, and his blood surged with an undeniable heat. She offered him a reticent smile, lifting her empty hand to wave at him. Sebastian smiled back, finding that the expression came more readily to his face than it ever had. Helena brought out the best in him, and for that, he wanted to offer her the world.

Soon, he told himself. In the very near future, he would have the power to wipe those worry lines off her face for good.

"Ladies," he murmured as the game paused, and they all turned to face him. "I trust you are enjoying yourselves."

"Very much," Helena replied, giving her racket a twirl.

"*So* very much," said Cecelia. "Thank you, my lord."

"Please, call me Sebastian, all of you. There is no need for formality among us. Any friends of Helena are friends of mine."

Wilhelmina Barrington gave him a sly look, her dark eyes appraising him from head to toe. The woman's gaze made him feel utterly exposed, like an errant pupil standing before a strict governess. He had only just met her but recognized that she was one to be reckoned with.

"He wants something," she teased. "What are you after, *Sebastian*?"

He held his hands up with a sheepish grin. "I have been caught. I had hoped for a moment with Helena alone."

The dark-haired Selina and the tall, willowy Euphemia traded glances and burst into giggles while Wilhelmina smirked.

"I knew it. Well, Helena? Do you wish to be alone with this man?"

Helena lowered her eyes, her lips quivering with amusement. "I suppose, but only if you all won't think too poorly of me."

Euphemia waved a dismissive hand. "Oh, pish! The two of you are practically engaged. Go, no one will say a word."

She pointedly turned her back and strode farther across the courtyard, and the others followed suit.

"We didn't see a thing," Selina declared, her racket held over one shoulder.

Sebastian promptly took Helena's hand and led her in the opposite direction—toward a small cluster of hedgerows that would offer them privacy. She giggled while trotting to keep up with his long strides, her racket falling to the ground.

"Sebastian! What on earth?"

"I haven't kissed you in three days," he grumbled as they rounded one of the tall hedges, which stood just high enough to conceal them from sight. "I'm dying."

"You've been counting?" she blurted with a full-throated laugh.

"Yes," he replied, spinning to face her once they had gone deep enough into the miniature maze to satisfy him. "Every hour.

Every minute. You don't have to tell me how pitiful I am, for I'm well aware."

Helena gasped when he spun her, so her back was to the hedges and caged her in with his body. "Oh, you aren't alone in that."

"Good," he rasped, grasping her waist and sinking into the soft warmth of her curves.

She tipped her head back to receive his kiss, and Sebastian went at her like a man starved. Foliage rasped against the sleeves of his coat as he pressed into her, his aching body yearning for closeness. Her breasts pushed into his chest as her back arched, causing her hips to undulate against him. Sebastian groaned and slid his hand lower to cup a handful of her luxurious, plump buttocks. She was a dream in the flesh, a tempting well of overflowing, sensual promise, and Sebastian's discipline was frayed to its snapping point.

He wanted her—all of her—so badly that illicit thoughts of her invaded his dreams and had him waking at all hours, hard and pulsing and sweating. Years of clinging to a rigid code of conduct kept him from pressing her into intimacies that should be reserved for their wedding night, but Sebastian was of the notion that it wouldn't hurt to sample the barest taste of her when she allowed it. These small samplings of her were the only thing keeping him sane.

"Helena," he whispered, kissing a path down her neck. "God, how I want you."

Her fingernails dug into his shoulders as she squirmed in his hold, whimpering at the flicks of his tongue against the sleek pillar of her throat. "I…I …"

Sebastian smiled against her shoulder, giving her bottom a firm squeeze. "Yes, sweet?"

"Oh," she moaned when he trailed his lips over the swells of her cleavage. The modest neckline of her day gown didn't offer him much access, but Sebastian would not be cowed. He dipped his tongue past the fabric, skimming it along the edge of her chemise and tasting supple, bare flesh.

He lifted his gaze to find her head resting against the hedge, lips parted and eyes closed. "You were saying something?"

She opened her eyes and peered at him, frustration darkening the blush in her cheeks. "What?"

He kissed her chin. "I said, I want you, and then you were about to say…"

Helena gasped when he cupped her breast, seeking the point of her nipple through layers of fabric. The erect organ in his breeches pulsed at the feel of it hardening between his fingers and the low mewling sound she made in reaction.

"I need to hear it, Helena," he prodded. "Tell me you want me as much as I want you."

"I want you," she whispered, thrusting her breast more fully into his palm. "I want you, Sebastian."

Satisfaction flared within him, heightening the intensity of his desire with the utterance of those words in her low, husky tones. He buried his face in her neck, working at the fastenings running down the back of her gown. She pushed away from the hedgerow to provide him better access, and he tore at the gown in a frenzy of desperate need. They were relatively alone and freed from the constraints of society for this encounter, and Sebastian didn't want to waste another moment.

Her gown loosened enough for him to pull it down, but Helena stood upright and clapped both hands over her bosom before he could manage it. "Wait!"

Sebastian dropped his hands, disturbed by the acute fear written all over her face. "I'm sorry. Perhaps I shouldn't."

"No," she said with a quick, vehement shake of her head. "I want you to, it is only…"

"Only what, sweet?" he asked, prying one of her hands off her breast and bringing it to her lips. "It's all right."

She lowered her eyes, unaware of the enticing picture she made—shoulders and the tops of her breasts exposed, her skin kissed by a warm glow.

"My undergarments," she whispered.

Sebastian frowned. "Yes? I assume you're wearing them, a chemise, stays, and the like. What about them?"

He felt as if he had been punched in the gut when she looked up at him with shame on her eyes, her chin trembling.

"They aren't in the best condition. You make me forget things, Sebastian, like the fact that I am not the kind of woman you are probably accustomed to. I don't want you to be disappointed."

Sebastian cupped her cheek and pressed his lips to her forehead. "Is that all? I feared you were hiding a third breast or some kind of unsightly growth under there. Though, I wouldn't be opposed to a third breast considering that the two you have are so magnificent."

"Sebastian!" she chided. "I'm being serious."

He pressed a kiss to her lips. "So am I. Do you think I care about what you're wearing? The package isn't nearly as interesting to me as what's inside it. Besides, undergarments are meant to be removed."

She shook her head in disbelief. "Sometimes I think you are too good to be true."

Sebastian grinned. "Sorry to disappoint you, but I am only a man, brutish and carnal and lusty. But I adore you, Helena. I would want you if you were dressed in rags, mostly because they'd be easier to remove."

He had expected a laugh and perhaps an ease in her rigid bearing, but Helena merely stared at him, looking mournful. "I don't deserve you."

Sebastian took hold of the hand still holding her gown up and gently moved it to hang at her side. He strummed his knuckles along her cheek and down her neck, pausing at the edge of her bodice.

"I am the one who is undeserving," he declared. "You are too hard on yourself, Helena."

"And you are too besotted to see that I am not as perfect as you'd like to believe." Her protest was a weak one, whispered out on a helpless sigh as he eased her bodice to her waist and began pulling at the stays laced up her back.

"No," he countered. "I am simply too enamored with your best qualities to care that they come with your worst. I accept you as you are, sweet. It's time you started accepting yourself."

There was no more arguing as her stays sagged open, offering Sebastian full view of a thin chemise stretched taut over the full swells of breasts that made his mouth water. His breath hitched as he used trembling hands to ease the fabric downward, his belly clenching as he revealed the smooth globes. Helena clutched at his lapels, staring at him while he drank her in with his eyes, the reality of her obliterating the imaginings of his mind.

"Just look at you," he murmured, trailing his fingertips down her chest, then tracing the underside of one full breast. "So perfect, so beautiful."

Any reply she might have made was smothered by the choked cry she emitted at the touch of his hand. Her skin was satin-smooth and warm, her nipple a hardened pearl. He rubbed and squeezed, teasing tiny moans of shocked pleasure from her.

He glanced up at her just before dipping his head toward the opposite breast and gave her the tried-and-true eyebrow lift. "You're going to have to be quiet if you don't want your friends to know what I'm doing. Something tells me they'll attack if they think I'm not behaving like a gentleman. And there's nothing gentlemanly about this."

Helena muffled another cry with the back of her hand as he took her into his mouth, gently circling her nipple with his tongue before sucking it between his lips. She shuddered and clutched at him as he tasted and consumed her with his mouth, while one hand tugged and teased a distended nipple. The sounds she made, trying and failing to silence them, drove him and heightened his desire, making him feel as if he'd fall to his knees before her then and there and beg her to marry him today, tomorrow, right now. As long as he could place a ring on her finger and make her his in the most elemental of ways. He groaned at the taste and smell of her—sweet and womanly and so addicting, he didn't think he would ever get his fill.

He couldn't resist exploring more of her, his other hand slipping down her body to caress her waist, her hip, the lower few inches of her belly. She stiffened when his fingers brushed across her mons over the fabric of her gown but then bucked her hips as he trailed a finger along the hidden cove. Heat emanated from that most intimate and sacred of places, beckoning to him with a siren's call. He didn't dare lift her skirts, knowing not to tempt himself to do anything irrevocable. And yet, he couldn't resist pressing his palm between her thighs, seeking the spot that would bring her pleasure.

She was writhing and panting in his arms, uninhibited and passionate, and Sebastian wanted to show her what the height of such desire could culminate into. He wanted her to know how thoroughly he could please her, how utterly enthralled he was with every part of her.

He muffled her sounds of surprise and ecstasy with his lips, engaging her in a deep, stirring kiss as he pressed his fingers against the furrows and folds of her quim and stroked with slow, precise movements. Helena moaned into his mouth, parting her legs wider to let him pleasure her. Sebastian ignored his nagging arousal, willing to wait to have his own satisfaction. This would be solely about her, an affirmation of his desire for her and a reminder that she never had to worry that matters as meaningless as her garments could stop him from wanting to strip her out of every stitch.

He tore his lips from hers and watched the play of emotion over her face as she was awakened, her eyes saying things her voice could not. She was stunned, undone, and unraveled, just as he was. He lapped at her nipple, then gently took it between his teeth and was rewarded by the clench of her hands in his hair and a sharp gasp. Her hips jerked, and her body went rigid, and the dark pupils of her eyes expanded as her mouth parted into a riveting circle of surprise.

"Oh, Sebastian," she rasped, her voice low and hoarse. "I'm…"

"I know, sweet," he soothed between drugging kisses. "Let it happen. Give into the pleasure. Yes, that's it."

She grabbed hold of his nape and mashed her lips against his as climax swept over her, groaning against his lips as he stroked her through the spasming waves tearing through her. Sebastian soaked in every detail, memorizing it for his moments of solitude when he could call them up and relive the poignant, erotic moment whenever he wished.

When she slumped against him, her breaths coming harsh and fast, Sebastian gathered her against him and held her tight, burying his face in her hair. Despite feeling as if he might explode from such restraint, he was satisfied with the results of their interlude. He wasn't above using every weapon in his arsenal to convince her that marriage must happen sooner rather than later—short of compromising her completely. It was a line he wasn't willing to cross, no matter how persistently his cock reminded him just how badly it wanted to be buried inside her. He was stronger than his urges, potent as they were.

Once Helena went still and quiet in his arms, Sebastian began setting her clothing to rights. They'd been away from the others long enough.

He had just finished closing her gown when footsteps sounded on the other side of the hedge. Helena remained where she stood, a faraway look in her eyes that was quite flattering to his manhood given the circumstances. However, it fell to him to put some distance between them before they were discovered. Just as he placed his feet clear on the other side of the gap between the hedges, a footman appeared, approaching him with a grim expression and determined strides.

The man didn't bat an eyelash at finding them alone, simply giving both him and Helena swift bows before giving Sebastian his attention.

"My lord, I do beg your pardon for the intrusion. The visitor you have been waiting for has arrived. He is in audience with Mr. Radcliffe right now."

Sebastian was instantly sober, the insistence of his aroused state doused and his mind turning toward the matter of his brother's attack. This wasn't the most convenient time for an inspector from Bow Street to pay a call, but the Runners were busy men. They were here now, at their own convenience, and Sebastian wanted this matter dealt with so that he could move forward.

"Very good," he replied. "You are dismissed."

The footman retreated, leaving Sebastian to tend to Helena. She had recovered and now watched him with a furrowed brow.

"Is everything all right?"

He took her hands and drew her close. "Yes, everything is fine. I'm sorry to do this, but there is an important matter that requires my attention. It shouldn't take long."

At her questioning look, Sebastian sighed and squeezed her hands.

"I didn't mention this because I don't want you to worry, but I know you'll fret even if I don't tell you."

"I will," she confirmed. "Just tell me. Has something happened?"

She was already overset at the idea of something being wrong, her hands tight around his and her expression one of wary curiosity.

"Felix was a victim of the highwaymen that have been in the papers," he told her. "Three nights ago, when he was on his way to Yorkshire to attend a house party. They assaulted him and left him with a concussed head and stole his baggage."

Helena withdrew her hands from his, pressing one against her belly. She staggered back a step. "Oh, that's terrible."

He took hold of her shoulders. "He's fine, sweet. His pride hurts more than his head, I suspect. Still, I have contacted a magistrate from Bow Street, and he has asked for our help with his investigation."

"I-investigation?" she stammered. "Are these highwaymen so dangerous, then? I hadn't realized."

"They're a menace," he said, anger steeling his spine at the sight of her distress. He hadn't wanted to frighten her but could see that the subject caused her distress. "But not so intimidating that they cannot be swiftly and efficiently dealt with. Felix will tell the Bow Street Runners his story, and we will do what we can to aid in the apprehension of these thieves. In the meantime, I must urge you not to travel anywhere alone at night—not even within the city. Crime is rampant within London, and now the roads aren't even safe. If something happened to you, I don't think I could be held responsible for my actions."

She nodded but still looked as if her mind were a world away. "Did Felix tell you anything about the thieves? I mean, anything that might be useful to the investigation?"

"No," Sebastian sighed. "Only that there were at least four or five of them and that they incapacitated the driver and footmen before bludgeoning him over the head. He was knocked unconscious, and I suspect it has affected his memory. I hope that a few days of rest have made things clearer to him."

"So do I," she whispered, folding her arms around herself and staring off down the path between the hedges. "You had better go. They'll be wondering where you are."

"Are you certain you're all right?" he asked, not liking how pale she looked. Perhaps he shouldn't have mentioned the highwaymen.

"Of course. I just need a moment before I return to the others. Go, I'll be all right."

Sebastian was hesitant but decided that he was worried over nothing. He hadn't taken the news of Felix's attack well either. Helena's worry was another reason to do what he could to help put a stop to these robberies. Her peace of mind was important to him, as was the safety of the people he cared for most.

He rushed through the garden and into the house, following

the murmur of voices to the closed door of his study. Pushing the door open, he found Felix seated near a window in comfortable half-dress, while a lone man paced back and forth, taking notes on a small, rough pad of foolscap. The man wasn't what Sebastian had expected, but he supposed that Bow Street Runners came from backgrounds of all types.

The man wasn't as tall as Sebastian, but the bulk of his frame filled out a rough, wool coat and a wrinkled, haphazardly buttoned shirt. He wore no waistcoat, and a pair of braces showed when his coat wafted open due to the air he stirred about as he tread the rug, back and forth, back and forth. Loose trousers and boots completed the man's unfashionable attire, and a cap was tucked under one arm, having been removed at his arrival.

The man possessed an anvil of a jaw, sprinkled with coarse, bright red hair—a match for the overlong strands falling into his eyes. Despite his disreputable appearance—or perhaps because of it—Sebastian decided this was a man he wouldn't want to cross in a dark alley.

At Sebastian's entrance, the man halted his pacing and turned to face him, offering a half-hearted bow before going back to his notes. "My lord," he said in the lilting accent of an Irishman. "I thank ye for joining us. I was just questioning Mr. Radcliffe on the events o' the night in question."

Sebastian looked to Felix, who looked better today, his coloring back to normal and the dark circles under his eyes all but vanished. "And?"

"Story matches up to the others I've taken down," the Irishman stated. "Oh, beggin' yer pardon. Devlin Connelly, at yer service. As I was saying, Mr. Radcliffe reports no less than four but no more than five thugs, all armed and wearing hoods, cloaks, and masks. The attack was coordinated, resulting in the assault of a coachman and a footman as well as Mr. Radcliffe himself. Do I have it right?"

"Yes," Felix replied. "But I am sorry that I cannot be of further help to you, Mr. Connelly. It was dark, and disguised as they were, I did not see anything else I might use to describe them."

"'Tis all right," Mr. Connelly said, flipping to a fresh sheet of paper. "But any small details ye might recall can help. Anything ye can tell me about the size o' them? Were they large men or small? What kind o' weapons did ye notice?"

Felix crossed his legs and shrugged, staring upward as if searching his thoughts. "I'd say they were fairly large, all of them. Noticeably so."

Connelly glanced up from his paper, his stub of a pencil hovering over his scribbled notes. "Indeed, sir? Others have reported they were small men, likely why they have to hunt in a pack."

Sebastian wrinkled his brow and looked to Felix, who shrugged. "I can only tell you what I remember. They appeared rather large to me, intimidating. Their weapons were a hodge-podge of pistols, nothing special, no distinguishing markings."

Connelly narrowed his eyes and stared at Felix for a few seconds but then returned to his task. "I thank ye for that. Anything else ye might recall?"

Felix pursed his lips and squinted as if trying to see through air. "Erm, no, I don't believe there is. I did warn my brother that the details were muddled. I took quite a blow to the head."

He touched a fingertip to his temple with an embarrassed smile, though Connelly didn't even look up from his pages.

"I understand, Mr. Radcliffe, and am sorry. If ye find yerself remembering anything else, don't hesitate to visit me at No. 4 Bow Street. No information is unwanted or untimely."

Sebastian stepped into the man's path before he could make an exit. "Wait a moment. Mr. Connelly, surely there is more that can be done. These highwaymen have terrorized nearly a dozen people by now and show no sign that they intend to stop."

Connelly's pinched lips curled into a sneer. "They're a scourge that needs dealin' with, that's for sure. As of now, I've been placed at the head of the investigation, and I've begun by interviewing all the victims. It's my aim to compose profiles of a sort on these buggers—pardon me language, yer lordship."

Sebastian waved him off. "No apologies necessary. In the meantime, is there anything the Runners can do to assure safe travel along the roads? What of the horse patrol?"

"Beggin' yer pardon, me lord, but the grants we receive from the Crown are only sufficient to cover so many costs. The horse patrols are worn thin as it is. We simply can't spare the manpower."

Sebastian took hold of Connelly's shoulder and guided him toward his desk. "I want to be of help. As a peer and a member of the House of Lords, I have a duty to be of service wherever I can. Would a donation of a few thousand pounds suffice to fill the ranks of the horse patrol and ensure the roads are being watched—at least until such time as the thieves are apprehended?"

Connelly stared at him in slack-jawed silence while Sebastian sank into his chair and retrieved a quill and inkwell before reaching for a booklet of bank drafts.

"Beggin' yer pardon, me lord," he said after clearing his throat. "While I'm honored ye'd trust me to accept such a donation, I must request ye deliver the funds to No. 4 yerself. No offense meant, but I'd rather not have the burden of its safekeeping placed in me own hands."

Sebastian paused, his quill hovering over the thick paper. "No offense taken, Connelly. I respect your position. Please inform Sir Highsmith that I intend to deliver the funds at my earliest convenience. I trust they will be put to good use."

"Ye can be sure of it, me lord. Thank ye."

Ignoring the man's bow, Sebastian stood and extended a hand over the desk. Connelly hesitated only a moment before placing his own large hand into Sebastian's, and the two exchanged a firm shake.

"I hope to be apprised of your progress when there is news," Sebastian said.

"Indeed ye will. Good day, me lord, Mr. Radcliffe."

Connelly donned his cap and strode from the room. Sebastian

turned to Felix, who had risen from his seat and crossed to the cabinet where crystal decanters of spirits were kept.

"How are you feeling?" he asked, noticing that Felix moved about without any trouble.

"Fine," his brother replied. "Honestly, Seb, I wish you hadn't done that."

Sebastian scowled. "Done what? Assured that those ruffians are made to pay for what they did to you?"

Felix scoffed, pouring himself a healthy measure of brandy. "They robbed me and left us relatively unharmed. You are making too much of this."

"I think you aren't making enough of it," Sebastian snapped. "I won't allow it to go unchecked. Men like them should not be permitted to go unpunished for their crimes."

"Has it ever occurred to you that desperation and need can make thieves of even the best of people?" Felix argued, turning to face him. "The world isn't entirely black and white, Seb. Sometimes people have no choice in the matter."

"If a man is desperate, he can look for good, honest work. Are you honestly defending these miscreants?"

Felix sighed, brushing past him toward the door. "No, but I'm simply stating that no real harm was done. Surely time of the Bow Street Runners might be better spent."

Sebastian stared incredulously at his brother's back, unable to believe what he was hearing. It made no sense considering that he had been the victim of this crime.

"There are hundreds of them," he argued. "And with my contribution, they will have the means to patrol the London streets *and* the roads. I cannot allow this to stand, Felix."

"Right," Felix huffed on his way out the door. "I had forgotten that your perfection has qualified you to dictate what qualities make a person worthy of your respect. Have a care you don't break your neck falling off that high horse."

Sebastian stared after him, baffled and annoyed. This entire situation grew more bizarre by the day. Whoever heard of highwaymen who conducted their business in groups or a victim who didn't care whether the perpetrators were punished?

With a shake of his head, he returned to his desk to finish preparing the bank draft. He would deliver it after seeing Helena home. Then, he would turn his mind to more important matters like planning a romantic and memorable proposal for his future bride.

CHAPTER ELEVEN

ELENA STARED AT the gentle waters of the Serpentine winding its way through Hyde Park, hands folded in her lap. She wasn't certain how long she had sat here, her thoughts jumbled and turning over one another in a whirlwind of chaos. Having not slept a wink the night before, she was weary and suffered a headache. She would give anything to take to her bed with a cold compress and perhaps a tincture for sleep—blocking out the world and all its uncertainties and troubles. Unfortunately, she didn't have that luxury.

In fact, she had *never* been able to lean on the fragility that was supposedly her due as a woman of a good family and some means. She had always been the dependable one, the smart one, the one others turned to when they needed help. She had helped Henry make sense of his philosophy books his first term at Cambridge and had spent an entire year teaching Harriett the ins and outs of a lady's first season. She had held what was left of their family together after the deaths of her parents, holding her chin up and saving her tears for when she could be alone. To let Henry and Harriett see her falling apart would shatter their faith in her, and she had been determined to be strong for them.

She was so very tired. All her efforts could turn out to be all for naught once she was exposed as a thief. No one would care that she had been in danger of going hungry or losing her home. Not one member of the upper crust would offer her sympathy over losing her parents and learning that the security she'd been relying on her entire life had been a lie. She would be ruined, and her siblings along with her.

And Sebastian—wonderful, perfect Sebastian—would hate her for deceiving him and harming his brother. She might not have been the one to strike him, but she was guilty all the same.

Helena hadn't seen Sebastian since the picnic in his garden nearly a week ago. Like the coward she was, she had avoided his company, sending notes to inform him that she wasn't feeling well and would call upon him once she was feeling better. In truth, she felt ill—wrung dry and exhausted and nauseous at the thought of what she would have to do next. She couldn't be certain exactly what Felix had told his brother and the constable about the robbery, but she was certain she hadn't been exposed just yet. If Sebastian had been informed of her involvement, Helena would know by now. If the Bow Street Runners had been told, she had no doubt she would have been dragged off to the gaol days ago.

There was still time for her to do the right thing and come clean. If nothing else, she could save Sebastian and his family the embarrassment of being caught up in the scandal soon to follow her arrest. She was glad to have encouraged him to take things slowly and not propose marriage right away. They had been seen together, but the lack of an engagement would make it easier for the Radcliffes to come out of this unscathed.

But her poor siblings. Helena wasn't certain what they would do, but perhaps their lives would be improved by her absence. If Viscount Amberly truly loved Harriett, he would marry her regardless of Helena's transgressions. A respectable marriage would salvage her sister's reputation, and Henry would fall under the same protection. They could move forward with their lives while she paid the price for her error in judgment.

No, it hadn't been an error. Perhaps participating in highway robbery hadn't been morally or lawfully right, but desperation had driven her to take the only avenue she could find toward security of any kind. She had kept her family clothed, sheltered, and fed, for several months and would do it all again for their sakes. If she could change anything, Helena would have refused Sebastian when he had confessed his feelings for her. She would have insisted that it was impossible for them to be together or even lied to him by declaring that she didn't return his affection. It would have hurt him, but it would certainly be preferable to what she was prepared to do.

Burying her face in her hands, she issued a deep sigh. Knowing what needed to be done and actually going forward with it were two different things. Every time Helena thought she had gathered the courage to go to Sebastian, she grew afraid of his censure and his scorn, afraid to watch him turn his back on her and take back all the love and adoration he had showered her with these past weeks.

"Christ, Helena," she berated herself aloud. "You are such an idiot!"

A voice from her side made her flinch. "Ah, I wouldn't go that far."

She dropped her hands and discovered she was no longer alone. Seated beside her on the wrought iron bench was Felix, dressed for riding and looking refreshed. A dappled gelding grazed in the grass nearby, and Felix turned his body so that he faced her, a riding crop resting against his legs. His green eyes sparkled with good humor as he gave her a tentative smile.

"I have always thought you were rather smart," he added. "Smart enough to take part in a gang of women acting as highwaymen, even."

Helena was seized with the craven urge to bolt, but she held her ground, having known this moment must come eventually. She had wronged Felix and was obligated to face him and answer for it.

"Felix," she said, her hands clenched so tight her knuckles ached. "I...I'm so sorry. I never meant—"

He cut her off with one raised hand and shook his head. To

Helena's surprise, he didn't seem angry or even affected by what had occurred by the side of the road that night. He was his handsome, charming self, reaching out to pat her joined hands.

"Steady, Helena," he murmured. "I didn't come here to castigate you."

Helena wrinkled her brow. "You knew I would be here."

"I have heard that a certain young lady takes a walk by herself every morning and that a certain earl is displeased with the idea of you not having a servant or some such to keep you safe. I thought it my duty as your future brother-in-law to see to your welfare."

At the genial concern in his voice and the kindness in his stare, Helena burst into tears. Her chest heaved with uncontrolled sobs, and hot tears ran down her face in an uncontrolled deluge.

Felix retrieved a handkerchief and offered it to her, lips pinched with sympathy. "There now, it's not so bad as all that. I'm perfectly all right, and no one knows I saw your face that night or that the Band of Brigands are actually women. A gentleman never besmirches a lady's name."

Helena sniffled, dabbing at her cheeks with his handkerchief. "You have every right to expose me. What I've done is wrong, it...it's unforgivable."

"I don't believe that. Do you want to know what I think?" When she merely nodded, he continued. "I think that you are a brave woman. I do not know much about your circumstances, but I've heard enough to understand why you participated in such a scheme. The loss of your parents left you with little recourse. For ladies of high society, options are few. You only did what you felt you must to survive. I've read the accounts of the other robberies, and no one was ever seriously hurt."

"*You* were hurt," she protested.

"Only mildly," he countered. "Besides, I might have hurt you worse had your companion not hit me over the head. I wouldn't be able to forgive myself had I done you harm."

"I would have deserved it."

Felix took her hand and gently squeezed. "Stop that. I won't hold a grudge. What's done is done. I also want you to know I don't intend to tell Sebastian that you were there that night, but I think perhaps you should."

Helena peered at him with watery eyes. "I know. I've been too afraid, but all this week I've been telling myself that I can't go on lying to him. He deserves to know who I really am, who he thinks he loves."

Felix took the handkerchief from her hand and used it to dry the last of her tears. "He does know you. He simply isn't aware of the entire truth. But I know my brother. You've made a noticeable change in him, Helena. I can honestly say I have never seen him truly happy until now. He does love you, and I think he would rather hear the truth from you rather than anyone else. He might even understand your reasons."

"You know Sebastian better than that. He will hate me for it."

"No. I cannot pretend to know whether he will wish to move forward with the engagement, but I do know that he prizes honesty above most other qualities. I also know that keeping this from him will eat you alive. You'll make yourself miserable."

Helena sniffed and settled against the back of the bench. Felix was right and had only confirmed what she had known to be true. Sebastian didn't deserve to be lied to, and she would never be able to go forward with an engagement knowing she was keeping a part of her life hidden from him. Her days of highway robbery were over, whether he wished to wed her or not. The harrowing moment she had been unmasked by Felix had shown her how easily they could be found out. She was terrified at the very thought of ever attempting it again.

"I'll tell him," she promised. "Soon."

Felix stood, stuffing his handkerchief back into his breast pocket. "I admire you, Helena, and I wish you the very best. Call on me if you have a need."

"I will," she said, though she knew deep down that she'd

never do such a thing.

Her actions, and her actions alone, had led her to this moment. It was time for her to accept the repercussions.

SEBASTIAN RAKED HIS fingers through his hair in frustration, staring down at the row of engagement rings resting on his desk. Each one came in its own cedar box and had been retrieved from the vault where the family jewels were kept. He had left his family after dinner to sit here and make a final decision over the one he would present to Helena. His plan to surprise her with a proposal had been set in motion. A ball was to be held at Stratford House in three days' time, no small feat considering his mother was inviting everyone who was anyone amongst the *ton*. However, Sebastian was too excited to have the engagement sealed and a wedding date planned that he had insisted on rushing the event.

His mother was so happy that her eldest son was finally settling down that she had spent every waking hour of the past few days making plans and ordering the servants about on this errand or that. Sebastian had been ordered to keep his nose out of the dowager's affairs, which was her brusque way of telling him his input on the decor, music, and food weren't welcome. So, he was left with only two tasks, and one of them was to select a ring.

The Stratford coffers overflowed with jewels, some dating back as far as 1215, others having been passed down by former earls. Every piece of it would be Helena's to wear once they were wed, but her ring would be worn every hour of every day. It had to be perfect—beautiful, but not ostentatious, yet still living up to the standards of the new position she would gain.

Lady Helena Radcliffe, Countess of Stratford. It had a nice ring to it.

Sebastian lifted the second ring in the line, a sapphire set in silver and ringed in diamonds. She always looked lovely in blue.

But then, his gaze fell to his other favorite of the lot, a row of diamonds in an intricately engraved band of pure gold. He held both rings up into the light and tried to imagine Helena's face when she saw this ring or that. Each time, he pictured her mouth dropping open in shock and a cry of wonder spilling from her lips. Both were spectacular, yet neither would do.

With a frustrated huff, he laid both rings back down and sat back in his seat. Staring at the ceiling, he contemplated calling on Helena tomorrow afternoon. She had sent a note this morning telling him that she felt better and wished to see him soon. Perhaps they could return to Gunter's. He had heard rumors of a new flavor—parmesan. It sounded diabolical to Sebastian, but Helena liked trying new things. Perhaps she would enjoy it.

He was sitting in his seat grinning like an idiot at the thought of watching Helena eat a mouthful of cheese-flavored ice when a knock sounded on his study door. Sebastian sat up and glanced at the clock on the mantel, noting that it was nearly ten o'clock in the evening. Felix had left for an evening of carousing with his friends, and his mother was wont to turn in early most evenings.

"Come!" he called out, bending to begin placing the rings back inside their respective boxes.

The butler appeared on the threshold. "My lord, you have a visitor."

Sebastian snapped the final box closed and straightened, bewildered. "At this hour?"

The butler's knowing look put him on high alert. Something was wrong. "It is Miss Montgomery. She insisted she must see you right away, and it could not wait. I placed her in the adjoining drawing room and offered her refreshment. She declined."

Sebastian looked to the door connecting his study to the drawing room. It was the best place for them to meet—removed from the front of the house where servants might overhear, and two floors below where his mother slept.

"See that we are not disturbed," he ordered.

When he opened the door, Helena rose from the settee she'd been sitting on and whirled to face him. Her face was pale and drawn, and dark circles rimmed her eyes. She wore a dark pelisse over her gown, and a matching hat lay beside where she'd just sat.

"Helena," he murmured, locking the door and closing the distance between them. "Are you all right? What's wrong?"

She fell into his embrace when he reached for her, burying her face against his chest. Sebastian held her tight, stroking her loosely bound hair. She was trembling and holding onto him for dear life, sending bells of alarm ringing through his head. Helena was too aware of the ramifications of being seen visiting him so late at night with no chaperone. She might be a spinster, which offered her more freedom of movement than her sister, but her reputation wasn't inviolable. There was a reason she had come, and wondering what it could be filled Sebastian with dread.

"Tell me what the matter is, sweet," he said, prying her away from him to look down into her eyes.

The look on her face bewildered him, as did her reticence as she slowly reached a hand up to cup his face.

"I must speak with you," she said, her voice low. "It is important. And also, I've missed you."

Sebastian took the hand that rested on his cheek and kissed the palm, then led her closer to the fire. There was a chill still clinging to her clothes, and the fire had been stoked to offer warmth. He bent to kiss her, allowing himself to linger and make up for their time apart.

"I've missed you, as well," he murmured against her lips. "Are you feeling better?"

She nodded. "I think so. I haven't been quite myself, but I will be all right."

"Good. Did you receive your invitation to the ball? Mother will be disappointed if you don't come."

Especially since the occasion was being hosted in her honor. During an opportune moment, Sebastian intended to lead her out into the garden for a private moment and then he would get down on one knee and ask for her hand in marriage. Once she accepted, Sebastian would lead her back into the ballroom and announce their engagement. It was the perfect plan, but only if Helena actually attended the ball.

"That is actually what I wished to talk to you about," she said, staring into the fire. "I must tell you, this is so difficult, Sebastian. You are such a wonderful man, and you've been so good to me."

He ducked his head to catch her gaze, his head spinning with the effort to puzzle out her odd behavior. "What's this about."

"I love you," she said in a rush, her eyes colliding with his. "I have been afraid to say it, but before I tell you the rest, I need you to believe that. Do you believe me, Sebastian?"

"Of course I believe you," he declared, coming forward until their bodies touched and his lips rested against her brow. "I love you, too, Helena. Surely you know that."

"I do," she said in a broken whisper. "It's why I…"

Her eyes filled with tears, and Sebastian felt a tearing sensation in his chest as if his heart were being rent in two. Seeing her weep made him feel things he'd never experienced—such as the need to destroy whatever had caused her pain. The impotence he endured at knowing he couldn't battle her low esteem or her doubts was crippling.

"That's why everything will be all right," he told her. "Whatever is wrong, we'll face it together."

She took a step away from him, her chin raised resolutely as she reached for the buttons of her pelisse. "I came here to tell you something but find I don't yet have the courage. But, I want, I need you to make love to me, Sebastian. Now."

He had been so intent watching her unbutton her coat to reveal she wore a thin, white gown underneath—one that flaunted her curves to perfection—that he almost missed the words that fell from her mouth. Now that he'd torn his gaze back to her face, Sebastian could see by her expression that he hadn't misheard her. He had been convinced that this was a dream or that she'd said something else. But there was fear in her eyes and determination setting her chin, and she was wearing a gown that buttoned up the front—which she began to unfasten as she held his stare.

"Helena," he croaked, his good sense battling with the torrent of desire making him all-too-aware of how close he stood to having what he'd craved for weeks. "What are you doing?"

"I'm tired of feeling as if I have no control," she said, shrugging out of the gown and letting it fall to her feet. The firelight made her chemise appear paper-thin, showing Sebastian the tempting silhouette of her body underneath it. Her frayed, worn stays barely contained the swells of her breasts, reminding him of how recently he'd had his hands and mouth on them. "I have spent my entire life waiting for things to happen to me and dealing with them as they come. Just this once, I want to choose, and I am choosing you. I love you. I want you. I want *this*."

Sebastian clenched his hands, his palms itching to take hold of her, his every sense screaming to experience this woman in every way possible. "We should wait," he argued, though without much conviction. The tightness in his groin was becoming unbearable, and he had never before experienced such a depth of feeling along with such powerful lust. He felt drunk on the power of it, wanting to know what it was like to join in body and spirit with someone he loved, someone who commanded the worship of the very ground she walked on.

Helena clutched her chemise between her fingers. He could see the apprehension all over her face and knew she thought of the countless rejections she had endured. "I know waiting is the right thing to do, but tomorrow shouldn't be taken for granted. Nothing is certain except for this moment. I don't want to throw it away, do you?"

Sebastian clenched his fingers until his nails bit into his palms, all the blood rushing away from his head and straight to his baser parts. He ached for her like he never had before, and now there was nothing standing in his way except for his own sense of honor. Would it truly be dishonorable to lay her on the nearest piece of furniture and give her what she wanted—what was inevitable? Within days she would be his betrothed, and in weeks, his wife. She had confessed her love for him, and she was willing and wanting and so completely his.

There was nothing left to do but give in.

"No," he said, reaching out for her. "No, I don't."

THIS WAS WRONG. She hadn't come here to seduce Sebastian; she had come to tell him the truth. As Sebastian consumed her mouth with a fiery kiss, Helena told herself she should put a stop to this. If she told him to stop, he would, of that she had no doubt. He would listen to what she had to say and then react. Whether the night ended with him forgiving her and picking up where they left off or casting her out of his life, Helena knew it was the honorable thing to do.

But then, he was yanking at the ribbons of her stays and backing her toward the settee, his lips finding that mind-numbing place just behind her ear where she most liked to feel his lips. Her legs weakened along with her resolve as her senses overpowered the rational thoughts of her mind.

Everything Helena had said to him was true. She did love him, and she was tired of being a victim of circumstance. She had been timid and quiet her entire life, as she'd been taught a lady ought to be, and it had earned her nothing. If Helena was going to lose everything and everyone she loved due to her own mistakes, then she would allow herself to have this one night.

One night of being loved by Sebastian and experiencing something wonderful, something she'd never thought she might know. This beautiful man could be hers for a little while longer, just long enough for Helena to create a memory to cherish in the cold, lonely nights ahead. It wasn't wrong of her to need this, to give herself to him and hope that it would be enough to satisfy her before she walked away from him forever.

Her stays fell to the floor, and Sebastian nibbled at her lips while loosening the buttons of his waistcoat. He had been without a coat upon coming into the room, and now another layer had been shed, leaving him as undressed as Helena had ever seen him. She raised her hands to his chest, marveling at the sight of him in only his shirtsleeves. It seemed ridiculous to think the sight so sensual when very soon he wouldn't be wearing anything at all—but she wanted to catalog every moment, every revelation. Here she was, a virgin at three and twenty, who had never seen a man without his waistcoat.

Sebastian seemed to sense her need to touch and explore him and went still as she ran her palms up and down the expanse of his torso. She had felt every inch of him pressed against her, but this was different somehow. Every masculine ridge of him could be felt through the fine lawn of his shirt, and as he snatched his cravat away, she locked eyes on the thick column of his throat and the tufts of dark hair protruding from the gap of his collar.

She pushed leather braces off his shoulders, her touch skimming the bulges of powerful arms until she reached his cuffs. Unbuttoning him seemed to take forever, but before long, he was helping her tug his tails from his waistband and easing the garment off over his head. Helena let out a breath of wonder as what she'd felt through the fabric was revealed—muscle and tendon, skin and black hairs in hypnotizing whorls. She drank him in with her eyes first, then timidly raked her fingers through the hairs on his chest. It was a thick, soft mat that grew sparser as she followed it downward, turning into a straight line that arrowed into his breeches.

Sebastian sucked in a sharp breath as she went on examining him, learning the places on his torso that made him grunt and his stomach tighten or that made low grunts emit from inside his chest. His nipples responded much the way hers did, puckering and growing taut when she strummed her fingers over them.

Feeling bolder as he closed his eyes and let his head fall back, Helena stood on tiptoe and pressed her mouth to his throat. His pulse was alarmingly fast against her palm as she kissed him as he had so often kissed her.

His hands shot up to clench around her arms, and he yanked her closer, tilting his head to encourage her ministrations. Helena inhaled his scent—a spiced aroma that sent her toes curling into the rug and made her feel warm in the deepest parts of her belly. She tested a stroke of her tongue at his pulse and grinned when his fingers ticked around her arms, his pelvis arcing toward her to push the intimidating hardness of his erection against her belly. She tried again, then kissed her way lower, nuzzling his chest and teasing one of his nipples with her lips.

"Christ," he moaned, tangling his fingers in her hair and tipping her head back, so they looked into one another's eyes. "You're killing me, Helena."

She peered at him with eyes unfocused, feeling as if she floated in a dream. His hands caressed down her back, then palmed her buttocks, pulling her tight against him. He kissed her again, this time with more force and ardor than she was used to. Helena accepted him, threading her fingers in his hair and opening her mouth to him, drowning in the taste and feel of him against her tongue. He plucked at the pins in her hair, sending them to the carpet and letting strands of hair uncoil down her back. His fingers snarled in a tangle here or there, and Helena was certain there were still a few pins lost in the masses of her heavy hair, but she didn't care. The way he looked at her when he pulled back to study her, arranging her loose tresses so they framed her face, made her feel like the most beautiful creature ever created.

He turned her so that her back was to the settee, then lowered her onto it before going to his knees. He pushed her hat aside, then reached for a decorative pillow. Helena followed the prodding of his hands as he urged her to sit forward so he could brace it at her back. Then, he took another cushion and slipped it beneath her bottom, lifting her up and creating a soft, comfortable resting place for her. She smiled her appreciation, robbed of words as he bent his head and went about divesting her of her slippers.

Shame momentarily intruded on the moment as his hands touched her tattered shoes, but she pushed it aside as ruthlessly as it had invaded her mind. There was no place for shame, not tonight, not with him. Sebastian hardly seemed to notice the state of the slippers as he tossed them aside, his gaze fixed on her exposed legs. Her chemise had tangled around her thighs, but he pushed it higher, revealing the pink ribbons of her garters.

Sebastian pressed his lips just above her knee while untying the first one, his deft hands gently easing them down. His lips followed them, stroking down her bare leg and sending shivers of delight through her. He repeated the ritual with her other stocking, but this time, he kissed his way back up her leg, his hand stroking along the back of her calf. She fell back against the cushion when he pulled her legs apart, spreading her in the most indecent fashion. Before she could fathom what he was about, he was nibbling along the inside of one thigh, his hand cupping her hips as he eased the chemise higher.

Her lips parted on a strained cry of shocked pleasure when he sank his teeth into the soft flesh, then soothed the stinging spot with his tongue. A sense of modesty prompted her to close her legs once she realized he didn't intend to stop, and that his lips were coming dangerously close to the apex of her thighs. Sparks of firelight danced in the green flecks of his eyes as he looked up at her, gently gripping her knees and easing them apart again.

"Don't hide from me," he murmured, dropping a kiss on the smooth patch of her belly just above the nest of curls blanketing her mons. "I want every part of you, Helena. There is nothing for you to be ashamed of. Let me look at you, let me taste you.

Helena gasped when he covered her with his mouth, the heat and warmth of his tongue caressing her inner flesh, nearly sending her up off the settee. The grip of his hand at her thighs anchored her when her back bowed off the settee, and her fingers rasped against the damask. She had never imagined making love would involve such scandalous intimacies. The explanation given by her mother years ago hadn't prepared her for *this*.

She should be shocked that he would wish to put his lips to such an intimate part of her, but then his tongue circled the sensitive nub at the heart of her, and all thought fled Helena's mind. Nothing that felt so good could be improper between the two of them in the privacy of this room. Helena relaxed into his hold, his fingers kneading her buttocks and lifting her to meet his hungry kisses and laps of his tongue. She let her head fall against the back of the settee, unable to help moving her hips in time to the rhythm he created. He stroked her toward something spectacular, the sensations similar to what he'd made her feel the day he had touched her through her gown. Only this time, the fluttering and pulsing of her inner core were more powerful, more all-consuming.

"Oh God," she whimpered, biting down on a knuckle to keep herself quiet lest they be overheard. She was spiraling, falling apart, unraveling so fast that there was no controlling it. "Sebastian!"

He made a low sound of approval against her slick, secret flesh, flattening his tongue against her nub and circling it in a rhythm that left her breathless. Helena clutched the back of his head and held him against her as she splintered, the tension in her core snapping in a storm of pulsing heat. Her hips jolted, and her throat burned with the effort it took not to wail in helpless ecstasy.

Sebastian kissed and licked her until she went still beneath him, her thighs shuddering and her breaths labored. He placed gentle kisses up her belly, adding electric aftershocks to the lingering pulsations of her climax. When he reached where her chemise had bunched beneath her breasts, he snatched the garment down, leaving it trapped beneath the weight of them. Helena was helpless in his hands, adrift on waves of euphoria, yet still yearning for the rest of what he would give. He showered her with kisses, his lips finding her nipples, the tops of her breasts, her throat, her lips.

He fell between her legs, his knees braced on the edge of the settee and the heavy weight of his distended cock pressing into her thigh.

"Do you want me to stop?" he asked, going still over her, his gaze probing and heavy with concern and care. "I want you, Helena, so much it hurts. But I can end this right now and take you home. I don't want you to regret this."

She hooked one leg around his hip and urged him closer, taking hold of his shoulders and raising her head to kiss him. It surprised her not to be disgusted by the scent and taste of her own climax on his lips, and a shiver went through her at the reminder of what he'd just done to her.

"I could never regret it," she said. "I want all of you, Sebastian. Now."

He lowered his head to her shoulder and let out a labored breath, muttering something that sounded like, "Thank God," bringing a smile to Helena's lips.

Then, he was working the buttons at the fall of his breeches, his gaze intently locked with hers. Helena choked down the anxiety that spiked through her as her gaze strayed to the protrusion of his erection, larger than she had anticipated and swollen, reddened at its tip. He took her hand and urged her to touch him, hissing through clenched teeth when her fingers wrapped around the length. She marveled at the feel of him, both hard and soft, vulnerable yet powerful. He thrust into the circle of her grip, panting against her lips and shuddering as beads of moisture leaked from his head to dampen her fingers.

His hand fell back between her legs, his thumb lazily strumming the hypersensitive center of her, stroking her need back toward its precipice. When Helena could stand it no longer, she angled him toward her opening and raised her hips, inviting him into her body. Sebastian braced himself over her, his forehead pressed against hers and his eyes boring into hers as he gave a tentative nudge.

Helena stiffened, finally realizing the difference in the size of him compared to the space he was meant to occupy. She had known there would be pain, but being confronted with the nature of the act sent a hint of apprehension through her.

"Shh," Sebastian soothed. "Look at me, and don't close your eyes. Stay with me, Helena."

She did as he commanded, keeping her gaze locked with his and forcing her body to ease from its rigid clench. Sebastian kissed her, his lips light and sweet over hers, his tongue lulling her into relaxed submission. Then, he surged and clamped his mouth over hers at the same time, muting the sharp cry that tore from her throat at the sensation. He filled her in a single thrust, the burning stretch of it taking Helena's breath away. She arched beneath him, her fingernails digging into his chest. The fullness of him inside her was as wondrous as it was painful, leaving her hovering on a precipice between rapture and agony. He never took his lips from hers, his eyes open and blazing with intensity and light as he rested within her, soothing her with his lips and the soft strokes of his hands over whatever bare skin he could find.

Helena unwound by degrees, her thighs falling open and her back easing against the cushion as he circled his hips, seeming to push against every part of her depths, touching places she hadn't known existed. She gasped into his mouth at the dueling sensations tearing her apart inside—all of it leaving her breathless and in utter awe. Was this what it was to become one with another person? Helena stared up at him as he gripped the back of the settee and began to move, hypnotized by the motion created by his hips and the way they made the taut sinews of his torso ripple and undulate.

The throbbing pain became overshadowed by something wonderful, something that pushed Helena back toward that precarious height. Only, this time she wondered if she would survive the resulting fall.

Her sheath clenched around him, each pulse of his pelvis

creating friction and heat, sending her up and up until she felt as if she'd taken flight.

"Helena," he ground out through clenched teeth. "God, Helena, I love you...."

She was incapable of speech and could only stroke his cheek and hold his gaze, hoping he could see what words were inadequate to express. Giving herself over to the inevitable end, Helena raised her hips, determined to take all of him, to feel him in every corner of her being as she flew over the edge. He tucked her head against his chest as she cried out her pleasure, her core constricting around him in convulsions so powerful she thought she might lose her grip on consciousness. His fingers tangled in her hair, and he held her to him, his legs shaking and his thrusts becoming more sporadic as he groaned and murmured unintelligible words that she somehow understood. He loved her, and he was nearing his own end. She was his, and he was hers.

Wrapping her legs around him, Helena clung to him as he thrust one last time and spilled inside her, a hoarse cry echoing from his lips. They lay that way for a long while, tangled in one another and a light sheen of sweat slicking their skin. Helena kept her face buried in his chest, afraid to look up and confront the world as it must now be. Alone without Sebastian. Him, leaving her behind and eventually finding another woman to give his heart to—someone better and more deserving.

Tears sprang to her eyes, but she blinked them back. These were her last moments of closeness and intimacy with Sebastian, and she wouldn't ruin it.

Morning would be soon enough for that.

CHAPTER TWELVE

SEBASTIAN PACED THE courtyard, hands folded behind his back as he practiced the words he would speak to Helena hours from now, in this very spot. The ball was set to begin in a few hours, and his future would be sealed with one final act. He had spent the past few days thinking of Helena, dreaming of her, reliving every beautiful moment after she had removed her clothes and asked him to make love to her.

He had feared waking to regret it but was surprised to find that there was none. This woman was his in his heart, his mind, his soul. All that was left was for a vicar to clear she was his by law, but that was a trivial, if necessary, circumstance. It didn't change the way he felt or the joy he'd experienced as he'd lain on the settee and held Helena in his arms in the aftermath of their joining. She had fallen quiet afterward, her head laid on his chest and her body warm and soft beside his.

"What did you want to tell me?" he'd asked around a yawn, almost *as an afterthought. Whatever it was, he might have been too drowsy and sated to hear it, which was fortunate because Helena simply replied. "It can wait. I just want to be with you right now."*

That had been just fine with him, and Sebastian had fallen asleep, his body spooning her and one arm keeping her against him. He had awakened in the dead of night, chilled by the loss of the fire, to find that she had left. Sebastian had found a note on his desk in the study, one that he had hidden in a secret compartment beneath the top of his desk.

I shall never forget what we shared. Thank you from the bottom of my heart.

Yours, Helena

He had not seen her since but had received confirmation of her attendance at the ball, along with Harriett. Henry was still away at university, but he liked to think the young man would approve of his marrying Helena.

All was in readiness, and Sebastian had been too anxious to wait another two hours to dress. He had hurried his valet through the toilet, donning his best tailcoat and silk cravat and even adding a diamond tiepin into his ensemble. Such fripperies weren't like him, but this was a special occasion, and he wanted to look his best. His hair was cut and his jaw freshly shaved. Even the garden was at its best this time of year—all the spring flowers in full bloom. The evening promised pleasant weather if the clear sky overhead proved any indication.

Yet, he couldn't contain the restlessness that made him pace or the anxiety that made his hands tremble. The sooner the festivities began, the sooner he could have this done with and feel more at ease. He didn't doubt she would accept his proposal, especially given what they'd done. She could be with child, a possibility that had him grinning from ear to ear. He could have a family of his own within the year, something he hadn't wanted in the beginning but now desired with every fiber of his being.

The sound of voices from beyond the hedges caught his attention, and Sebastian went still to listen. He had been fairly certain that no one was in the garden but him, but as he crept closer to the greenery, he distinctly heard a voice that sounded an awful lot like Felix's.

He cocked his head and held his breath, instinct telling him that he wasn't supposed to hear what was being said.

"What are you doing here so early?" Felix hissed, his voice

holding a sense of urgency. "The ball doesn't begin for hours!"

Sebastian's heart dropped when the answering voice turned out to be that of a woman. Helena.

"I know, but I need to see him. I have to tell him, Felix. It's driving me mad. I tried to the last time we saw one another, but I lost my nerve."

Sebastian frowned, recalling yet again that Helena had been about to tell him something that night in the drawing room. What the devil did his brother know about whatever she was hiding?

"You haven't told him?" Felix practically bellowed. "Helena, you should have told him before now. Now, by God, this isn't good."

"What?" Helena probed, her voice quavering. "Why can't I tell him tonight?"

"You haven't puzzled it out yet?" Felix replied. "Sebastian hates balls, but he convinced Mother to throw one at the height of the season with only a few days' notice. He's fretted over the details and worked himself into a state because everything must be perfect for you. Don't you see? He plans to ask you to marry him tonight."

A heavy silence fell between them, and even without being able to see Helena or Felix, he could feel the tension winding through the air.

"Oh, God," Helena whispered. "No, I cannot let him do that. It wouldn't be right. He has to know the truth before he decides if he still wants me after what I've done."

He felt as if he might retch, his insides a maelstrom of confusion and suspicion. What was going on between Helena and his brother? Why did he know things about her that Sebastian did not? And more importantly, what exactly did Sebastian need to know before marrying her?

He fought back the urge to go tearing around the corner and demand the truth. He wouldn't risk being lied to or fed some half-truth. If he waited and listened, Helena might reveal it herself.

"I told you, he loves you," Felix soothed. "He can be uncompromising, but the way he feels about you—"

"Will not change the fact that I'm a wanted criminal," Helena blurted. "Or that I accosted his brother and that my actions led to your injury."

"I've already told you, it hardly qualified as an injury. I am fine and hold no ill will toward you for acting out of desperation. You aren't a bad person Helena, you only…"

Sebastian ceased hearing them, the sound of his rushing blood filling his ears as he stood there feeling like the biggest idiot in all of Christendom.

It made no sense, and if someone had made such an accusation, he would have called them out for the smudge to Helena's name. But she had said it herself. *She* was one of the highway robbers who had stolen from his brother and left him lying unconscious on the side of the road. *She* and the four others, whom he assumed had to be her friends, had been picking the pockets of unsuspecting people for months with no one the wiser.

As he stood there grappling with the unwelcome truth, shock gave way to anger, cold and steely. He couldn't feel anything anymore, not even disappointment at learning that Helena wasn't who he'd thought she was. Sebastian had never thought such pain could be possible, but then he had never placed his heart into the hands of a lying, scheming seductress, either.

While he stood there wrestling with whether to confront them or walk away to lick his wounds in solitude, the blur of movement caught the corner of his eye. He whirled to face Felix and Helena, who had been about to depart the garden when they'd stumbled upon him. Felix swore and ran a hand over his jaw, while Helena froze in her tracks, devastation crossing her lovely features.

Even now, Sebastian thought her achingly beautiful. The foolish, besotted part of him wanted to go to her and demand she stop her illegal activities and marry him. But the part of him that had just been stabbed in the heart rebelled, hardening his resolve.

He couldn't marry this woman who could look him in the eyes and smile and play the innocent, all the while hiding a secret, criminal life he'd known nothing about.

"Sebastian," Helena croaked, one hand pressed to her middle. "I…I was just—"

"There is no need to explain," he snapped, refusing to fall prey to her manipulations a second time. He had been fooled once; he'd be damned if he allowed it again. "I think I've heard quite enough, Helena. Or should I call you the vipress you are? How about liar? Thief?"

"Sebastian, that's enough," Felix interjected, moving to stand between him and Helena. "She wanted to tell you everything. She just never had a chance."

"She has had every chance," Sebastian scoffed. "Now, get out of my way."

Felix clenched his jaw, his raised chin announcing his intention to remain right where he was. Sebastian clenched his hand, on the verge of planting his brother a facer, but Helena placed a hand on Felix's shoulder and moved him aside.

"It's all right, Felix," she said. "This is my fault, and I must accept the consequences."

Sebastian crossed his arms over his chest and raised his eyebrow, waiting for her to try to explain herself. He wouldn't go out of his way to make this easier for her. Helena surprised him, not cowering in the face of his wrath. She squared her shoulders and looked him in the eyes.

"Sebastian, it was never my intention for anyone to get hurt, least of all you or your brother. The highwayman scheme, it was the only way. After my parents died, I discovered that there was no money left, not enough to see us through in the long term. My brother and sister are still so young, and it was my responsibility—"

"To rob carriages to provide for them?" he challenged, unable to remain silent any longer. He was so angry he felt sick with it, heat and bile churning in his gut and threatening to spew up through his throat. "Were the options of finding a husband or seeking work not available to you, madam?"

Helena faltered, hands folded in her skirts as her gaze flitted away from him.

"Look at me!" he bellowed, causing her to flinch and raise tentative eyes to him. "At least look me in the eyes while you tell me the truth about who and what you really are! Will you have me believe that a woman as intelligent and cunning as yourself couldn't find some other way to support her family. Harriett has been a smashing success this season and has her pick of husbands. Was that not enough for you to better your situation? You couldn't be satisfied with that, so you took to stealing what didn't belong to you!"

"It wasn't that simple!" Helena fired back, her shocked stupor melting away in the face of indignation. "My God, you really are as arrogant as everyone says. Of course, you would know better than I what choices were available to a woman in my position, wouldn't you? Find a husband, you say. From among which men, my lord? The ones who never gave me a second glance or who used me to make their way to the ladies they truly wanted? Find employment, you say. With what qualifications? Perhaps you have failed to notice that this realm of society does a pitiful job of preparing young ladies to make their own way in the world. I know how to play the pianoforte, stitch a sampler, dance, and speak French. What job would you have me take with such skills, my lord? Oh, I know! I should simply have walked down to Covent Garden and sold the only wares at my disposal to the passing men. I'm certain they would have condescended to look at me then!"

Sebastian strode forward until they were almost nose to nose, infuriated that she would try to paint herself as the victim in this situation. "At least whoring is honest work," he hissed, staring down his nose at her. "Though I'm certain you realize that. Isn't that why you parted your legs for me the other night, hm? Perhaps you thought if I had a taste of your cunny, I would wed you even after you revealed your sins to me. A form of currency, bartered to get what you want. Well, I hate to disappoint you, madam, but even the feel of your thighs around me isn't enough to erase what you've done."

Helena struck out at him before he could blink, her palm cracking against his cheek with more force than he would have found her capable. Sebastian staggered back, only to be caught up by Felix, who took him by his collar and shook him until his teeth rattled.

"Have you gone mad? You've no cause to speak to her that way!"

"No," Helena protested. "Let him speak."

Felix kept a tight hold on Sebastian's coat, but his gaze was on Helena, who stood before them magnificent in her fury, eyes blazing. "No," he said. "You don't."

"She does," Sebastian spat. "But I have nothing more to say to you. I want you out of my sight, and you had better hope I can be convinced not to go straight to the nearest magistrate and reveal the identities of the so-called Band of Brigands."

Helena turned as if to leave, but then faced them again, hands braced on her hips. "You might not have more to say, but I do, and you will listen. I love you, you idiot! And you could tell me that you had stolen the royal jewels, and I would still love you. But you would never do such a thing, would you?"

"No," he growled. "Because I have honor—something you are so obviously lacking."

She scoffed, shaking her head at him as if he were as big a fool as she felt. "Is that what you think? Perhaps you can tell me how far your honor would go if everything you owned vanished overnight and if you couldn't afford the valet who manicures your nails and cuts your hair, if your clothes were frayed so badly, they were falling apart. Tell me, my lord, if your honor would be enough to feel the grates with coal for warmth, or put food on your table, or keep your mother and brother safe and living in their beloved home. I'll tell you how far it would go, about as far as I could throw you. I would wager that once your precious honor ran out, there isn't a thing you wouldn't do, a person you would cheat or rob in order to provide for those you love. But you wouldn't know anything about hunger or desperation, would you, you spoiled, pampered brute!"

This time, when she turned her back on him, she didn't look back. Sebastian sagged in Felix's hold, all the wind knocked from him by her stunning exit. Once she disappeared through the gate leading to the alley between his house and the neighboring one, Felix released Sebastian and turned on him, face reddened and a vein in his forehead pulsing.

"I cannot believe you did that," he accused. "The things you said to her. Sebastian, you were needlessly cruel."

Sebastian shoved Felix away from him, snorting like a bull and feeling as if he might commit an act of violence at any moment. "I will tell you what's cruel," he snarled. "Letting me make a fool over myself for that woman, when you knew what she was! I'm your bloody brother! If she wasn't willing to tell me, you damn well should have."

Felix crossed his arms and pinned him with a pointed look. "You're wrong. The real cruelty was me convincing Helena that if she told you the truth, you would try to understand. I told her that you truly loved her, and even if you were disappointed, you would forgive her because that is what you do when you love someone. Now, who's the fool? I suppose I am for thinking so highly of you. As it turns out, you're just like *him*."

Sebastian lost his hold on control and closed the distance between them. He hauled Felix up by his lapels, rage and hurt spiraling through him. "Don't you dare. Don't you ever compare me to Father."

"Or what?" Felix challenged. "You'll hit me? That was how he liked to settle his disputes, wasn't it? And when you're done, I suppose you'll drown yourself in liquor and plow through every whore in London. You may as well because, for all you've striven to avoid his behaviors, you've still managed to grow into an arrogant, uncompromising bastard. That woman never did anything but love you, and now you've gone and destroyed her."

Sebastian trembled with impulses barely held in check. If he swung his fist now, he'd prove Felix right, and if there was one thing he couldn't abide, it was being compared to their father in any way.

"She lied to me," he argued. "She played me for a fool."

"People are imperfect," Felix said, his voice gentling as he pulled himself out of Sebastian's hold. "Even you. Perhaps you could stop trying to reach impossible standards long enough to realize that if you cannot allow a person to make mistakes and learn from them, you will never find anyone who meets your requirements. You are going to die alone."

With that, Felix strode away, his steps long and determined. Sebastian slumped against the nearest hedge, feeling as if he'd been pummeled from head to toe. His gaze strayed to the path Helena had taken out of the garden, and for a moment, he experienced guilt over some of the things he had said. He certainly shouldn't have mentioned their night together in front of Felix, but in his pain, he had lashed out. He had wanted her to hurt as he was hurting, to know how it felt to have the person she loved wound her deeply.

Did Helena even love him? That Sebastian even had to wonder whether her devotion was real rekindled the flames of his ire. Perhaps he had been misguided to think her perfect, but Sebastian didn't think he was asking too much for her to have been honest with him. Her lie hadn't been a small one; it had shaken the foundations of his regard for her, making him question their every interaction and wonder whether any of it had been real.

He might never know whether she had truly loved him, but Sebastian did know that he would never allow himself to go down this road again. He had taken a chance and acted impulsively and was now reminded of why he had always ordered his life with such standards. Felix might scoff at them, but until now, they had kept him relatively safe. They had protected him from the kind of agony that went beyond skin and bone and pierced the soul.

He never wanted to feel this way again, and the only way to heal was to return to what he knew. It was time for the practical, stoic earl to resume his place and get on with his life.

HELENA SWEPT A critical eye over the items she'd packed in her valise. Near the door to the bedroom she had been sharing with Harriett for the past several months sat a trunk filled with all the things she would need during her time away from London. Inside the valise were a collection of books, her embroidery tools, various colors of thread, and a smaller, more precious items she didn't want to risk to her trunk. At the top of the pile were the miniature portraits of her parents she would never want to be without. Her father stared up at her, somber and disapproving, while her mother appeared grieved. Of course, it was all in her imagination. These portraits of her parents were lovely and showcased what warm and loving people they had been, even if they'd had their flaws. Her own disappointment in herself was what she saw when she looked into their faces, knowing that she had failed them.

No, she realized, as she glanced to where Harriett sat on the bed watching her. She looked downright despondent while watching Helena prepare for their first prolonged separation since Harriett had been born. However, the twinkle of a modest but lovely diamond ring on her left hand gave Helena such pride. She had not failed her parents, who had entrusted her with seeing to her sister's welfare.

In the fortnight that had passed since that fateful encounter in the garden at Stratford House, very little had changed, and yet Helena felt as if the world were shifting beneath her feet. Viscount Amberly had proposed to Harriett, who had gleefully accepted. Helena planned to return to town for the wedding, which was planned three months from now. Meanwhile, Helena had been left with nothing but time in which to consider her future. She had asked her friends over for tea and tearfully told them that she could no longer join them on their highway adventures.

Not wishing to frighten them, she had refrained from divulging the facts surrounding the robbery of Felix, whom none of them had recognized in the dark except Helena. Despite being worried at the sudden change in her demeanor, as well as news that she and Sebastian wouldn't be getting married, her friends were loving and supportive. They had patted her hand and crooned over as she wept, confessing that she felt she had no choice left but to flee London. Her job with Harriett was done, and the last of their savings from the last heist would be left for the maintenance of the house and Harriett's trousseau until the wedding day.

Mina had pulled her aside and made the offer that would save Helena from a life of loneliness and uncertainty.

"There is plenty of room with Mama and me," she'd said. "I would very much love it if you would come to live with us. Please, I will not take no for an answer. We are comfortable, and perhaps you might look into teaching at the county schoolhouse, or, oh, you've always been so good on the pianoforte. I'm certain many of our neighbors would pay you to give their daughters lessons."

Helena had fallen onto Mina in tears and thanked her for the offer. She didn't have too much pride to accept it, as there were few options left to her. There was her family's impoverished estate and a manor house with a leaking roof and a crumbling foundation, but not much else. Sharing a home with a close friend sounded like heaven, and Helena was even willing to help Mina care for her mother. Feeling useful in that way would give her a purpose. In time, her heart would heal, and perhaps she would be happy again. For the time being, she would settle for being safe in the knowledge that Harriet's future was secure, and thereby Henry's as well. Amberly had already promised to put money in trust for Henry and ensure that he was taken care of. Helena was free to forge a new life.

"Must you go?" Harriett asked as Helena closed her valise. "Surely, Sebastian doesn't mean to let you go. He loves you, Helena."

The mention of his name sent pangs of longing through the far reaches of Helena's being. In the days following their falling out, she had been so angry with him that there had been no room for grief. However, she'd had no choice but to face the truth. Sebastian might have hurt her with his words, but she had wounded him first with her lies.

He had lashed out at her in his anger when he might have done far worse. She had been terrified that a magistrate would turn up on their doorstep any day, but after a few days, she began to hope that he might have had mercy on her. Now, she was all but certain that he didn't intend to see her hanged for her crimes. Perhaps love was what stayed his hand, or maybe he didn't want a dead woman's soul on his conscience.

"I think he did love me," Helena said, sinking on the bed beside Harriett. "But sometimes love isn't enough. He has decided that we do not suit, and I agree with him. It would never have worked, Harriett. So, I have to let him go, and now you have to let me go."

Harriett leaned her head against Helena's shoulder with a sigh. "But I don't know how to go on without you."

She rested her head atop Harriett's and laughed. "Of course you do. Mother taught you all you needed to know, and I picked up where she left off. You are a woman now, and soon you will be married. I cannot tell you how happy I am to see you going on to create your own life. It was going to happen regardless, and it's the way things should be."

Harriett sighed. "I suppose you are right, but I don't like you being so far away."

"I'll only be in Kent, less than a day's travel. And I will return before the wedding to help you prepare, and I will be there for you every step of the way. And when you have children, I will be their doting aunt who spoils them despite your protestations."

Harriett looked up at her and smiled, but there was sadness in it. She didn't have to speak for Helena to discern her thoughts. She, too, had hoped that perhaps there might be an uncle to help her spoil nieces and nephews and perhaps children of her own to play with them. But Sebastian was finished with her, and her monthly courses had come and gone within the weeks since their one night together. Her dreams would have to remain locked away, where only she could mourn them.

"Come now," she prompted, getting to her feet. "I'm not set to leave until tomorrow, and we shouldn't waste our last day together in tears. What do you say we find ourselves some amusement for the day? I know! Gunter's has unveiled an interesting new flavor of ice. Let's go sample it."

Harriett wrinkled her nose. "A parmesan ice doesn't sound very appealing."

Helena laughed and hauled her sister up by her hand. "Then you enjoy your usual lemon while I live adventurously. Come on, I want to spend the day with my sister."

Harriett looped an arm through hers. "I would like nothing better."

CHAPTER THIRTEEN

SEBASTIAN SLOUCHED IN his seat and stared morosely into the half-empty glass of brandy before him. He had been nursing the same measure for over an hour now, finding that the strength of spirits wasn't enough to soothe the ache in his chest. He'd been walking about in a daze for weeks now, wrestling with his damnable heart and his contrary, rational mind. The two did battle through his waking hours as well as through the night, making him toss and turn as his dreams haunted him with mistakes that couldn't be undone.

He'd been awful to Helena and couldn't take it back. Every time he convinced himself he must at least apologize for the way he'd spoken to her, Sebastian hesitated. Once she forgave him—if she could even be convinced to do so—what was he to do then? Was he willing to push aside the seriousness of her trespasses and ask her to marry him as he had intended to?

Those thoughts inevitably brought him back to the night of the ball, which he had spent sulking in corners of the ballroom and avoiding the company of others. He hadn't danced and had barely touched his food at dinner. His mother's concerned glances had been met with morose silence, and as the evening wore on, the dowager seemed to sense that something had gone wrong. He had told her nothing, other than the bare fact that he and Helena were not to be married. If she wanted to probe further, she refrained, though she had been quite vocal over the rift that had formed between him and Felix. His brother hadn't spoken a word to him since their argument in the garden, and when the dowager inquired as to the reason, Felix defiantly told her to ask Sebastian before leaving the room.

He had never felt so alone in his life. His mother tiptoed around him as if afraid he might shatter if she spoke louder than a whisper, and his own brother despised him. And Helena…

He missed her so much he could hardly breathe. It was an unpleasant feeling, turning about when he thought he heard her voice only to realize it had been his imagination, or fantasizing he saw her face from a distance only to find she wasn't really there. How was a man supposed to nurse his anger and get on with his life when he felt as if his heart had been broken? How was he supposed to grapple with the fact that the state of his heart might have nothing to do with Helena's lie and everything to do with the fact that he'd let her walk out of his life without giving chase?

"Bloody hell," he muttered to himself, taking up his glass and taking the rest of his brandy in one swallow.

"Dear God, you look awful."

Sebastian's head jerked up at the sound of Derek Thorne's voice. His friend had just arrived at Whites and discovered him seated near the bay of windows overlooking St. James Street.

"Go away," he groused, snatching up the decanter he had asked the attendant to leave for him. He had hardly touched it but now felt the need to drown his sorrows. "Can't you see I'm dying?"

Derek ignored his command and took a seat near him, prizing the brandy out of his hand. "You aren't dying. You're just an idiot."

Sebastian glowered at his friend, who he currently considered making his *former* friend. "What the devil are you talking about?"

Derek shifted the decanter out of Sebastian's reach when he tried to take it back and rolled his eyes. "Oh, I don't know, it might have something to do with the fact that you were ready to marry Miss Montgomery not a fortnight ago and now sit here sulking. Word travels fast, my friend, but I was willing to give you time to come to your senses. I can see that what you need is intercession. So, here I am."

Sebastian sank further into his chair, his legs splayed before him. He looked a right vagabond, a few days' worth of stubble shadowing his jaw and his skin sallow from weeks cloistered indoors.

"There is nothing anyone can say to fix this," he grumbled. "And even if there were, I certainly wouldn't take advice from *you*, a man so averse to marriage he is willing to stake three hundred pounds on a wager that he won't marry."

Derek grinned, and the fact that he looked so impeccably put together while Sebastian was suffering aggravated him all the more. "I might not want to marry, but that doesn't mean I'm ignorant on matters of love. No one knows more about how you're feeling than I do."

Sebastian felt like an ass as he remembered Derek's broken engagement and the humiliation and pain it had caused. If anyone knew how he felt just now, it was certainly Derek.

"Apologies."

Derek waved a hand. "Forget it, it's in the past. Besides, we're talking about you right now. Tell me what you did, and I'll tell you how to fix it."

Sebastian stared across the room, the club only half-filled at this hour of the afternoon and mostly quiet. He was silent while he ruminated over what to tell Derek and what to keep to himself. In the end, he posed the first question that came to his mind.

"Do you think me pompous?"

Derek snorted. "Everyone thinks you're pompous, but it's part of your charm. You're an annoyingly likable person."

Sebastian straightened, leaning forward as he realized Derek was the perfect person to help him. He hadn't thought of it until now, but no one knew what it was like to face hardship like his friend, who had worked for everything he had.

"What I mean to ask is, do you think I am so arrogant that it makes me ignorant to the plight of those in need? Do you think that I am so privileged that I cannot fathom what it is like to be truly desperate, desperate enough to do something that is morally wrong for the sake of survival?"

Derek frowned. "What is this about, Seb?"

"Just humor me, please. And I want an honest answer."

"Very well," he replied, still seemingly confused by this line of questioning. "In short, yes, I think you are that arrogant, but it isn't an insult, it's a simple fact of your position. You were born into this world, and while I know it comes with its share of responsibility, it also comes with a great deal of privilege. We were schoolmates, so I know how hard you worked at university, how much you wanted to make yourself into something respectable and worthy of admiration. I think the world of you, but…well, you have no idea what it is like to worry where your next meal will come from or face the possibility that a single incident could cause you to lose everything. It's a problem a man like you will never face."

Sebastian shifted uncomfortably in his chair, echoes of Helena's words resounding in his head. She had accused him of not understanding, and Derek had said much the same thing. They were both right, loathe as he was to admit it. He could never fathom sinking to such depths of hopelessness that he was left with few choices.

"Tell me something," he said. "If you ever faced the threat of losing your home and seeing your mother and sisters starve, and there was no work or no money for you to invest, none of it. What would you do to care for them? Would you steal or kill or cheat?"

Derek pursed his lips and gave Sebastian a sly look. "What makes you think I haven't done those things."

Sebastian blinked, taken aback by the ease with which such words fell from his friend's lips.

Derek chuckled and uncorked the brandy decanter and took

up Sebastian's empty glass, filling it and keeping it for himself. "I will admit to never having committed murder, but there wasn't much else I wouldn't do if the occasion called for it. How do you think I managed to have spending money during our years a Cambridge?"

"I thought you were simply good at cards!"

"Not *that* good. You would be surprised how far a card up a man's sleeve can go toward earning him a few shillings here and there. That money made the difference between being presentable for classes and being dressed in rags, between being able to purchase coal for the grate in my room or tapers to study by in the evenings. I'm not proud of it, but as a boy, I picked a pocket or two. That was before Father's business became profitable, and we did what was necessary to keep from starving."

Sebastian ran a hand through his disheveled hair, guilt and helplessness swirling through his gut in a toxic combination. "I'm so sorry. I had no idea. Why didn't you ever tell me? I would have helped you."

Derek lifted his stubborn chin and took a sip of his drink. "Even the poor have their pride, Seb. I am better for my hardships, even if the things I did might have landed me in goal or on the end of a noose. I will not tell you that wrongdoing should go unpunished, but I will assert that not everyone who commits such acts does so because they are a terrible person. Sometimes, breaking the rules is all a person can do when they have no other recourse."

Sebastian opened his mouth to reply when a sharp rap against the nearby window startled him out of his wits. He turned to find a lady framed in the glass, one hand on her hip and the other beckoning him outside. Narrowing his eyes, he realized that it was Harriett. If looks could kill, he would be incinerated where he sat, Harriett's displeasure with him as clear as day. Behind her stood a confused Viscount Amberly, who appeared to try to convince her to continue on their way, but the chit would not be moved.

Derek laughed as Harriett's motions toward him grew more determined, the set of her mouth indicating she didn't intend to leave until Sebastian complied. "That would be the other Miss Montgomery, yes?"

"Yes," Sebastian replied, slowly getting to his feet. "I shouldn't keep her waiting."

Derek frowned. "But you still haven't told me what you did. I am owed a riveting story."

Sebastian was already making his way to the door, his mind racing as he thought over all the reasons Harriett might accost him, and they all had to do with Helena. His heart lurched at the thought that something had happened to her, proving that he could never be angry enough to stop loving her. He'd been a fool for ever thinking it.

"Another time," Sebastian called over his shoulder. "For what it's worth, you've been a tremendous help."

"You're welcome," Derek replied, his voice fading away as Sebastian stepped outside, his eyes burning from the sudden exposure to the sun.

"Harriett?" he murmured as she descended on him, her expression murderous. "What are you doing here?"

She jabbed a finger at the center of his chest. "The question is, what are *you* doing here?"

Sebastian gazed helplessly about, finding that Amberly stood nearby, giving him an apologetic look. Apparently, the man wasn't sorry enough to take his fiancée in hand. "Having a drink?" he replied, at a loss as to what else to say.

"You're letting her get away, you stubborn man," Harriett retorted. "I don't know what happened between you and Helena, but if you don't come to your senses, you are going to lose her forever."

"What are you talking about?" he demanded, certain he had already lost Helena forever. Was Harriett trying to tell him that he still stood a chance? "Where is she?"

"Preparing to leave London first thing in the morning."

Sebastian staggered, that announcement nearly knocking him off his feet. "What? Where is she going?"

"To Kent," she replied. "She thinks it will be too difficult to remain in London because you are here. She seems to be under the impression that you no longer care for her. What did you do to my sister?"

Sebastian held his hands up in defense, afraid she might bludgeon him with her parasol and him too tired and worn thin to defend himself. "Harriett, there are matters that, it's complicated."

"No, it isn't. Either you love her, or you don't. Either you want to marry her, or you don't. She has her things packed and a carriage ready to take her to Kent, and just what do you intend to do about it?"

Sebastian stared off down the busy street, the noise and bustle of the people around him fading into nothing. In his mind, he could see clearer than he had in weeks, the path to his destiny, the future he had nearly let slip through his fingers.

"I'm going after her," he declared.

Harriett, who had been prepared to continue dressing him down, clamped her lips shut and looked at him as if he'd gone mad. "You are?"

Sebastian grinned and took her hand, giving her knuckles a quick, affectionate kiss. "Yes, I am. Thank you, Harriett."

He didn't stay to hear her reply but faintly registered her shouted, "You're welcome!" as he barreled down the lane, dodging the women and their servants coming and going with shop packages and gentlemen out for their strolls.

Once he had cleared the busiest portion of St. James Street, he broke into a run and didn't stop until he found a hackney coach. He had walked to Whites, but there was no time for a walk home. There was much to do before tomorrow, and Sebastian would need help setting his plan in motion.

It was risky, ridiculous, and so romantic, he was impressed with his own genius.

None of it would matter if Helena refused him. But even then, Sebastian would walk away knowing he had tried.

The hackney couldn't move fast enough to suit him, and he paid the driver and flung open the door before they rolled to a stop before Stratford House. He dashed through the entryway and tore through the corridors, calling out to his brother.

"Felix! Felix, are you here?"

The door to the dining room stood ajar, and therein he found Felix, seated before his luncheon, with a napkin tucked into his collar. He glowered at Sebastian while biting into a bit of cheese.

"May I help you?"

Sebastian leaned against the doorframe, out of breath. "Listen, I don't have time for your dramatics. I was wrong, and I'm sorry. There, now will you help me win Helena back? She's leaving London tomorrow, but not if I can convince her to stay and marry me."

Felix dropped the hunk of cheese and ripped the napkin from his shirt. "Finally! What took you so bloody long?"

HELENA SHUT THE book in her lap, unable to concentrate on the words. She was disappointed not to have Mina's company for the journey to Kent, but her friend had sent word this morning that an urgent matter had arisen, and she would have to follow Helena to Kent a day after their planned trip. She had left her carriage at Helena's disposal, writing that she would simply take the post-chaise when she was ready to depart.

It wasn't like Mina to abandon her friends, so Helena supposed the urgent matter must be something truly important. She hadn't relished being left alone with her own thoughts and nearly opted to remain in London to wait for Mina. But, if she didn't leave now, she never would. Even as she sat in a carriage taking her farther from town with every passing minute, Helena longed to call out to the driver and tell him to turn around. She was running away like a coward but could see no other way forward.

In order to heal, she had to remove herself from the source of her heartbreak. She would never persevere living in fear that she might cross Sebastian's path at any time and be forced to relive the hurt all over again.

It was time to begin anew, starting right now.

With a sigh, she placed the book back inside her valise and retrieved the embroidery she'd begun working on last night. She had just threaded her needle with a lovely thread in a shade of marigold when the carriage lurched. Helena's things went flying across the carriage as the horses slowed, and the clamor of voices came at her from outside. She gripped the edge of her seat, her heart racing, and she tried to make sense of what was happening. The coachman was shouting at someone, and a man's voice came back, thin and muffled by the carriage doors.

Dear God, were they being accosted? And in the middle of the day, at that! What sort of highwayman robbed carriage in the clear light of day?

She almost laughed at the irony of her situation but realized she must be ready to defend herself. A highwayman wouldn't have mercy on her just because she was a woman traveling alone. Throwing herself out of her seat, she searched the compartment beneath it, where she had stashed her blunderbuss. Mina had insisted she carry it while traveling, and Helena was grateful for it.

Footsteps crunched over the ground outside, and the men had gone silent. Helena's hands shook as she cocked the pistol and pointed it at the door, prepared to fight for her life if need be. Her assailant wouldn't be pleased when he learned she had nothing of value for him to steal.

The door swung open, and a flash of sunlight temporarily blinded her, and all she could make out was the bulky silhouette of a man.

"Stop right there!" she bellowed at the exact same time that the man called out, "Stand and deliver!"

Helena froze with her finger braced on the trigger as her vision cleared to reveal Sebastian—looking windblown and deliciously tousled, a black cape draping his shoulders.

"Your heart," he finished, his eyes widening when he noticed the pistol leveled at her. "Dash it all. That isn't how it was supposed to play out! Would you point that thing somewhere else? I'm trying to be romantic."

Helena gaped at him, slowly lowering the weapon and easing the hammer back in place. Realizing what a sight she must make, she pushed the skirts of her carriage dress over her legs. "Sebastian? What are you doing here?"

Sebastian waited until she had climbed back onto the squabs before hauling himself in and closing the door. Sitting across from her, he pushed the cloak off his shoulders and sighed.

"Correcting the worst mistake of my life," he said, reaching out to take both her hands.

They were solid and warm, a clear indication that she wasn't dreaming. He was really here in the flesh, looking as if he'd just stepped out of her dreams and into reality. His hair had been mussed by the wind, or perhaps nervous fingers. His eyes glittered with promise and hope and, most of all, love. Helena wanted to weep. She had never thought she'd have him look at her this way again.

"You were right to be angry with me," she began, her words tumbling out. "I should never—"

"Wait, let me say this," he cut in. "I've been thinking of what words to use when I found you, how to convince you to forgive me for the way I acted. Yes, what you did was illegal and wrong and so dangerous I'm tempted to take you over my knee for it. But I have had time to examine my heart and consider all the things you said, and you were right. I don't know what it is like to be faced with such dire choices, to be forced to consider sinking to lowly means to justify my ends. It disturbs me to know you ever faced such choices. I was angry, yes, but I should have listened to you and tried to understand because, as a wise man once told me, that is what you do when you love someone."

Helena really was on the verge of weeping now. Her throat constricted, and her heart soared as her eyes filled with tears. "Oh, Sebastian."

"I'm not finished," he rushed on. "I'm sorry, but if I don't say it all now, I'll forget something, and you deserve the best I have to offer. Another wise man once said that in the achievement of one's goals, a man should do three things. Firstly, have a clear, definitive, and practical ideal. Second, have the necessary means to attain the ends, and lastly, adjust all your means to that end."

She smiled as he sank to one knee on the carriage floor, unable to believe that this was truly happening. "Aristotle," she said with a laugh.

"Yes," he confirmed. "And I've decided that what I want is you for the rest of my life. That is my clear and practical ideal—you as my wife, by my side, the mother of my children, the driving force behind my every success. And I do have the means to make it so. I have my heart, which I place in your hands without condition, and I have the money to see you pampered and catered to for the rest of your life, though I'm certain you won't grow spoiled because you are such a wise and wonderful woman. And last of all, I am adjusting my means to meet the end. I am begging your forgiveness and putting myself at your mercy because I cannot live without you. I tried it for two weeks, didn't care for it at all. So, Helena Katherine Montgomery, will you do me the honor of marrying me?"

He reached into his coat pocket and presented her with a cedar box, which he opened to reveal a beautiful silver ring graced with a perfect, oval-shaped stone of yellow topaz. Helena let out a soft breath of wonder, her hands coming over her mouth as she studied the ring.

"Oh, Sebastian, it's—"

"Wait, there's more," he said, shoving the box into her hands and going back into his pocket. "I couldn't decide, so I decided to leave it up to you. There is also this one."

Helena burst out laughing as he offered up a second ring, this one shining gold with a sapphire. A third was produced from his opposite breast pocket, and Helena balanced the other two in her lap as he thrust a silver band boasting a row of perfect diamonds. Finally, a fourth ring appeared, and her mouth dropped open at the sight of a fiery ruby, large and square and heavy enough to send her sinking to the bottom of the Thames if ever she should fall in.

"You can have your favorite, hell you can have them all, and I'll choose three more, and you'll have a ring for every day of the week," he said, gathering her hands in his, along with the ruby ring. "Just tell me you will be mine and that you can forgive me for abandoning you when what I should have done was insist that none of it matters. Because it doesn't. I love you, and I will do anything, give you anything if you only say yes."

Helena glanced down at the ruby, the diamonds, the topaz, and the sapphire. In the end, they all clattered to the carriage floor as she threw herself into his arms. "Yes, Sebastian. Yes to all of it, to the rings, to marriage, and to you!"

Sebastian hauled her into his lap and sought her mouth for a kiss, which she gave him without restraint. In it, she could feel his longing and the pain falling behind them. She could feel the depth of his love and the sorrow of their separation. She accepted it all and gave it right back to him, sealing it all with the joy she felt at being in his arms again.

By the time they pulled apart, Helena was breathless from the kiss, as well as battling with dual urges to laugh and cry.

"You went through all this trouble for me?" she asked, shaking her head in disbelief.

"Yes," he said, kissing the tip of her nose. "Though I cannot take all the credit for it. Felix helped me come up with the idea, and Mina agreed to stay behind in London so I could have you to myself."

"That sneaky little minx!" she exclaimed.

Sebastian grinned at her, looking like a little boy who'd just been caught doing something naughty. "None of this would be necessary if I hadn't handled your revelation so abominably. Can you ever forgive me?"

"You already have been," she assured him. "And do you forgive me for deceiving you?"

He raised his eyebrow at her, sending more peals of laughter through her. Helena had nearly forgotten how good it felt to laugh, to simply be happy and free. "Yes, but we will have to discuss that spanking at some point," he quipped, grabbing a handful of her bottom and giving a playful squeeze. "I am uncertain that you have truly learned your lesson."

She squealed with delight as he gave her a light swat, finding that the flush on her cheeks wasn't due to embarrassment but arousal. Sebastian's eyes grew wicked as he seemed to realize she was in a state, and he leaned closed, resting his forehead against hers.

"Your coachman is currently taking a walk while enjoying one of my finest cigars," he murmured.

Helena returned his impish grin and helped him lift her skirts while he positioned her so that she knelt over him on the squabs. Their lips crashed together in a tangle of lips and tongue and teeth, her hands tearing at his fall while his skimmed up her thighs, finding their way beneath her skirts.

"I missed you," he murmured as she freed him from his breeches, his lips seeking her throat, her chest, the crest of one breast. "I burned for you the entire time we were apart. Never leave me again, even when I'm being an ass."

"I won't," she panted, leaning closer to allow him to unbutton her dress. "As long as you promise never to leave me, even when I'm being a shrew."

He groaned as the head of his prick found her wet and ready opening. At the first touch of his hand, Helena's body had flared to life, and now she was desperate to have him inside her, to relive that first soul-shaking moment of becoming one with him.

Now they truly were one, never to be separated from him.

"I love it when you're shrewish," he replied, cupping her hips and easing her down to accept his length. "God, yes, you beautiful, vexing shrew. That feels magnificent."

It truly did. Helena lost the will to banter with him as pure pleasure took over, sweeping through her like wildfire as he thrust upward, then moved her hips, showing her how to move, how to make love to him in this provocative and intriguing way. The tight fit of their bodies created to most intriguing friction between them, sending her hidden bundle of nerves pulsing and aching with the building intensity of her need. She wrapped her arms around him, gasping and moaning as he tore open her stays and latched onto her breast through her chemise.

Her sheath pulsed around him, his way eased by the slick heat of her arousal. His fingers dug into her hips as he guided her, his head resting against the squabs but his eyes open and fixed on her. Helena seized the power and control he placed in her hands, testing different motions of her hips and learning what she liked, what Sebastian liked. His harsh breaths came out hoarse and strained, tangled with deep and guttural moans that spoke of his pleasure. He cupped her breasts, toying with them as she swiveled and circled her hips, her cries echoing off the walls of the small space as her pleasure built and built until she could no longer contain it.

Sebastian held her close as she climaxed, nibbling at her breast and taking over setting the rhythm when she became too boneless and weak to manage it herself. He pumped into her, his face buried between her breasts, and his strokes becoming harder and faster. He was a mad man, going over the edge and driving her there with him, stoking another stunning, breathtaking climax from her before she'd even recovered from the first.

They collapsed in a heap together, hair mussed and clothes askew, the warmth of the carriage creating the perfect cocoon. Helena tried to move, but Sebastian stilled her with a tight arm around her back and a kiss.

"Don't go yet. I need to be close to you right now."

With a sigh, Helena rested her head on his chest and listened as his heart lowered to its normal rhythm by degrees. "Hmm, all right. We will eventually have to move, though. Frank should be finished with that cigar about now."

He made a low sound of protest, toying with a loose strand of her hair. "I suppose you are right. Besides, we should really pick up those rings. They're antiques, you know."

"In a moment," she murmured. "Just a little while longer."

Sebastian kissed the top of her head and whispered drowsily, "How about forever?"

EPILOGUE

London, three months later...

DEVLIN CONNELLY FOLLOWED the footman through the well-appointed corridors of Stratford House. He hadn't thought to return here after his initial audience with Mr. Radcliffe and his brother, the earl. However, he had received a mysterious message months ago from Stratford, with the man claiming to have new information regarding the identities of the Band of Brigands.

He snorted aloud as he considered the ridiculous name for the vigilante highwaymen who had reached levels of fame in London unprecedented among their sort. But then, no one had ever heard of multiple highwaymen working in tandem. It was a sensational story, one that helped to sell papers.

"I beg your pardon, sir?"

Devlin drew up short, realizing he had nearly trampled the footman because he hadn't been paying attention. He also realized that the man had heard his rough snort and was now staring down his long nose at Devlin as if he gave off a noxious odor. He had washed this morning—as he did *every* morning—but he was used to such treatment from the ton. Out of his livery, the footman was no better than he was. He'd likely come from some unsavory background, entrenched in poverty and desperation, just like Dev.

The difference was, this footman bowed and scraped to the nobility, while Devlin did no such thing. He had worked his way up the ranks of the Bow Street Runners by relying on instincts that had been honed in the slums of St. Giles. He'd been spat upon, sneered at, and called every filthy name one could think of, and still, he'd risen to become one of the most trusted and respected constables at No. 4 Bow Street.

"Nothing," Devlin replied, giving the footman an acerbic look. "Are ye going to open the door, man? His lordship's expecting me."

With a delicate, highhanded sniff, the servant opened the door, announced him, then turned on his heel to stride away, muttering something about 'bloody Irish' under his breath. Devlin sneered at the man's back before going inside to find the man he'd come to meet awaiting him.

The Earl of Stratford had seemed eager to aid his investigation, and the generous bank draft he had delivered to Sir Highsmith had been enough to fill out the ranks of the horse patrol with more men and, even better, more horses. From now on, all roads out of London would be safeguarded by these men. All had been quiet for the past few weeks, but Devlin understood the mind of a criminal better than most because he'd once been one.

It was only a matter of time before they surfaced again, making it inevitable that they would be caught.

However, when Devlin had come to Stratford House to answer the earl's summons, he had been informed that the man was away on his wedding trip—a sudden ceremony and resulting honeymoon having happened with little to no planning or noticed.

His sources revealed that the man was back in town, and Devlin had arrived at the first opportunity to find out what the man knew.

"Mr. Connelly," the earl said, rising from behind his desk. "What a welcome surprise. What brings you here. Oh, where are my manners? Darling, come meet Mr. Connelly, he is a constable from Bow Street."

For the first time, Devlin noticed the woman sitting quietly near the fire with a pile of books spread on the sofa to either side of her. She set down the one she'd been reading and approached, a smile lighting up a winsome face. She was lovely and full-figured, with honey-brown hair and hazel eyes.

"May I present my wife?" the earl announced proudly. "Lady Stratford, Countess of Stratford."

The lady offered her hand, and Dev took it, not daring to touch his mouth to it. He'd learned long ago with their sort to merely grace the air above a lady's hand with a kiss. These fancy lords were possessive of their women.

"It is an honor to meet you, Mr. Connelly," Lady Stratford said. "Might I send for tea?"

Devlin removed his hat as an afterthought and inclined his head. "No, me lady, thank you. Yer lordship, I had hoped to speak with you about the message I received shortly before you left London with yer wife. Ye said somethin' about information about these highway brigands."

The countess had left them to return to her seat, but to Devlin's eye, she didn't appear to be reading the book she had picked up. Her neck was stiff, and her head tilted just enough that Dev knew she was eavesdropping. The earl seemed not to notice.

"Ah, yes…that," he said with a sheepish smile, rubbing the back of his neck. "I must apologize for wasting your time. I came to realize that I was mistaken. I believed I had discovered the highwaymen's den of operation. However, it turned out to only be a regular house of ill repute. I quite forgot to send word, given the wedding and all."

Devlin frowned but said nothing. The man was clearly lying. He was good at it, but Dev had questioned enough liars and thieves to know when someone was bamming him. However, in the earl's words, he heard what went unsaid. The man would say nothing else on the matter.

Likely, Stratford had grown bored with playing at inspector and throwing his money around on his brother's behalf. It was so very typical of the lords of the *ton*, who were often fickle and flighty.

"I see," Devlin stated, his gaze flickering once more to the earl's bride. "It is an honest enough mistake, to be sure. Ye'll be certain to send for me if ye or Mr. Radcliffe remembers anything else."

The earl smiled, but it wasn't genuine. It struck Devlin as dubious and false, concealing some truth he couldn't yet figure out.

"I will," Stratford said. "I wish you a good day, Mr. Connelly."

"Good day to ye, yer lordship, me lady."

Devlin turned to leave, slapping his worn cap back over his unruly curls and ignoring the stares of servants as he made his way out of the house. He had been hopeful that the interest of an earl would be enough to accelerate his investigation, but now he'd arrived right back to where he'd started—with more questions than answers.

But he wouldn't take this as a defeat. There were other matters that needed his attention—including a hotbed of seedy activity going on right here in the city. The ridiculously named Band of Brigands was sure to misstep someday, for all criminals were eventually caught due to their own foolish mistakes.

And when that day came, Devlin would be ready and waiting.

About the Author

Elise Marion is a lover books and has a special place in her heart for sweet and sensual romance. Writing about love across all walks of life is her passion, as is reaching people through the written word. The Army wife and stay-at-home mother of three spends most of her time taking care of her children. Her second job includes writing stories about characters that people can fall in love with. When the Texas native isn't caring for her family or writing, you can usually find her with her nose in a book, singing loudly, or cooking up something new in the kitchen.

www.elisemarion.com
Facebook: facebook.com/elisemarion86
Goodreads: goodreads.com/author/show/5239954.Elise_Marion
Book Bub: bookbub.com/authors/elise-marion
Amazon: amazon.com/Elise-Marion/e/B005PIRY24